PILGRIMS

PILGRIMS

by M. R. Leonard

BLUE
CASTLE
PRESS

This is a work of fiction. Names, characters, places, and incidents either are the product of the author's imagination or are used fictitiously. Any resemblance to actual persons, living or dead, events, or locales is entirely coincidental.

Copyright © 2024 by Michael R. Leonard

BLUE
CASTLE
PRESS

All rights reserved. No part of this book may be reproduced or used in any manner without written permission of the copyright owner except for the use of quotations in a book review. For more information, email Blue Castle Press at: bluecastlepress@gmail.com.
First paperback edition November, 2024
Blue Castle Press
Boston, MA

Cover design and interior formatting by Cover Kitchen

Library of Congress Control Number: 2024912895
ISBN 979-8-9910-1560-8 (paperback)
ISBN 979-8-9910-1561-5 (hardcover)
ISBN 979-8-9910-1562-2 (ebook)
ISBN 979-8-9910-1563-9 (audio)

www.MRLeonardauthor.com
10 9 8 7 6 5 4 3 2 1

To my wife
my rock and my heart
without whom none of this would be possible

PROLOGUE

SAINT INNOCENT OF RIYADH

Great art Thou, O Lord, and greatly to be praised, who, in Thy power and in Thy infinite wisdom, hast created me, but a particle of Thy creation, to humbly extend Thy mercy into this hospital, that, through Thy perfect will, I might save these children from the killer robots, slow the alien hand of death wreaking destruction across the land.

The lights flickered as the hospital backup generator began to give way.

Jumping over dead bodies, Monsignor Innocenti raced down the hallway to the hospital nursery, the infant squirming in his right arm. A lone doctor stood inside the nursery, a group of school-age children trembling behind him—the first survivors the Monsignor had seen in far too long.

Between him and the innocents was a killer machine, its spiderlike body arched back, poised to launch itself through the tempered glass of the nursery door. Ignoring the pain that radiated up his left arm toward his chest, the Monsignor focused on the machine. He raced to close the distance, but before he could reach it, the machine burst through, landing inside the nursery in a rain of glass.

I beseech Thee, O Lord, commend my failing body into the nursery, that I may grab the killer machine and cast it back into the corridor, so that the people inside might be saved.

Monsignor Innocenti stepped through the now-shattered nursery door, glass crunching beneath his feet. The machine was getting back up, preparing to strike. Tucking the child closer to his chest, the Monsignor reached for the machine with his left hand, praying the crushing pain in his chest would not make his aim any less true. Before the machine could fully rise, the Monsignor grabbed it and threw it back into the hall.

I praise Thee, O Lord, who hast graced me with swiftness, that Thou has heard my entreaties, delivered me to these innocents in the hope that they may be saved.

"You're alive?" Like many men in Saudi Arabia, the doctor spoke English with a British accent. Huddled behind him were a dozen young children and perhaps a dozen more newborns crying in their bassinets.

"The machines will not harm me," the Monsignor said in his heavily accented English. Grabbing fresh linens from an empty bassinet, he threw them onto the ground at the foot of the nursery door.

"Because you're a priest?" the doctor asked, his eyes focused on the Monsignor's Roman collar.

"Si." Monsignor Innocenti placed the infant on top of the sheets, arcs of pain shooting down his left arm from his chest.

O Lord, who in Thy providence had me find this child along the road to administer Thy sacramental mercy unto him, if I may beseech Thee further, let the child be as a holy wall, let him keep the wicked machines at bay outside the nursery until I can administer Thy salvation to the souls whom Thou hast spared in this room.

"What are you doing?" the doctor asked. "Those things will be back in here any second. They'll kill the baby."

"The child will protect us." Leaving the infant, the Monsignor limped to a sink on the far wall and turned on the tap, letting the water run until it was cool and clear.

"Protect us?" The doctor held out his arms as the children quivered behind him. "How?"

"The child has a halo of protection. The machines will not bring him harm, nor will they dare cross a threshold he lies at." The doctor tilted his head, no understanding on his face. "I can save the other children," the Monsignor pressed. "Make it so the machines will not hurt them, either."

The doctor looked at him skeptically, seemingly unwilling to trust the priest, but his gaze was broken by a child's shriek.

Four more machines had gathered at the entrance, their small metal bodies motionless, their spindly legs gripping the doorjamb like spiders in wait.

O Lord, who created earth and stone through Thy all-loving dominion, turn these machines to stone now, keep them still, if only for a few minutes, that I may deliver Thy mercy before the Diplomats arrive, my toil made fruitless by their steely hands.

"Now bring the bambini to me," the Monsignor said, gesturing at the bassinets. "There isn't much time."

The doctor said something to the children in Arabic before grabbing a bassinet and wheeling it over. As soon as the bassinet was next to the Monsignor, he picked up the newborn and began the rite.

"Amen, amen, I say to you," the Monsignor said in his native Italian. "No one can enter the kingdom of God without being born of water and Spirit. And so, I baptize you in the name of the Father." The Monsignor brought the child's head under the faucet and let the cool water run over her. "In the name of the Son." The newborn cried as the water flowed over her head again. "And in the name of the Holy Spirit." He put the newborn's head under the water for a third and final time. His task done, the Monsignor returned the newborn to the bassinet.

"Where does this halo of protection come from?" the doctor asked, pushing over another bassinet.

"The child is Christian." The Monsignor picked up the

new infant, a baby boy, and lowered the child's head toward the running water.

"But the child is Saudi, no?"

O Lord, Thou art true, and being Truth, I conform myself to Thee. So that even now, even in this darkest moment, I shall not lie, poison Thy creation with the falsehoods of the enemy.

"Si," the Monsignor admitted.

The doctor's eyes grew wide. "You're *baptizing* them?" Grabbing the Monsignor, he pulled him away from the sink.

"It's the only way to save the children," the Monsignor pleaded, unable to lean forward and get the child's head under the water.

"How dare you?" the doctor seethed. "These are Muslim children born to Muslim parents. It's apostasy!"

A searing pain shot down the Monsignor's left arm, his aged body failing; he could not go on much longer. "All of Arabia is in ruin," he cried. "These bambini are orphans now— their parents surely dead. I must protect them while I still can."

"No." The doctor pulled with renewed strength. "I won't let you."

O Lord God, the Creator and Disposer of all things in nature, of sin the Disposer only, grant my earthly vessel one last thrust of vigor, that I may have the strength of Samson before my end.

Monsignor Innocenti dug deep, summoning all his power. Somehow countering the might of the much-younger man, he stretched himself forward and dipped the child's head under the running water. "I baptize you in the name of the Father."

"Stop!" the doctor yelled, redoubling his strength and pulling the Monsignor away from the sink.

O Lord, even before a word is on my tongue, Thou knowest it. Thou knowest that I am terrified, tormented by the slaughter of these innocents. But I would die a thousand deaths, undergo any trial, that just one more child might live. So I beg Thee, intercede for me now, do for me what I, Thy lowly servant, cannot.

The Monsignor shifted so that the child's head was again positioned under the flowing water. "And in the name of the Son."

Adjusting his grip, the doctor pulled the Monsignor away from the sink with even surer strength. He yelled something in Arabic, and the huddling throng of children descended on the Monsignor with terrible speed.

"Please," the Monsignor pleaded. "It's the only way."

The little hands grasped at him, determined to snatch the newborn away. He struggled to hold on to the baby, but the children were smothering him, endangering the little one, so he let them take the boy, thrusting the infant into the arms of an eight-year-old girl.

"We don't have much time," the Monsignor cried. "The Diplomats will be here soon."

The doctor continued to restrain the Monsignor like he was a robber in the night.

My God, please show me a way to save these children. I beg Thee.

A child let out a scream. The Monsignor and the doctor turned in unison. Looming in the doorway was a Diplomat, its metal body gleaming, its crimson head drenching the nursery in a deathly glow.

The Monsignor gasped. "We're too late."

Moving its robotic torso through the shattered doorway, the Diplomat picked up the infant wriggling at the threshold and cradled it with the gentleness of a mother. The child in its steely arms, the Diplomat carried the infant to an empty bassinet and placed it down softly, making sure no harm came to the little boy.

O Lord, in Thy mercy, keep those infernal machines still. Strike sense into Thy wayward Pilgrims, that they may see their error before it is too late.

With no barrier holding them back, the killer machines leapt forward, unleashing their fury into the room. The doctor released his grip on the Monsignor as the children scattered in every direction. They fell to the ground as the machines caught up to them, their eyes wide, a look of waking death seared onto their faces.

The doctor's fists flew at the machines in a desperate attempt to protect the two children cowering behind him. Yet no matter how swift his punches, the machines were swifter still, overwhelming the doctor until he was face down, limp on the floor.

The Monsignor dove toward a young boy whose little

hands were trying frantically to dislodge a machine clinging to his hip. The Monsignor swiped the machine onto the floor, immobilizing it under his foot.

O my God, my loving God, who has known me since before I knew myself, let my body shield this child, let me remain here as long as it takes, let my flesh turn to dust before this child sees any harm.

Wrapping the little boy in his arms, the Monsignor checked the child's back to ensure there were no machines lurking there. But as he beheld the child's face, the boy's eyes grew wide, and his body went limp. A little machine scurried away from his ankle, its work done.

Monsignor Innocenti laid the child down, the nursery his final resting place, and surveyed the room. The eight-year-old girl was still breathing, the newborn alive in her arms. Kneeling at the feet of the motionless Diplomat, she sobbed, rocking back and forth.

Monsignor Innocenti rushed toward her, but he wasn't fast enough; a small machine leapt up to her neck before he could stop it. She fell backward, her lifeless gaze fixed on the security camera above.

The infant twisted in the girl's dead arms.

Please, Lord, let me save him. I beg of Thee.

Monsignor Innocenti grabbed the newborn from the girl before the nearest machine could strike. He sprinted toward the sink as the little machines climbed into bassinets, extinguishing the unbaptized newborns' cries like candles, one by one.

"And in the name of the Holy—" the Monsignor said as he thrust the child's head underneath the flowing water, one word away from salvation.

Before he could say the final word, the child went limp, its little eyes wide open, its tiny body still. A glint of metal flashed in the corner of the Monsignor's eye, skittering away across the floor.

Hand clutching his chest, the Monsignor fell to his knees with a cry, still cradling the deceased child with his other arm.

My God, my God, why hast Thou forsaken me?

The Monsignor slumped over, his consciousness fading, his fragile heart finally giving out.

As the cries of the two surviving infants filled the Monsignor's ears, the Diplomat approached him. Kneeling beside him, it made the sign of the cross with its steely hand and began to pray, its deep bass voice echoing throughout the room.

It was the last thing the Monsignor would ever hear.

PART I

1

FIFTY-SIX HOURS UNTIL ARRIVAL

In two days, Austin would be dead along with everyone else—including Aurelia. But he still had one last chance to be with her, to smell her golden hair, to kiss her perfect lips. It all came down to the phone in his pocket, the phone he wasn't allowed to be carrying, the one he was caressing as he marched through the night in a drunken haze.

Mr. Washington shot him a concerned look. "You all right, Austin?"

"I'm fine," he managed to reply, the cheap hooch he'd plied himself with threatening to come back up.

Mr. Washington nodded, but the look of unease remained on his mahogany face. Ignoring it, Austin stared across the high school football field to see the last neighborhood civil defense platoon taking its place on the visitor end zone. In a few moments, the Regulars would call the muster to order and his chance to see Aurelia's post in time would vanish.

"Attention!" The sergeant stalked along the first row of men. He was clad in full battle dress, his regalia a sharp contrast to the civilians gathered on the field, half still in their pajamas. Behind him on the running track, his commander, a lieutenant, stood with a half-dozen Regulars on either side.

"Let's go!" the sergeant yelled. "Move it!"

Austin peeked at his phone as the formation came to order: still nothing.

"The Pentagon estimates the aliens will enter Earth's atmosphere this Friday around noon eastern time," the lieutenant stated with a firmness that contrasted with her petite frame. "For now, we assume the Premise is true, but—"

She cut off as a black Humvee rolled onto the track.

Two figures exited the Humvee. From their steel-toed boots to their tactical helmets they were clad in black, the only hint of color being the remorseless eyes that peeked out from their balaclavas.

The Black Shirts were here.

"But," the lieutenant continued, her voice betraying a slight quiver, "we must always remember General Fergusson's words: 'The Corollary is only as strong as our bravery.' "

She nodded to the sergeant.

"Okay, you maggots!" the sergeant shouted. "Let's see how

well you've been studying your civil defense manuals." Planting his feet in front of a middle-aged man on the ten-yard line, he said, "You! What's the First Assumption of Alien Capability?"

"Ah, well . . . it's that—"

The sound of a broken rib cage washed over the muster as the man fell at the sergeant's feet.

The lieutenant's gaze shot to the Black Shirts, as if in search of approval, but they betrayed nothing. Returning her attention to the man writhing on the ground, she said, "We give you those manuals for a reason, militiaman. You'd do well to study it closer."

Austin's stomach curled, the swill ready to come back up, when he felt his phone vibrate.

Aurelia.

"You!" The sergeant pointed at another man. "Go!"

Austin wondered whether the Black Shirts could see his hand from where he stood in the second row. They could. Easily. But in two minutes her post would disappear, and the password it contained would be gone forever. This was his only chance for a bit of happiness before the end. This is what he'd risked bringing his phone for.

"Sir!" the militiaman shouted. "The First Assumption of Alien Capability is that the aliens have cyber dominance, sir!"

Before Austin could stop himself, his hand turned, revealing the phone. His body was taking over, giving in to the urge to see the password despite the feeble protests of his booze-dulled brain.

TRIUMPH.

The nausea disappeared. *Triumph.* How apropos. Three years of following her socials, paying for her all-access content. She had been his only ray of brightness in a cold and dying life. But now, with the password, it was all about to pay off. Just one paycheck stood between him and her in-person fee. Just one more boring class to teach before he could hold her in real life, wrap himself up in her purple sheets, and wait for the end of the world.

"That's correct, militiaman," the lieutenant said. "All things digital or electronic are to be considered intelligence liabilities or attack vectors. That's why military formations have to be able to operate low-tech; take the aliens' advantage away."

Austin covered the phone with his palm, wondering if he'd been noticed. The Regulars and the Black Shirts were all focused on the lieutenant; Austin's gamble had paid off.

"It's not enough to simply know the First Assumption of Alien Capability. You have to *follow* it." The lieutenant gave the sergeant a nod.

"Tech check!" the sergeant bellowed. "First row, arms out!"

The nausea returned in a heartbeat. Suddenly his phone felt like an anchor, dragging him to the bottom of a dark sea. It had been three years since the Regulars had called for a tech check at a muster. Austin had been sure they didn't bother with those anymore. But he hadn't counted on a surprise visit from the Black Shirts.

"Lieutenant, I got something," the sergeant yelled, clutching a chubby militiaman who was shaking uncontrollably.

"Let's see it."

Sweat erupted on Austin's brow as the chubby militiaman pulled up his shirt, revealing a small plastic rectangle on his abdomen. "It's my insulin pump, ma'am," the militiaman said. "I need it."

The lieutenant's face fell. She glanced at the Black Shirts, taking a second before turning back to address the militiaman. "Do you think your diabetes is more important than the planet's defense?"

The chubby man's mouth quivered.

"Some time in the stockade will help you sort out your priorities," she said. "Take him in." The man sobbed as two Regulars dragged him off the field.

"First row, fall out," the sergeant barked. "Next row, arms up."

When the men in the first row turned ninety degrees to their left and began marching away, Austin's heart pounded as panic overtook him. In a few seconds, he would be in the front row, his phone exposed for all to see. And Aurelia would be gone forever. Rather than in her beautiful arms, he would spend his final hours in a sweaty, throbbing cell.

He cursed himself for bringing the infernal thing, wishing with all his being he could just be rid of it.

That was when he felt a hand on his, prying the phone

from him, absolving him of his misery. Austin forced himself not to turn around to look his salvation in the face. Instead, he let the phone go from his grasp moments before it was his turn to stretch out his arms.

The sergeant manhandled him, his palms sweeping over Austin's body with the gentleness of a bulldozer, but there was no contraband to be found. After a moment, the sergeant moved on to pat down Mr. Washington, who stood next to Austin in line.

The nausea he felt lifted, and he exhaled in relief. Aurelia really would be his, one last pleasure before the eternal blackness, some unknown stranger to thank.

A bump on Austin's thigh made him freeze—all his muscles tensing in unison.

His benefactor was trying to return the phone to Austin's pocket, but his aim was off. He kept fumbling on Austin's leg, the whole clumsy spectacle impossible to hide.

"Hey, you!" The sergeant raced toward Austin; his face twisted in fury.

Austin tensed, preparing for the worst, but to his surprise, the sergeant charged past him and grabbed the man behind him. As the sergeant dragged the man forward, Austin saw his savior for the first time: he was old, probably in his early seventies, with a thick head of shock-white hair and a mustache to match.

"Ma'am," the sergeant said, shoving the old man in front of the lieutenant. "This man was trying to hide his phone in the pocket of a militiaman I'd already searched."

Though the old man stood a head taller than the lieutenant, he seemed to shrink under her scrutinizing gaze.

"Please, ma'am," the old man stammered. "I'm forgetful in my old age. When I realized I had the phone on me, I got scared. I didn't mean to do it. Please have mercy."

Bile clawed at the back of Austin's throat. This kind old man had saved him, and even now he was lying to protect him.

The lieutenant stole a quick glance at the Black Shirts. They loomed ominously by their Humvee, their narrow eyes hunting for disobedience. "Forgive you?" she said after collecting herself. "Do you think the aliens will be so forgiving?"

The old man trembled.

Austin's mouth opened to confess, to spare the old man, but no words came to his lips.

The lieutenant's cold command cut through the air. "Twenty lashes," she declared. "Sergeant, get my whip."

A pain shot through Austin's heart as the Regulars forced the old man to his knees and ripped off his shirt. The man's back was spotted and pale, so pallid it nearly glowed in the predawn murk. Without ceremony, the lieutenant got behind the old man and took the whip from the sergeant's hand. Her gaze once again went to the Black Shirts, their heartless eyes still and unmoving, before she turned back to the kind old man.

"One!" She hurled the leather tongue onto his back, leaving a trail of broken skin in its wake.

The night echoed with the old man's scream.

"Two!"

Austin's stomach squeezed, the booze threatening to make itself known.

"Three!"

The whole formation shuffled as the old man's agony crested over them. Austin tried to distract himself by focusing on the lieutenant's patches, reading and rereading them over again: "Lieutenant Wu—US Army, Twenty-Second Mechanized Battalion."

"Fifteen!"

It didn't work.

The sight too gory for his stomach to bear, he let loose, retching and then retching again until all that he heaved was air.

By the time he finished, the old man was lying wasted, bloody on the ground, and the sergeant was storming toward Austin, fists clenched in rage.

2

FIFTY-THREE HOURS UNTIL ARRIVAL

She stood in the doorway like a wraith, her nearly translucent skin complementing the pale blue of her nightgown, the garment so threadbare it looked as though it were made of tissue paper. His mother stood a foot shorter than him, her thinning hair at eye level, the gray roots climbing out of her skull like a creeping obsolescence. To a stranger, she might have looked like a nutjob, but she was just poor, the money for luxuries like hair dye and new nightgowns having long since run out.

"Austin?" She scrunched up her face. "Are you okay?"

Struggling to close the front door to the apartment with his unresponsive arms, he said, "What time is it?"

She pointed at the vomit stain on his shirt and frowned.

For breaking attention, the sergeant had made him do one hundred push-ups on top of his own sick, but he didn't have time to explain.

"Mom," Austin insisted, "what time is it?"

"It's seven thirty-eight."

Austin's heart sank through the floor. He rushed past her, down the hall, and into his bedroom, where he turned on his Jurassic laptop, the whir of its barely functioning hard drive filling the room.

He was late.

Eight minutes late.

Those eight minutes could be all the difference between him dying alone or in the arms of Aurelia.

As the machine booted up, he tore off his soiled shirt and grabbed another one from atop the pile of dirty clothes on his bed, just managing to get it on before the videoconference loaded.

"Come on. You know you want to."

The sound of Austin's class spilled out of the tinny laptop speakers. The kids were scattered about the classroom, some perched on desks, others leaning by the window—evidently taking full advantage of what they thought would be an unscheduled free period.

Miraculously, an administrator was nowhere to be seen.

"Everyone will be there," Kevin continued, his Southern drawl cutting through the chatter. He was standing next to

Nicole, who was seated at her desk, trying not to let her gaze linger on Kevin's canyon-esque dimples. "It might be your last chance to have some fun."

"*Salve discipuli!*" Austin summoned his best teacher's voice. "Let's all take our seats so we can begin."

Getting a bunch of teenagers to focus on Latin was challenging in the best of times, but it was nigh impossible to do so when aliens were set to arrive on Earth in two days, and the teacher himself showed up almost ten minutes late. Austin, however, had no choice but to proceed. Administrators often checked in on the classes of remote teachers, especially substitutes like Austin. While he was lucky that none had decided to stroll in before he logged on, they would still be none too pleased with the classroom's current state of disarray.

"Salve discipuli," Austin repeated, his tone sterner.

"Salve magister," the class half-heartedly replied, ambling back to their seats.

This was Austin's last class before the Arrival. The school would be closed the next day and the day after that. He just had to get through this lesson to receive his final paycheck, the last thing he needed to book his intimate session with Aurelia.

"Let's pick up where we left off in Book III of the *Aeneid*," he said, "with Anchises's death in Sicily. Who wants to start?"

"Why were you late, Mr. D?" Adam's drawl was even thicker than Kevin's, seemingly a prerequisite for admission to this private academy in Savannah, Georgia—a veritable assembly line of southern gentlemen and debutantes.

"Muster ran late," Austin said, the image of the old man's bloody back floating through his mind. "Now let's look at line six hundred ninety-two," he said, shoving the vile image down. "'Sicanio praetenta sinu iacet insula contra Plemyrium undosum; nomen dixere priores Ortygiam.'"

"Do you think it'll work, Mr. D?"

Adam was still looking at the front of the classroom where Austin's head was displayed on a huge monitor, his copy of the *Aeneid* noticeably unopened.

Austin frowned. "Do I think what will work?"

"The musters, the mobilization, the nuke stockpiling?" Adam said. "All of General Fergusson's plans?"

No. It was a pipe dream—a parody of hope.

"We're not here to talk about the Arrival." Austin tried to sound gentle but prodding. "We're here to translate the *Aeneid*."

"Oh, come on, Mr. D," Kevin chimed in, his desk pulled conspicuously close to Nicole's. "You're the only teacher trying to teach anything today. The rest are just showing movies."

Austin grimaced. The other teachers were full-time and tenured, but he was a substitute—one slipup away from being fired and his pay withheld (a consequence Principal Madison never tired of reminding him of). "I'm not responsible for their classrooms. I'm responsible for mine, and it's important we learn this stuff."

"Important?" Kevin laughed. "Not when the world is going to blow up on Friday."

Trying to slow his racing heart, Austin took a deep breath.

Kevin was right, of course. This was all pointless. School was nothing but a way to keep kids from running amok as the clock ticked down to the end of the world. But the school had a clear policy for when the kids started saying that all hope was lost—"Arrival Anxiety" they called it. Teachers were to remind students of the Premise, try to convince them everything would be okay, and then get them back to their schoolwork.

"The aliens aren't going to blow up the planet," Austin said, trying to sound like he believed what he was saying. "That's the point of the Premise. If the aliens wanted to kill us, they would have attacked Earth at range years ago as they traveled here. They haven't, so we operate under the premise that they're peaceful."

"Maybe they've got to get up close to use their weapons," Kevin replied.

"No," Austin said with a shake of his head. "When the alien ship lit up the night sky five years ago with its deceleration burn and set off the Great Panic, it was traveling at almost ten percent the speed of light. If the aliens had simply dumped their sewage and let it crash into Earth, the kinetic energy would have been enough to blow the crust off the planet. So, no—they don't have to get close. Their spaceship is basically a weapon already."

Austin felt his stomach churn. He'd heard some government flak deliver that exact explanation in a press conference a few days earlier. He hated doing the same, but he had to do what it took to be with Aurelia.

"But what if—"

"Kevin, we need to get back to work."

"No, hear me out, Mr. D. What if the aliens change their minds and decide to stop being peaceful? Have you ever thought of that?"

Austin winced. He'd thought of nothing but that. "They won't."

"I don't know, Mr. D. They've been making their way to Earth for five years, and they haven't replied to a single communication. Seems kinda suspicious to me."

It didn't seem "kinda" suspicious. It seemed *incredibly* suspicious.

But all Austin said was "I'm sure they have a good reason for not responding."

"Maybe they do. But what's going to stop them from saying 'You know what? These human meatbags suck. Let's blow 'em up.'"

"The Corollary," Austin said through clenched teeth. "It follows from the Premise that the aliens believe peace is more profitable than violence, so humanity can ensure peace by increasing the cost of conflict. That's why governments worldwide have expanded their militaries, trained citizen militias, and built up weapons stockpiles. If the aliens become hostile, they'll get sucked into an endless guerrilla war. That's how we'll make sure the aliens stay on their best behavior."

Even though he was repeating, nearly verbatim, the justification the Regulars often gave at the musters, Austin knew better: militia duty wasn't about protecting the planet—it was about keeping the population too tired and afraid to disobey.

"Random dudes with rifles are going to scare the aliens? I don't think so, Mr. D."

"Kevin, that's enough, now—"

"He's messing with you, Mr. DeSantis," Julia said from the front row, a scowl parting the sea of freckles on her face. "I saw his dad on TV saying his hedge fund was going to make a killing betting against all the worriers who think the world ends on Friday. He's just pretending to be afraid of the Arrival so he can convince Nicole to hook up with him before the 'world ends.'"

"Shut up, Julia!" Nicole shouted.

The classroom shattered into laughter, and Kevin sat at his desk with a self-assured smile on his face.

"That's enough!" Austin yelled. "I *need* you all to stop."

His pleas fell on deaf ears as the class collapsed into a series of individual conversations.

Aurelia's image floated into Austin's mind—her symmetric face, her perfect skin. He'd come so close to having her: surviving a tech check, keeping his mouth shut as they tortured an old man, and completing one hundred push-ups in his own vomit. Now he was being thwarted by a bunch of sixteen-year-olds, kids too young to drive, too carefree to have tasted true failure.

"Guys!" he shouted, but not one person looked over. It was hopeless. Trying again, he said, "Listen up."

Frustration burned in him when not so much as one head turned toward the front of the class. Austin's cheeks flushed. "You want to know the truth?" His voice filled with acid, a tone so caustic it cut right through the din. "Kevin's right: this Friday, we're all dead."

The room went silent.

"The aliens traveled across the galaxy in an asteroid so big it could house the entire US population with room to spare. Do you realize how much power that takes?"

The students stared at him, a few mouths going agape.

"A shit ton!" Austin focused on Kevin, glad to see his self-assured smile had evaporated. "There's no way an alien race capable of that level of staggering power has any time for humanity. We're like insects to them, and the first thing they're going to do when they get here is clean house."

Feeling his blood pressure rising, Austin took a breath to calm himself. Running a hand over his head, he said, "I don't know why the aliens haven't killed us already—I really don't. But come Friday, it's all over, no matter what Kevin's dad and all the government lackeys think. So can we please just translate the *Aeneid* for the next hour?" All eyes were locked on him as he pleaded with them. "It might be a waste of time, but I need the money to buy one last moment of pleasure in my life before we all die. And after today's class, we'll never have to see each other ever again."

The second the truth slipped from his lips, he thought he'd feel better, but, instead, he felt awful.

Austin inhaled deeply, staring at his students, who'd all gone quiet. The hangover, the indignity of being disobeyed by teenagers, the vision of the kind old man being whipped . . . none of it had been fixed by his outburst, but at least his class was under control. It was a start.

But then Austin noticed something: the students weren't looking at him. Their gazes had all turned to the side of the classroom. Before Austin could figure out what they were staring at, a figure emerged into frame. Principal Madison stared back at him, a look of horror on his face.

3

FIFTY HOURS UNTIL ARRIVAL

That one?" The bartender pointed his meaty hand at the bottle of high-end scotch. "It's forty grand a shot."

Austin nodded. There was no point in saving his pennies anymore. His last chance at getting what he needed had gone out the window when Principal Madison had let him go—without his last paycheck.

Instead of going for the scotch, the bartender went for the Fedcoin machine and then plonked the heavy metal box in front of him. "Pay first, then I pour."

Austin sidled onto a barstool that tilted on the uneven floor. "Let's keep it open. I'll be drinking all day. I don't want the Feds to cut me off."

The bartender leaned over the bar, bringing his basketball-sized face close to Austin's. "Do I look stupid to you?" The bartender let the question hang. "The aliens arrive in two days and every lush in Virginia wants to rack up a tab drinking top-shelf whiskey they think they'll never have to pay for. I'm not falling for it. Cough it up now, or get out."

In no state to argue, Austin pressed his thumb to the fingerprint reader on the Fedcoin machine and then entered his six-digit PIN. It rewarded him with a green flash and a soothing ding, letting the bartender know he had sufficient funds.

That Austin had sufficient funds came as no surprise. The last time he'd looked at his Federal Reserve account, he'd had almost five million dollars. More than enough for a glass of expensive scotch, but about 150 grand short of booking his session with Aurelia; almost exactly how much he would have been paid for today's Latin class if he hadn't been fired.

He'd been saving up for five months, scrimping every penny, forgoing every comfort. He'd even unsubscribed from her all-access social feed to save some cash. All so he could be with her in person at a luxury hotel in Washington, DC—an extravagance she reserved solely for fans dedicated enough to catch one of her disappearing passwords and wealthy enough to pay the steep price for four hours of her time.

Now it would never happen.

The bartender set the rocks glass in front of him, and Austin wasted no time in slugging the scotch down. He gagged as he sucked it in, memories of his retching from earlier this morning still fresh on his stomach's mind. But as the crisp, clean booze settled into his bloodstream, he could feel his body equalizing, the scotch smoothing out his comedown from the cheap swill he'd drunk the night before.

Pushing the empty glass forward, Austin asked, "How much for the bottle?"

The bartender shot him a skeptical glance. "Just shy of a million."

"I'll take it," he said with a nod.

The bartender hesitated, his arms locked across his chest. A bottle of bathtub hooch would cost a tiny fraction of that sum and be just as effective at getting him lit.

"Feds can't cut me off once I already have the bottle," Austin explained, gesturing at the Fedcoin machine. "And I might as well drink the good stuff before I die."

Seemingly satisfied with the explanation, the bartender relaxed his arms. "You're not gonna die, kid." He began to type in the new purchase amount. "You ain't that lucky. Your problems are still gonna be here come Saturday."

Austin nodded politely, unwilling to disabuse the barman of his false hope, and placed his thumb back on the reader. As he entered his PIN, he braced himself for the red light and the jarring denial tone, but, to his surprise, it flashed green.

It wasn't long after the aliens had been detected coming toward Earth that society broke down. Riots, price spirals, cops walking off the job. Order didn't really make sense when you thought the world was going to end in a few years. But the governments that did survive fought back, and, while the Black Shirts did their part, it was the digital dollar that put them firmly back in control. With cash eliminated and all deposits held at the Federal Reserve, the government could see all purchases in real time and tinker with people's balances at will. Shoot your mouth off at a cop? Your Federal Reserve account gets debited on the spot. Go to the bar a bit too much? Next time you go out, the machine will flash red when you want to buy a drink. Do right by Uncle Sam by ratting on a neighbor who skipped muster? You might just find a life-changing sum waiting for you in your account. Only those smart enough to buy bitcoin before the Great Panic had been able to get off that vicious ride, and Austin hadn't been smart enough.

The bartender handed him the bottle, and he pulled the cap off and took another slug, trying to drown his regret. As the scotch rolled down his throat, he began to feel a warmth in his stomach. He languished in relief as the scotch carried his troubles away, only to have Principal Madison float back into his mind. He hadn't just robbed Austin of a paycheck when he'd fired him; he'd taken away his last chance of happiness in this world. And for what? A little yelling? For telling the kids the truth for once?

When Mr. Hanlon had stormed off the job six months earlier, Austin had come to Principal Madison's rescue, allowing the Latin class to continue uninterrupted. Madison had been lucky to find Austin—a once up-and-coming classics professor—the most overqualified substitute Latin teacher in the country. Yet all it took was one slipup for Principal Madison to cast him out.

Austin poured some of the overpriced scotch into the cloudy glass. Madison had been merciless, just like Lieutenant Wu. That man, that kind old man, he'd made just one mistake, and rather than cut him a break, she'd cut his back open. If only Lieutenant Wu could feel the same pain.

As soon as the thought crossed his mind, he winced, berating himself.

Austin abhorred violence. Always had. The idea of Lieutenant Wu's small back being ripped apart by a whip—it was too much. No one should have to suffer that, not even her. But he allowed himself the joy of imagining her being discovered with a cell phone by her superiors. The feeling of helplessness she would experience knowing her fate was out of her hands. She deserved it, and in Austin's fantasy, he was the one who made that happen.

He smiled.

The scotch was working, dulling the pain. With any luck, he would be able to drink the bottle dry while he hid from the aliens in this dingy hole.

"Breaking news," the TV blared, shaking Austin from his drunken wanderings. "We're receiving reports Ghana has just detonated a nuclear device. We go live to our Pentagon correspondent for more."

The bartender was standing a few feet from the dilapidated flat-screen TV, a remote in his hand.

"Hey!" Austin was already beginning to slur. "I came here to get away from that crap!"

The bartender turned his barrel-chested frame in Austin's direction. "I always watch the morning news. You have a problem with it, get out."

Austin shrank back in his stool as the bartender turned the volume up.

"Early this morning, satellites detected a two-kiloton nuclear explosion in Mole National Park, seventy-five miles west of the Ghanian city of Tamale." The correspondent was standing in the Pentagon briefing room, the creases on her pantsuit so sharp that they almost looked like a military uniform. "This makes Ghana the ninety-third nation to become nuclear capable. I was able to sit down with General Fergusson to get his reaction."

The image cut to General Fergusson sitting across from the correspondent in an aircraft hangar, a giant American flag covering the wall behind. His face was long, like an airport control tower, and his irises were so thin it was as if his face were populated by two black holes. When he spoke, he moved his head with a subdued vitality, the small movements enough to make him look like a man twenty years his junior. Yet his face was woven with wrinkles, their edges so sharp they looked like cavalry sabers held aloft for a charge.

"The Corollary"—General Fergusson's voice pulsated like war drums in the distance—"is only as strong as our bravery. And now, through the valiant efforts of our Ghanian brothers, another nation has smashed the atom and added themselves to the nuclear family so that the human race may ensure that humans and aliens shall remain at peace, the threat of a brutal asymmetric war the price to pay should the aliens' reason and comity ever fail."

The poetic confidence, the martial appearance straight out of central casting . . . Austin could understand why he'd become the "Face of Earth's Defense." But it was a false hope, the ballad of a lost cause. It didn't matter how many nukes humanity stashed secretly around the world to fuel a nuclear-armed insurgency. Friday would be the end of all things, of that Austin was sure.

"Thank you," the news anchor said as the shot returned to him in the studio. "In other news, UN Secretary-General Rochana called on China to cease further tests of their orbital nuclear launch platform, reminding the Chinese general secretary that such tests were inconsistent with the Premise, which China affirmed along with other nations in the Helsinki Accords."

It was all the news Austin could take. Grabbing the bottle, he stood up from his stool on his scotch-soft legs and carefully made his way over to the booth at the far end of the bar. The sound of the TV faded to a drone as he nestled himself inside the wooden booth and poured himself another glass.

"Cynthia, it's no use," a man said, his voice cutting into Austin's solitude. "It'll never work."

"Why wait, then?" Cynthia responded, and Austin heard something slam onto the table in the booth next to his. His eyes shot to the right, trying to see, but the walls of the booth were too high. His own private enclave. "Just pull the trigger and end it now, Liam."

"Are you crazy?" Austin heard Liam scrambling. "If the bartender—"

"If *nothing*!" She cut him off. "It won't be long before your boss figures out the money is gone. And if we don't get the last five million for the Coyote, you'll be in jail for embezzlement before the weekend. I'm not raising our daughter on my own. You promised me you'd be there for her."

Austin's ears perked up, and he waited in breathless silence for Liam to respond. When he finally did so, his low voice was full of surrender. "What's the difference?" Liam asked. "We're all dead Friday anyway."

Austin braced himself for Cynthia to respond in a rain of slaps, but she only said, "You and I both know this shitty world is still going to be spinning come Saturday. You're just giving up—taking the coward's way out."

Liam took a defeated breath. "I know you're right, my love, but everyone is trying to get to El Salvador. I had the whole thing planned down to the last penny. But that rat raised his price at the last minute. Now my plan is toast. We'll never cover the shortfall in time."

"There's ten million in that store," she said calmly. "More than enough to cover the gap."

Even in his scotch-infused haze, the words "ten million" traveled through Austin's ears with a supernatural clarity. That was double what he'd managed to save in five months of brutal scrimping. He put the scotch down and leaned closer, an ember of hope sparking to life inside him.

"The store might be a dump, but it has eyes. We won't get ten miles away before the cops nab us. It won't work."

"You're making excuses," Cynthia snapped back. "Cameras don't run without a hard drive."

"Do you know how to take a hard drive out of a computer?"

"You know I don't." There was a brief pause. "Let's just take the whole computer."

"Store computers have a GPS in them now. If we try and move it, the alarm will go off and ping the cops. Then you'll be in jail, too."

"So we smash it." Cynthia sounded desperate. "This is our child we're talking about."

"I know. But if I mess with the wrong part, it pings the cops. The only thing you can take is the hard drive. And I have no idea how to remove one of those without just pulling the whole thing apart. I'm sorry."

Aurelia was there again in Austin's mind, her golden locks, her sapphire eyes. She could be his after all. He grabbed the bottle of scotch and approached the neighboring booth.

"I think I can help," Austin said.

"Were you listening to us?" Liam said, his face compressed in anger.

Austin's eyes widened as the man let go of Cynthia's hand and grabbed a gun from the table.

Even though Liam was seated, Austin could tell he was as tall as Cynthia was short, easily over six feet, and his forearms bulged, so much so they threatened to tear the rolled-up sleeves of his dress shirt. He had straight hair that parted right down the middle and clear green eyes that were at once both sultry and disarming.

Cynthia made for a beautiful terror—sharp brown eyes shining with fury, long brown hair billowing down her shoulders. Not even her pregnant belly could soften her, make her look any less fierce. But now that Austin could see them together, he saw how each's beauty magnified the other, the type of couple whose photo would populate the frames in a frame store.

"My laptop was old even before the Great Panic," Austin quickly explained, "but I've managed to keep the thing chugging along ever since. Gone through four hard drives and two motherboards. I can handle what you need done."

Cynthia looked Austin up and down. "You a cop?"

"No," Austin said, "just desperate."

Her eyes narrowed at him. "How desperate?"

"I'll do what you need for two million."

Cynthia shot Liam a look, letting him know his last excuse was finally exhausted. He held out for a few moments before he nodded, assenting to the ferocious woman's will.

"Go home and sober up. We hit the store tonight." Liam took the bottle of scotch from Austin. "We'll pick you up in the parking lot across the street at midnight."

Austin nodded as his eyes lingered on the million-dollar bottle in Liam's hands. Letting him have it was worth it if it meant he'd get to be with Aurelia.

"Thank you so much, stranger." Cynthia looked at Austin with great affection, like he'd grabbed her stroller before it was run over by an oncoming bus. Then her eyes hardened. "But if you do anything to risk my baby's life, so help me, it'll be the last thing you do."

4

THIRTY-THREE HOURS UNTIL ARRIVAL

Liam's crowbar hovered inches from the door, hesitating.

"Is there an alarm?" Austin asked, eager to get the show on the road.

"No," Cynthia said, her voice low. "The owner practically lives here. He doesn't need one."

"Where is he now?" Austin asked. The question had rolled around in his head ever since he'd left the bar that morning. How did they know the store would be empty, or even what valuables the owner had?

"Who cares?" Liam said dismissively before wedging the crowbar deep into the doorjamb.

The answer didn't sit right with Austin. Sure, during the Great Panic many people had fled to the countryside, but that was mainly to get away from marauding humans. Why, after almost five years of the status quo, would someone make a break for it now? It wasn't like trees and wilderness would offer any protection against an advanced interstellar race.

Before Austin could follow up with another question, Liam said, "We're in!" and entered the shop.

Austin was quick to follow. The predawn October air was cold, and even though they had parked behind the shop, he was still worried someone might spot them.

Cynthia flipped on the light switch, revealing a short hallway. To their right was a small lavatory, and to the left a door marked "Office." Austin moved down the hall toward the beige curtain that separated the back hall from the main shop.

Liam had described the shop as a dump, and, from the outside, it had been hard to deny. The brick facade was crumbling, and there were no windows save for the one foggy pane of glass on the main door. Now that Austin was inside, however, he could see the store was immaculately kept. The cheap linoleum floors were spotless, and each product was placed with its label pointing perfectly outward on the shelves.

"There's one." Liam pointed at the ceiling.

Austin looked up to see a camera aimed at a Fedcoin machine on the counter. The machine would be zero use to them. It had been only five years ago, but it felt like another lifetime when stores had cash in their registers or stashed somewhere in a safe out back. Now, with the government-imposed adoption of the digital dollar, Liam and Cynthia would have to stalk through the store like antiquers at a fair, assessing which goods would fetch the most in resale.

"Go find that computer and make sure the cameras are down," Cynthia instructed Austin before making her way over to the shelf closest to the beverage cooler. Austin nodded but had to catch himself from staring. He couldn't remember the last time he'd seen a pregnant woman, birth rates having fallen off a cliff shortly after the aliens had been detected.

The office in the back was small, no wider than a hallway, and contained only a filing cabinet, a metal desk, and a small cot. Austin slid himself in until he reached the desk lamp at the farthest point from the door and turned it on. In its dim light, he could get a good look at the cot. It had been well used over the years, confirming what Cynthia had said: the owner really did seem to spend all his time here.

A photo on the desk showed an older man kneeling next to a young boy in a Little League uniform. They were both smiling happily, but something about the photo unsettled Austin. The little boy looked familiar, but that made no sense, given the photo must have been taken decades before he was born based on their clothes. He frowned, an uneasy feeling snaking down his spine. Something wasn't right, but he was too far in to back out now. There was only one way out of this mess, one way to get Aurelia, so he refocused on the task at hand.

It took a second to find the computer tower; it was

crammed under the desk, and to Austin's delight, it was made by the same manufacturer as his laptop. Just as he was about to open it up, the sound of a bottle shattering rang in his ears, making him jump.

"Hun, are you okay?" Cynthia called.

"I'm fine, my love," Liam shouted back as he walked by the office door carrying an overflowing crate of liquor bottles. "Just dropped a bottle on my way to the car."

"Take your time. Each one of those bottles is worth a few hundred grand."

All the noise was compounding their chances of being caught. After a few deep breaths, Austin managed to calm himself enough to remove the case of the computer tower. Its side wall was held on by only two screws, so he pulled out the small screwdriver set he'd brought with him and figured out which one was the right size. It took him only a minute to take out both screws, and he quickly found the hard drive, disconnected the cables, and pulled it from its slot, leaving the rest of the computer undisturbed.

Success.

Now it was just a matter of grabbing the goods and getting out of there before anyone was the wiser. He reattached the computer tower case, slid out of the narrow office, and went back into the main part of the store.

"I got it," Austin said, holding up the hard drive.

Cynthia was sitting on a stool behind the cashier's counter, furiously scratching a lottery ticket. "Good," she said without looking up. "Grab the cigarettes."

Austin put the hard drive in his coat pocket and began grabbing cigarette cartons from the shelf, hoping his speedy compliance would expedite things.

"Hey," Liam said from behind Austin, "what are you doing?"

Austin spun around to find Liam holding a wooden crate in his arms.

"I know a guy who'll buy a roll for three hundred grand a pop," Cynthia said as she shifted on the stool to face Liam. "But if there's a winner, I'm keeping it for our daughter. I want her to ride horses."

Liam laughed. "My love, that's crazy. We won't even be here to cash it. Put those down."

Cynthia pointed to the crate in Liam's hand. "What's that?"

"I found this under the cot in the office."

"Pry it open. Let's see what he was hiding under there."

Austin finished gathering the cigarettes, stacking the cartons like firewood in his outstretched arms. While Liam put the crate on the counter, Austin jogged past him to the car out back. Upon returning to the store, he found Liam and Cynthia puzzling over the crate's contents.

"Know anyone who would want these?" Liam asked in a confused voice.

"No." Cynthia tilted her head. "Some rich jerks are throwing an end-of-the-world blowout. They put the word out to keep an eye out for strawberries, but I don't know about this."

"Even with aliens arriving, these rich a-holes always find a way to be on top," Liam seethed.

Austin approached the cashier's counter but kept his distance. He wanted to see what was perplexing them, but not enough to get within arm's length of Liam, whose face was turning flush.

"I know, hun," she said. "I heard they're spending a whole bitcoin on the party, too."

"A whole bitcoin? On *one* party?" Liam grabbed something inside the crate and flung it at the wall, sending it splattering in a pale yellow mélange.

"Those parasites"—he scowled as he grabbed another fruit from inside the crate—"can eat . . ." Liam sent the fruit flying against the wall, where it exploded in a fibrous splash. "Reprocessed grain . . ." Liam took two more fruits from inside the crate and smashed them on the floor. "Like the rest of us!"

The racket was horrible. Austin wanted to flee, but Aurelia drifted back into his mind, and he stayed put.

"Are we going to take those?" Austin asked, hoping to refocus his accomplices on their escape. The injustices of the world could wait, not that they'd matter past Friday anyway.

"It's up to you, hun." Cynthia looked to Liam.

Austin, too, reluctantly turned his gaze toward Liam, who

was still boiling with anger. Instead of answering, Liam closed the distance with Austin and slapped a pear into his hand.

"Smash it," Liam said in a way that was devoid of optionality.

Austin held the pear in his hand, the first one he'd touched in five years. Austin sympathized with the man. Most orchards had been plowed under and turned into grain farms to fill massive grain stores. If the aliens ever poisoned their soil, they would still have food. As a result, fruit was nigh impossible to come by—except for the rich.

He'd forgotten what pears tasted like, and as he stroked the greenish skin, he considered what would happen if he took a quick bite. But with Liam on top of him, he thought better of it. He took a last look at the pear and then sent it sailing across the room into the wall.

"Nice one." Liam patted Austin on the back with his weighty mitt.

Something about just letting that pretty thing fly, seeing it break open as it impacted the wall, felt good. It felt good for the wrongness of it, to break something so valuable just because he could. Grabbing another, Austin let it fly with the enthusiasm of a child, letting out an exultant laugh when it splattered onto the far wall in a brilliant display.

He became lost in the glee of destruction, enjoying the act for itself and not for any gain it would bring him. He let a third one sail.

"Cynthia?"

The voice nearly caused Austin to fall over in shock, all the muscles in his body squeezing at once.

Standing by the curtain that led to the back hallway was an old man with a hospital bracelet on his wrist and a look of unvarnished pain on his face.

"My pears!" the old man cried.

Recognition thundered through Austin's body, and for the second time that day, he thought he was going to be sick. It was the old man from the muster, the one who had taken his phone.

"Liam?" the old man asked, his voice trembling with hurt and betrayal. "Why?"

Liam looked down, unable to meet the man's eyes. Austin had his answer as to how Liam and Cynthia seemed to know so much about the store: they knew this man and knew that something had happened to him. But they didn't seem to know his dedication, that he would get himself to the store straight from the hospital, despite the awful fate that had befallen him at the muster.

The old man then turned his gaze to Austin. "And you?" he said with a mixture of confusion and recognition.

Austin readied himself to speak, to beg for forgiveness, to let the man know that he wouldn't have come if he had known this was his shop, but before he could, there was a loud thud and the old man fell to the ground, a splatter of blood landing on Austin's shirt.

Cynthia appeared behind him, the Fedcoin machine in her hands, blood dripping down its side. She looked toward Liam, who stood there drooping, seemingly too shocked or ashamed to do anything.

The old man flailed on the ground at Cynthia's feet. "Help, please," he said, reaching his hand toward Austin as blood poured down the back of his skull.

Cynthia lifted the Fedcoin machine over her head, her pregnant frame poising itself for another blow.

Austin's gaze darted to Liam's waistband, where the black metal butt of the handgun glinted in the dim light. The same weapon Liam had threatened him with at the bar was mere inches from Austin's grasp, and its owner was so distracted that it could be Austin's if only he'd reach for it. But a paralyzing fear gripped him, rooting him there like a tree.

His heart pounded, echoing in his ears, but he couldn't make himself stop her as she sent the Fedcoin machine flying, its heavy metal case soaring downward until it stopped with a deathly thump, crushing the old man's skull like a pear.

5

TWENTY-NINE HOURS UNTIL ARRIVAL

Black Shirts—the thought of them haunted Austin as he entered his building lobby.

He'd run all through the night to get home as soon as the kind old man had been killed, dashing out of the shop before Liam and Cynthia could stop him, ducking down alleys and over fences to throw them off the trail, ditching the hard drive in a random trash can as the sun peeked over the horizon.

He hadn't made a penny from the robbery, the whole misadventure being for naught. But the money was far from his mind, replaced with thoughts of the Black Shirts coming for him. Homicide was military jurisdiction, which meant they would be after him as soon as the old man was found dead. For all he knew, they were already on the hunt.

Bounding up the building stairwell, he covered the six flights of stairs to his mother's floor in record time. He needed to get out of his blood-splattered shirt, then he could figure out what to do next.

His mind raced as he approached the apartment. His phone had been destroyed at the muster, so he hadn't brought that to the crime scene, and he had no known connections to Liam and Cynthia. Even the Black Shirts wouldn't be able to track him down instantly. But they'd find him eventually; they always found who they were looking for.

"Auss?" Austin was fumbling with his key when his mother opened the door. The air spilled out of his lungs as he rushed to cover the blood on his shirt. "What are you doing?"

"I couldn't sleep," Austin said, pushing into the house and making his way to the kitchen sink.

"You went out?"

"Yeah." Austin turned on the water and began scrubbing his hands raw, his back to her so she couldn't see the stain. "What are you doing up? Don't you usually have breakfast with Mrs. Armstrong on Thursdays?"

"She canceled." His mother came up behind him. "The pharmacy called and told her they finally had her heart medication in stock. She has to run out and pick it up before they're out again."

Austin squeezed dish soap onto his shirt and stretched it until it was under running water.

"Hand that shirt over. I'll wash it."

"No, Mom, I'm fine." Austin couldn't unsee the store: the blood-covered floor, the old man's shattered skull, Cynthia's swollen belly.

What if he had grabbed the gun? Cynthia would have had to stop, and the old man would be alive.

But Liam was much bigger than Austin, and distracted as he was, he would have noticed if Austin had gone for the gun. Austin couldn't have done anything. They would've attacked him, too.

That was why he froze.

They killed the old man, not him.

His mother touched his elbow, shocking him back to reality with a jolt that sent water from the tap flying.

"Auss!" She stepped back. "You splashed water on me!"

Austin clumsily reached for the paper towels and handed his mother a pile.

"What's gotten into you?" she asked. "Where were you just now?"

Backing up against the kitchen counter, he tried to come up with a plausible explanation, but all he could think of was the old man's skull, bleeding on the floor, and the Black Shirts coming after him.

He couldn't have stopped it, not even with the gun. This wasn't on him; it was Cynthia's fault. If it were up to him, he would have made sure the old man had survived. Of course, he would have been turned over to the police, his last chance with Aurelia ruined, but the old man would be alive. Surely he didn't want the old man to die. That couldn't be the reason he'd done nothing. He had to believe that.

A sharp, shooting pain raced through Austin's heart.

"Austin," his mom demanded again. "It's like you're in space. What's going on?"

Austin emerged from his fog enough to realize that, with every passing second, he incriminated himself further.

"Sorry, Mom. I'm just tired," he mumbled as he looked back at her, silently begging that she would accept his throw-away answer. He thought he saw her face soften, the tightness around her eyes fade, but it lasted only a moment.

"What's that?" she said, pointing at his shirt. "Is that blood?"

Austin's head felt light. "It's nothing, Mom."

"Are you hurt?" she pressed.

"Oh, yeah, that's right. I am. I mean, I was. But I'll be fine."

"What happened?" she said, coming closer.

"I cut myself," he said, backing away.

"Where?"

He wrung his brain for answers, desperately trying to find some way out of this mess. "It was really more of a nosebleed," he stammered.

"A nosebleed?"

The futility of the moment bore down on him, and he felt

himself regressing to a child, tears brimming in his eyes. His mother's expression shifted again, her face softening all the way. It was part reflex and part pattern. Austin had learned long ago she couldn't bear to see him distraught, her one true weakness being her son in pain.

"It's okay, Auss," she soothed. "I'll take care of you."

"I'm fine, Mom," Austin choked out.

"Did I tell you I had good news?" she said in an obvious effort to cheer him up.

"No, what is it?" he replied, grabbing her lifeline eagerly.

"It's the government, Auss." Her voice rose an octave. "People are getting nervous about the aliens, so they declared a jubilee."

Austin tilted his head, still processing how lucky he was that his mother had let him off the hook.

"Do you know what this means?" she pressed when he didn't reply.

"No. What?"

"I got a deposit in my Fed account," she said, a genuine smile spreading across her face. "It's equal to two months' rent. Can you believe it? They're doing that for all heads of households in the country—two months of housing costs as a present. Aren't we lucky to be Americans?"

A tingle went down Austin's spine as the significance of the news dawned on him. This was the other side of the digital dollar, the way the government bought loyalty from a scared public with a fire hose of spending, inflation be damned.

"What do you think we should do with it?" she asked.

His mind immediately went to Aurelia, all concern for the Black Shirts gone. He could have her. It would take each and every penny in his mother's account, but two months' rent would be enough.

Swallowing the guilt down, he said, "I don't know, Mom. I'll think about it," and walked past her toward the bathroom.

"Of course," she said as he closed the bathroom door. "I love you, Auss."

An "I love you, too" sat immobile on his lips, so slow to emerge that he had closed the door before he responded.

He would shower off any other traces of blood, and then he would hide out in his room. The Black Shirts would be hunting him, but it was the day before the Arrival and there would be a lot of scores being settled, a pile of bodies for them to work through. It might take them two days to track him down. Swift justice any other time, but not now—Austin would be saved by the end of the world.

6

TWELVE HOURS UNTIL ARRIVAL

Austin held his breath as his mother rolled over with a grunt and pulled the covers over her pale blue nightgown. When he was sure she was asleep, he reached his hand toward the nightstand with a deliberate steadiness, going for his mother's phone, the only thing that stood between him and Aurelia. Just a few swipes, and she would be his.

He tried not to think about the robbery and the fact that it had had been totally unnecessary. If he had just drunk himself stupid at the bar and stumbled home to sleep it off, the money would have arrived in his mother's account—no need to rob a store. The kind old man would be alive, and the specter of the Black Shirts would just be a bad dream. But he couldn't help it; the thought consumed him, spiraling in his brain endlessly, even as his fingers clasped the icy blackness of his mother's phone.

Without warning, the bedroom filled with light.

"This is the Emergency Alert System," the TV blared. "This is not a test. Please stay tuned for a government message."

Austin was used to the television switching on when the government had an announcement, but the timing of this message could not have been worse.

"What?" his mother slurred.

Austin threw himself to the ground, the phone still clutched in his hand, and pressed his body against the side of her bed. All it would take would be for her to roll over and look down at the floor to see her larcenous son.

"The president has asked me to speak with you about the alien mother ship that has settled into a cislunar orbit halfway between Earth and the moon."

From his position on the floor, Austin could see Secretary of Defense Ramirez on the screen. She spoke with a grandmotherly calm, her matronly stillness a sharp contrast to General Fergusson's martial bravado. It was a trait that made her much beloved by the public, who took her mere presence in such a prominent position as proof positive humanity had nothing to fear.

"Smaller crafts have also been detected heading for Earth's atmosphere. They should be here around noon eastern tomorrow. Now, the nice folks at NASA tell me the small crafts are tethered to the mother ship and that they could be the way the aliens land."

The mattress shook as his mother moved to the edge of the bed.

"But we don't know for sure. All we know is that coming down to say hello doesn't violate the Premise. I mean, if I were an alien, I'd be champing at the bit to say hi to all you fine folks in this great country of ours. So let's give them a warm welcome and be on our best behavior because any citizens who show hostility by shooting off a gun or any such thing will be declared an enemy of the state and will be prosecuted to the fullest extent of the law."

Austin shrank himself further as his mother put her feet down on the opposite side of the bed. She walked toward the TV, the remote in her hand, and was pressing the power button to turn the TV off. It didn't matter that Austin had told her a thousand times the power button was disabled during an EAS message.

"Now, you might have heard that the Chinese general secretary has put his nuclear forces on maximum alert. I want to assure you that I've reached out to my colleagues in China to let them know this is against the spirit of the Premise and risks provoking an unnecessary war. Instead, we should be extending a hand of welcome. As my abuela used to say, 'More is achieved by licking than biting.'" The secretary chuckled. "I assure you, it sounds much better in Spanish."

His mother pulled the plug from the wall, and the room was cast into darkness. Austin lay perfectly still as his mother made her way back to bed. He waited there silently, breathing just enough to stay conscious, until he heard her snores fill the emptiness of the room.

From his spot on the floor, he pressed the "on" button on her phone, and the screen burst to life, a wave of blue light washing over his face. He waited to see if the new light in the room would stir her. When it didn't, he proceeded to type in her PIN.

It didn't work.

He typed in the code again.

No luck.

He began to breathe heavier as an overwhelming desire to scream grew within him. He'd come so far, and now a six-digit number blocked his path. He tried one more time but got the same result; he was one failed attempt away from locking the phone for six hours.

She'd used the same pin for years. Now, of all times, she'd changed it. He wondered if she knew he would try to take the money, but he dismissed it outright; she wasn't that perceptive.

In the end, though, it didn't matter. He'd risked every-thing, and it had all been for naught. His dream of Aurelia had been destroyed.

Standing, he looked at his mother, her face pointed at the ceiling, mouth agape. She looked like a hospital patient lying there—sallow, making a racket with every breath.

He was about to put the phone back and go find some leftover hooch to drown his misery when a thought crossed his mind. Lifting the phone, he inched it closer to her face, bracing himself for the second the light would be too much and she would wake up. Just as he was about to pull back and admit defeat, the phone shuddered in his hand and the home screen appeared.

The facial recognition had worked.

He was in.

He scrolled past the EAS message and deftly navigated to her Federal Reserve account, where he saw the meager offering from Uncle Sam. It was a pittance meant to buy the pliability of a frightened public. But it was enough for Austin, enough for him to have Aurelia.

He transferred the entire balance to his account, put her phone back, and went back to his room. After logging on to his laptop, he finally booked his in-person session with Aurelia—emptying his account as well.

He was now ready to face Armageddon, and he would do it in a Washington, DC, hotel room, where he could die in the arms of his beloved. He'd leave first thing.

As he crawled into bed, he tried not to think about how his mother would react when she awoke to find her account emptied and her son gone.

7

FIVE HOURS UNTIL ARRIVAL

Austin hadn't been clothes shopping in years, but after scouring his closet, he found the clubbing shirt he'd worn in his grad school days. Unfortunately, it had been crammed into his closet so tightly it looked like he was wearing a crumpled-up piece of paper. He pulled the fabric on the black button-down shirt taut, but as soon as he let go, the wrinkles reemerged.

He considered ironing the shirt, but thought better of it. He'd never ironed a shirt before, and he was more likely to ruin it than make it look better. Besides, only his mom knew where the iron was stored.

Running his fingers over his face, he carefully checked for any spots he might have missed while shaving. His razor was old, dulled by a year of continuous use, a replacement blade practically impossible to come by. He felt little bumps of scruff here and there, but it was the best he could achieve with the rusty old thing.

He tried to remind himself that he had succeeded; he'd gotten what he'd wanted. He'd braved the surprise muster, survived a botched robbery, and stolen the money off his mother's phone unnoticed, besting every calamity the universe could throw his way. And in the end, he was going to get the girl.

Yet, despite everything, he still felt unhappy.

The feeling worried him. If he wasn't happy with Aurelia, how unhappy would he be without her?

He tried not to linger on the question, the notion of going without her so bleak he didn't even want to entertain it.

Maybe this was all life was, a battle to stay close to zero rather than to fall further and further into negative numbers. If that was all there was to life, then surely he would be better off wrapped up in her purple sheets. A few hours of bliss to mark his final hours.

With a sigh, Austin glanced at himself in the mirror. He was as ready as he ever would be.

He opened the bathroom door and stepped out.

"Austin! You can't go out like that."

His mother stood outside the bathroom door. "Come on, take that shirt off so I can iron it." She reached for his shirt, not even waiting for a response.

"Mom, I'm fine," he said, pushing her hands away. "Why

are you up so early?"

She stopped, her eyes welling up with tears. "I couldn't sleep, Auss. I couldn't sleep a wink."

Austin felt a tightness in his chest. She had found out what he'd done. He should've known better than to try and hide it from her. And now *he* was the one who'd caused *her* pain.

"I tried to put it out of my mind, but it just kept swirling, flying around my brain like a bat trapped in an attic."

She was holding her head now, the strain on her forehead showing. He was waiting for the crescendo where she told him how disappointed she was, how she was losing sleep because of what her boy had done to her.

"What do they want? Why are they coming? What will happen to us?"

She pulled her hands away to reveal the panic in her wide eyes. Austin realized he was wrong: it wasn't the money that had her upset but the ever-present dread of the Arrival, the existential angst of the ticking clock. He had always assumed she was just too simpleminded to let it get to her, that she'd managed to distract herself with the banality of daily life. Now he could see it had been eating away at her for years, and like Mount Vesuvius, the pressure was being released in one cataclysmic burst.

"After your father left, I swore I would protect you, but I don't know if I can, Auss."

She reached back, straining for the wall, her knees buckling. Austin darted toward her, catching her before she hit the floor.

"Oh Auss. I'm sorry, I just . . ."

"Shhh, it's okay, Mom. I've got you."

If she had been a much larger woman, he would have had to lower her to the ground, as her legs were barely holding up any weight, but he managed to walk her the few steps from the hallway to the living room and then maneuver her into her usual sitting position on the sofa.

"I'm going to get you some water."

"No, just stay here with me."

He took a seat on the couch next to her as she clutched his hand.

"I didn't know you were so scared about the Arrival, Mom. You never talked about it."

The morning sun was coming in the window now, making her tear-streaked face shiny. She sniffed deeply before answering him.

"I didn't want you to worry about me. I know what these aliens took from you." The tenderness in her voice made his heart feel tighter. "You were going to make such a great professor. You were so close." She was looking at him now, regret etching lines of sorrow on her face—not regret that he was her son, but that she couldn't do more for him. "Did you know Dean Edwards told me the spoken-Latin program you started was one of the most impressive things he'd ever seen in all his years in academics? You were a shoo-in for the next faculty opening. He told me that at the Classics Department Christmas party you brought me to a few months before the Great Panic."

She reached for a box of tissues on the end table and dabbed her eyes.

"Then the aliens showed up, and you had to move back in here with me when the university cut your department. I know how much that hurt you, Auss. I knew how much pain you were in. And I didn't want you to have to deal with a wreck of a mom as well."

Austin put his other hand on top of hers. He had brought so much unhappiness into the house when he'd moved in, and he knew it. Broke, no prospects, abandoned by what few friends he'd had. He was like a dark cloud in her life, constantly avoiding her so he could wallow in front of his laptop to leer at women who didn't even know he existed.

"I'm scared," she said. "I know the government says the aliens would have already destroyed us by now if that's what they wanted to do, but I can't help it. I just keep wondering why they would come all this way to Earth. Then I get this terrible feeling I'm going to lose you." She grabbed a few more tissues and blew her nose. "Then I'll be alone. I don't know what I'll do then."

It had been just him and his mom for as long as he could remember, his dad having left before Austin was old enough to talk. The last thing she had in this world was him, and he was about to leave her to face the Arrival alone.

"You're probably better off without me," he said quietly, his voice trailing off as the truth finally slipped out.

"Oh, Auss! Never say that! You're my whole world. I love you so much!"

Austin lowered his head, unable to meet her gaze. "You wouldn't say that if you knew what I did."

She grabbed his face and turned it toward her. "No, never, Austin. I mean it. You can't do anything that will make me stop loving you. Not even emptying my bank account."

A wave of dizziness swept over him. She'd known what he was up to this whole time, and even then, she hadn't brought it up until he did.

"How can you say that? I betrayed you, Mom."

"I know you did, but I forgive you." She had stopped crying, her mouth upturned in a soft smile.

"How can you do that? You gave me everything. And still I wanted more."

Her smile only grew, radiating a warmth he felt he didn't deserve. "It's easy, Auss. Love. It's not just some sentiment. It's the greatest thing in the universe." She leaned her head on his shoulder. "I know you think I'm being cheesy, but it's true. I love you more than life itself. And I hope with all my heart you'll come to understand love like that someday."

They sat in silence, Austin's hand resting on his mother's.

The pain in his heart was still sharp, but it was dulling ever so slightly. Their quiet togetherness was interrupted by the chime of the wall clock, the sound a reminder that Austin had an appointment to keep. Austin's mom stood up and started smoothing out her pale blue nightgown.

"Now give me that shirt. You can't go out looking like that."

Austin looked up at her, wondering if she had any idea where he was going, that he was about to leave her—the woman who clearly loved him more than anything else in this world—to be with a woman who, in exchange for a small fortune, would love him for only a few hours.

Perhaps, just like with the money, she *did* know.

She was clearly more perceptive than he gave her credit for. She must have noticed him on his phone, looking at Aurelia's profile. Yet here she was, willing to do anything for him despite all the pain he caused her.

Running a hand through his hair, he let out a breath. "It's okay, Mom. I'm not going anywhere."

She tilted her head. "I'll be fine."

"No, really, Mom. I'm staying here with you."

Her smile grew wide as if he had said the most touching thing in the world. Without words, she leaned over and hugged him. She squeezed tight, as though if she loosened her grip he would float away. This time he didn't play any games. He embraced her as well. He couldn't remember the last time he'd hugged her like that.

"Thanks, Auss," she said, pulling away from him. "Now hand over that shirt. I can't stand looking at those wrinkles."

Austin began to protest, but he was cut off by the television in the living room snapping on.

"This is the Emergency Alert System. Alien crafts have entered Earth's atmosphere," the television blared. "Stand by for an important message."

8

TEN MINUTES UNTIL ARRIVAL

Austin's finger settled on a photo of his father. "Do you hate him for leaving us, Mom?" he asked.

Her smile faded.

They'd been having such a good time all morning—ignoring the TV, flipping through old photo albums, telling stories about happier days; there were even moments when the two of them lost themselves completely, forgetting that they were in their living room waiting for the apocalypse—but Austin knew so little about his mom's relationship with his father and this was his last chance to ask.

"No." She took the photo album and put it on her lap. "Hate just eats you up inside. It doesn't do any good to hold on to it." She chewed her cheek. "Though, sometimes, I wonder what it would have been like for you if you'd had a father around."

Austin touched his mother's hand. "You were a good role model, Mom."

"I did my best." She sighed. "But a mother can only do so much."

She turned the page and put her finger on another photo. "This was your first trip to Ocean City. All you wanted to do was make sand castles. I couldn't even get you in the water."

Taking the hint, Austin resumed the pose of the dutiful son. He had more questions about his dad, but there was no sense in picking at old wounds, not when they were trying to squeeze as much happiness as they could out of the little time that remained.

"Remember the cotton candy, Auss?" His mother's eyes were distant, back in a memory. "You couldn't get eno—"

A grinding noise interrupted her thought.

Austin shot up from the couch, straining the buttons on his newly ironed shirt.

"It's the EAS on your phone," Austin said, once he realized the origin of the noise. "I'll shut it off."

His mother's lips quivered. They'd both agreed not to look at any news. They wanted to be present, to enjoy each other's company, not fixate on the end. But their apartment was like a deep-sea submersible plunging into the depths, the pressure of the outside events building until they inevitably came pouring in.

"Austin," his mother said as he picked up the phone. "Just tell me."

Austin turned the phone off, marveling at how perceptive his mother was. He'd barely glanced at the alert.

"There's a craft over DC," he said. "That's all I saw."

Closing the photo album and placing it on the couch, she said, "Is there any chance the Premise, the Corollary—all the stuff the government says—is true? That we're going to be okay?"

Austin opened his mouth, but no words came. Even though his urge to comfort her was strong, he didn't want to lie and tell her there was a chance when he was sure there wasn't.

Instead, he shrugged helplessly. "Whatever happens, we'll be together."

She smiled back, the always-grateful recipient of even the most trivial gifts he gave her.

"Do you want something to eat?" Austin asked, trying to change the subject.

As his mother opened her mouth to answer, a deafening wail assaulted their ears, causing Austin to double over in shock. It was as though an oil tanker had blown its blast signal right into their living room.

"Austin!" his mom shouted after the horn stopped. "What was that?"

Austin rushed to the window and looked out. He couldn't

see anything but the cloudy noon sky above and the cracked asphalt of the street below. It was like the horn had come from the air itself, every molecule vibrating in unison.

"Was it them? Was it the aliens?" His mother's voice trembled.

Closing the shades halfway, Austin returned to the couch, taking her hand in his own. "I don't know."

A few seconds later, their apartment filled with sound again. Austin pulled his mother to him and hugged her, his muscles tense. His grip loosened, however, when the next sound to fill the apartment was spoken words.

Pater noster, qui es in caelis, sanctificetur nomen tuum.

"Austin, what is that?" his mother hollered over the noise.

"It's . . . Latin," he said, convinced his mind was playing tricks on him. The look of confusion on his mother's face was a perfect reflection of his own.

"It is?" she said as the sound stopped. "What did it say?"

Austin paused, unsure if he was imagining things. "'Our Father,'" he said, "'who art in Heaven, hallowed be Thy name.'"

"You're praying, Auss? That means this is it, doesn't it?" Tears flooded out of his mother's eyes. "I love you. I love you so much. I love you more than anything else in the world."

"No, Mom. I'm not praying," he said. "I'm translating. That sound was the Lord's Prayer—in Latin."

Her mouth twisted. "The last church around here closed two years ago. And none of them ever had loudspeakers that could do something like that."

"I think . . ." he replied. "I think it's the aliens."

Her face tensed, a dark thought seemingly having entered her mind. "Your great-uncle Lewis liked to pour cola on the ground. The ants would swarm, thinking they'd hit a bonanza. That's when he'd pull out the magnifying glass." She looked him up and down. "They couldn't be doing that, could they?"

Austin's stomach turned as he pictured it: his great-uncle laughing as he rained fiery destruction on the unsuspecting ants, who, only minutes earlier, had been graced with a sugary wind-fall. Now it was the aliens' turn to mock, to fill humanity with the false sense of security of the Lord's Prayer—crazy creeds the gullible clung to—right before they finished them off.

Austin hesitated as his mother nudged him for an answer. She wanted him to tell her that the aliens weren't a bunch of psychopaths out on an interstellar joyride, that they weren't going to get their jollies by taunting humanity before they destroyed them, that everything was going to be okay, but he couldn't; he was through lying to her.

"I'm sorry," he said, bringing her close.

They sat in silence, the only noise the sound of his mother's stifled weeping. He wondered when the blackness of death would overtake him. Would he feel anything? Would he know he was dead? Or would it be as inaccessible as the time before he was born? He hoped so. Life was so full of pain, and he saw the kind old man every time he closed his eyes. He'd be glad to be rid of that image, glad for the nothingness of it all.

The horn sounded again, and Austin covered his ears, his hands doing very little good. Then the living room window went dark. It was like the daylight was gone, instantly replaced by night. It made the apartment so dim that Austin could barely see save for the trickle of light coming from the microwave clock.

"Austin! This is it!" his mom shouted in the darkness. "I love you!"

"I love you, too!" He held his mother tight, bracing himself for the end.

A few moments passed by, and, to his surprise, the apartment became bright again, daytime reemerging as quickly as it had disappeared.

"Was that it?" she asked. "Is it over?"

Austin's mind was running too fast to answer. He thought about plugging in the TV to check the news, but he didn't want to subject his mother to images of worldwide destruction before she died. Instead, he went back to the window. She followed, seemingly too afraid to be even a few feet away from him. They approached the window and leaned over to see what was going on outside.

Nothing.

No alien troops, no massive conflagrations in the distance.

Just a cloudy Virginia day.

They were still bent over looking when the horn sounded

again, rattling Austin's insides as if he were next to an amplifier at a concert. He covered his ears and looked up to the sky. The clouds turned black as nightfall descended again, no time for his eyes to adjust.

By pure reflex, they both bolted away from the window. Austin reached out in the gloom and steadied himself on the end table near the sofa, holding himself there, waiting for his eyes to adjust, but his mother cried out and hit the floor with a thud.

"Mom!" he yelled.

When she didn't reply, he frantically searched through the darkness, trying to feel for her, hold her again so that she would not die alone.

After a moment, his hand touched a waft of her thin hair. He followed her hair up to her scalp, and there he felt an unmistakable warm and runny liquid: blood.

9

THEY'VE ARRIVED

M r. Washington pounded on the door. "Austin! Are you in there?"

Austin was sitting on the floor with his mother's head in his arms. Every time he removed his hand, blood leaked from the wound.

"Help!" he shouted back, his heart racing in a panic. "I need help in here!"

"Okay, I'm coming in! I'm using my spare key." Within seconds, Mr. Washington was barging into the front hallway dressed in his militia clothes, green canvas cargo pants with a green button-down shirt. "Austin, what did they say?"

"Get Mrs. Armstrong!" Austin said.

Mr. Washington entered the living room, looking at Austin

and his mother in confusion.

"Tell her to bring her nurse supplies," Austin added urgently. "Go quick!"

His mother stirred. "Harold?" she asked in a foggy voice.

A wave of relief crested over Austin. He had no idea how hard she'd hit her head, but he took it as a good sign that she was recognizing people. If he could just get the wound closed, she would be in a much better place. Unfortunately, despite Mr. Washington's quick entry, he was still immobile.

"Monica?" Mr. Washington asked. "What happened?"

"She fell when the sky went dark," Austin said, trying to maintain a semblance of patience. "Now can you please go get Mrs. Armstrong?"

"Okay." Mr. Washington nodded, but remained still. "First, can you tell me what they said?"

"What *who* said?" Austin asked through gritted teeth.

"The robot. What did it say to the pope?"

He searched Mr. Washington's face, trying to detect if this was some sort of poorly conceived joke, but his expression was earnest. "I don't know what you're talking about," Austin said, barely managing to suppress his irritation. "Please, just get help for my mother. She's hurt bad."

"Haven't you been watching the news?" Mr. Washington grabbed the remote from the coffee table. "You must be the only two people in the world who haven't seen it." He attempted to turn on the TV.

"It's unplugged," Austin said, too dumbfounded at Mr. Washington's seeming lack of interest in his injured mother to tell him off.

Mr. Washington shot Austin a puzzled look, but rather than ask any questions, he went over and plugged in the TV. The screen burst alive with a newscast.

"That's where they came out." Mr. Washington pointed to a live feed of Saint Peter's Square in Rome.

A silver cylinder occupied the entirety of the eastern portion of the square. It was unlike anything Austin had ever seen before. Smooth as glass and rising into the sky and out of the camera's frame, it dwarfed all the buildings around it, including the structure Austin recognized as Saint Peter's Basilica.

"The wall just folded away," Mr. Washington said. "There wasn't a hinge or a crack or anything. One second a solid wall, the next a giant hole where the alien came out. Never seen anything like it."

"An alien came out?" Austin said, scanning the screen.

Despite being as smooth as a polished mirror, the cylinder did not reflect any of its surroundings.

"Uh-huh. And you should see the ship the tower came down from," Mr. Washington said, marveling at the live feed. "It must be a mile wide if it's a foot. It's made from the same material as that cylinder. It just dangles there in the sky over Rome, nothing more than a tether back to the mother ship to keep it from crashing into the ground. It looks like a giant Hershey's Kiss suspended up in midair. These aliens have them over twelve cities around the world, including right up the road in DC!"

Austin noticed the pope and several clerics sitting at an altar table on the steps of Saint Peter's Basilica. Before he could ask Mr. Washington what the pope had to do with any of this, his mother stirred in his arms.

"Are we under attack?" she asked weakly.

Her question pulled Austin's attention back to the task at hand.

"Can you go get Mrs. Armstrong, please?" Austin pleaded. "This cut won't stop bleeding."

"But . . ." Mr. Washington protested.

"Fine," Austin huffed, out of patience. "Stay here and hold my mom. I'll go get her." Before he could get up, though, Mr. Armstrong charged through the apartment door.

"Austin . . ." Mr. Armstrong said, breathless. "What did the robot say?"

"Mr. Armstrong, where's your wife?" Austin said. "My mom's hurt."

"Monica?" Mr. Armstrong gestured toward Austin's mom on the living room floor. "Is she okay?"

"She fell when everything went dark," Austin said. "Where's your wife?"

"She's down pulling the car around," Mr. Armstrong said,

still breathing heavily. "She wants to make a run for it. She thinks Pope Stephen killed the alien. I can't convince her otherwise. I thought you might be able to tell me what the robot said."

"A robot? What are all of you talking about?" Austin demanded.

"The robot spoke Latin, Austin." Mr. Washington knelt on the floor and took one of his mother's hands in his own. "The news said they're having trouble finding someone who can interpret spoken Latin. Isn't that your whole thing? Speaking it?"

Austin couldn't believe it: the aliens were here and they spoke Latin. The prayer they broadcast was not a one-off. "If you want me to translate, I need to hear what they said."

"We'll have to wait for the news to do a replay." Mr. Washington squinted at the TV in disapproval. "Right now, they're just showing the live feed of the square."

"You're such an old man, Harold." Mr. Armstrong pulled out his phone. "It's already on the internet."

Mr. Armstrong propped his pudgy frame on the floor next to Austin, resting his back on the coffee table. The four of them leaned in close and trained their eyes on Mr. Armstrong's phone.

For the first time, Austin laid eyes on one of the creatures that had instilled terror on Earth for the past five years.

It was a long and grotesque thing, over forty feet tall even with its three legs bent and curled backward, as if posed in a kneel. It knelt a few dozen yards in front of Pope Stephen, who was holding a golden chalice in the air. As the pope mouthed some words, the whole sky went dark, save for the altar, which was bathed in a light so bright that Austin thought it would sear the phone's screen.

"We went dark at the same time here in Virginia," Mr. Armstrong said. "According to the news, it happened each time the pope did that thing Catholics do with the bread and the wine."

Austin could barely hear him; his attention was entirely focused on the alien. The three long, slender legs met at a torso surrounded by a skirt of tentacles that seemed to hide the part where the genitalia would be on a human. Each tentacle wriggled independently, like the chaotic motion of a centipede's legs—it was disgusting, but Austin couldn't look away.

Directly above the skirt of tentacles were two eyes, and midway around the circumference of its torso were two holes where human ears would be. Austin concluded that this must be the alien's face. Which was strange because the torso continued upward for another fifteen feet, meaning the face was in the center of the body's mass, not at the top like a human's.

"How much longer until the robot?" Austin asked.

"Just a little bit longer," Mr. Washington replied.

"People on the internet are calling them 'Pilgrims,'" Mr. Armstrong said. "They traveled across the whole galaxy just to go to church."

"What a name." Mr. Washington laughed. "No way I can think of turkey and the Mayflower when I hear that word now."

Two long, slender arms jutted out abruptly from the alien's side near the top of the torso. They were so thin compared to its bulbous body that they looked like the twig arms of a snowman. Each arm terminated in a hand made up of three fingers. Its skin was a pale white with gray shapes that appeared and disappeared in some sort of pattern.

The creature was hideous, so unlike man, but Austin was mesmerized, his brain filling with questions. What kind of world would create these creatures? How had they managed to journey across the stars?

"Here it comes," Mr. Armstrong said.

The alien began to writhe, its entire body moving in violent jerks. It fell to the ground in a heap as if it were having a seizure.

"What happened?" Austin asked, his brow furrowing. "Why is it seizing like that?"

"We don't know," Mr. Washington said. "It looks sick, right?"

In an instant, the wall to the cylinder folded open and seven robots came charging out. The robots were human-sized, about six feet tall and made from the same shiny metal as the cylinder. They were bipedal, with two jointless legs that connected to a shiny metal torso, elliptical in shape and devoid of grooves or features. The torso had two proportionate arms sticking out that terminated in a hand with five fingers. At the top of the torso was a faceless glass dome that glowed a deep crimson, casting a red shade on the darkened ground of the square as dusk set in over Rome. The robots moved rapidly across the square, so gracefully it looked like they glided rather than walked.

Six of the robots grabbed the alien, taking it back to the cylinder, while the seventh robot walked up to the altar and knelt, its domed head bent low.

"Beatissime Pater."

Austin was taken aback by the deep bass of the voice, which sounded pristine even on the phone's tiny speakers.

"Da veniam petentibus. Missa dicta hic maneas quaeso, mox redibo."

"How is the sound so good on this video?" Austin asked as he watched the robot glide back to the cylinder and disappear inside.

"Are you kidding?" Mr. Armstrong said. "Every microphone in Rome is pointed at those things right now!"

"What did it say?" Austin's mom asked faintly, surprising him.

"It said 'Holy Father, our most humble apologies. Please wait here after the Mass, I will return very soon.'"

"I told her!" Mr. Armstrong exclaimed. "I told her the robot didn't accuse the pope of killing the alien."

"Okay, that's great," Austin said as his mother stirred in his arms. "Now can you please go get your wife so she can help my mom? We could really use a nurse's help here."

His plea finally seemed to get through to Mr. Armstrong, who got up, putting so much of his generous weight on the coffee table Austin feared it would give way.

"That wife of his," Mr. Washington said as Mr. Armstrong exited through the apartment door, "she scares so easy. I tried to tell her that everything would be all right, that the world wasn't coming to an end today. But she just wouldn't hear it."

As Mr. Washington's words sank in, a cold sweat pooled on Austin's back.

The Black Shirts.

They would be coming for him, the end of the world no reprieve.

"Monica!" Mrs. Armstrong called from the doorway, her nurse's kit in hand. "Oh, Monica, what happened?"

"She fell when the light went out," Mr. Washington explained. "When Pope Stephen did the bread and wine thing at the Mass."

Mrs. Armstrong gently nudged Austin aside and took over supporting his mother's head. She pulled out a pair of nitrile gloves from her bag and began dabbing the wound with hydrogen peroxide as her husband hobbled back into the apartment.

Dazed, Austin retreated to the sofa to get out of the way.

"Why is it taking so long for the news to translate, Austin?" Mr. Armstrong huffed as he leaned against the wall.

Austin stared. He'd counted on annihilation, almost like

a fantasy, the only way he'd escape the consequences of his crimes.

"Austin?" Mr. Washington prodded. "What's wrong with you?"

"What?" Austin asked.

"The news," Mr. Armstrong said. "You translated the Latin instantly. Why can't they do that?"

Austin took a breath, trying to compose himself. "Most Latin scholars only ever learn to translate the language in its written form. Speaking is a whole other skill. I guess the news just doesn't have someone who can do it."

"You should work for the news, Austin," Mr. Washington said excitedly. "I bet they'd pay you a lot."

The sentiment hit Austin like a grenade. He finally had a marketable skill, but it wouldn't do him any good now.

"Look!" Mr. Armstrong pointed to the live feed on the television.

A robot had emerged from the cylinder and was approaching Pope Stephen, who was still at the altar. The robot kneeled, its domed head bowed low. "Sancte Pater, Vicarius Christi," the robot said in its deep bass voice, "Pricipis Apostolorum Successor, Pontifex Supremus Ecclesiae Catholicae, humiliter te oramus ut nobis audientiam concedas, ne iter nostrum, trans immane barathrum spatii et temporis frustra sit."

"Austin, help us out," Mr. Washington said.

Austin cleared his throat and began translating in real

time. "'Holy Father, Vicar of Christ, Successor of the Prince of Apostles, Supreme Pontiff of the Universal Church, we humbly beseech you for an audience so that our journey across the vast chasm of space-time may not have been in vain.'"

"My goodness, Austin," Mrs. Armstrong breathed. "You're amazing."

With the aid of two clerics, Pope Stephen rose from his seated position. Once standing, he replied as loudly as his raspy voice could, "Fratres in Christo . . ."

"'Brothers in Christ,'" Austin translated. "'In the words of our Savior, "ask, and it will be given to you; search, and you will find; knock, and the door will be opened to you."'"

The robot bowed even lower, touching its domed head to the ground, and spoke. "'Blessed Father,'" Austin translated. "'Whatever is said unto me shall be heard by our brothers, for I am their emissary built specially for this world.'"

"I get it now," Mr. Washington said, his voice filled with wonder. "The robot, it's like some sort of diplomat."

"Oh, that's good," Mr. Armstrong said. "I'm going to post that on the news forums."

Pope Stephen nodded and turned, shuffling up the steps into the Basilica, the robot following behind.

"Austin, it sounds like poetry when you translate," Mrs. Armstrong said. "It's wonderful."

"What does this all mean?" Mr. Washington asked no one in particular. "The aliens came to see the pope?"

"It's in the name, Harold: they're Pilgrims," Mr. Armstrong replied.

"Does that mean we're safe?" Austin's mom asked softly, but with an unmistakable glimmer of hope.

"I think so, Monica," Mrs. Armstrong said, letting out an audible sigh of relief. "We're all going to be okay after all."

There was crash at the doorway.

"Austin DeSantis!" a voice bellowed, the words as coarse as bark. Two Black Shirts stood in the front hallway, rifles in hand.

"What's the meaning of this?" Mr. Washington approached them. "We were just watching—"

The Black Shirts stormed into the living room, shoving Mr. Washington out of their way. Hurtling backward, he raised his old arms to steady himself but, instead, stumbled into the TV before collapsing to the floor in a heap. A final glimpse of the Vatican flickered on the screen as the TV teetered back and forth and then fell from the stand, crashing down on top of him.

"Harold!" Mrs. Armstrong yelled.

The two Black Shirts grabbed Austin, dragging him off the couch and slamming his face down onto the coffee table, perilously close to Mrs. Armstrong, who was still tending to his wounded mother.

"Austin!" his mother screeched.

Pulling his arms behind his back, the Black Shirts

restrained Austin with zip ties so tight he thought they would sever his hands. His arms secured, they hauled him to his feet and toward the exit, elbowing Mr. Armstrong as they pressed by.

Before they took him through the door, Austin glanced back and caught a glimpse of his mother: a look of pure anguish was on her face, her worst fear having come to pass.

PART II

10

Help me, someone," a man nearby said, his voice high like a child's, even though his gray hair betrayed him. "I'm not supposed to be here."

Austin wasn't supposed to be here, either.

He was supposed to be dead.

Killed in a world-ending fireball.

Instead, he was in a waking nightmare, kneeling on the floor of a disused warehouse, with his arms bound behind his back, a solitary light overhead to illuminate him and the twenty other similarly restrained wretches kneeling all around him. The light was an island of brightness in the vast emptiness of the warehouse, the rest of the cavernous space drenched in impenetrable shadow. In those shadows lurked the Black Shirts, the only warning of their approach the clomp of their boots.

"I was just trying to get some noodles," the man blubbered. "He was dead when I got there. I tried to tell them . . ."

Austin shifted his knees, but they cried out in pain at the slightest movement; there was no comfortable position on the cold and dirty floor.

"I was hungry. That's the only reason I was at the restaurant." A fresh round of tears streamed down the man's face. "I don't even know who he was."

"Shut up," a long-haired prisoner kneeling behind the crying man whispered. "You'll bring on the Black Shirts."

The man continued to sob. "Why won't they listen? I told them it wasn't me."

"Shut up."

"I'm a good man. I've never hurt anyone."

"*Shut up!*" The long-haired prisoner's voice strained above a whisper, a reeking desperation in his tone.

"I'm not supposed to be here . . ."

"Psst, hey." The prisoner to the right of the crying man was whispering now. He looked different from the others; while everyone else wore crumpled street clothes, he wore a well-pressed suit.

"The Black Shirts like to torture criers," the well-dressed man said into the crying man's ear. "Especially ones who say they're innocent. They take it as an insult, like you think they don't know how to do their job."

The crying man fell silent, his face turning an ashen white.

Austin felt his skin crawl as images of torture filled his mind. He wanted to run, sprint into the darkness, anything to get out of this place.

The clomp of boots filled the air, and five figures appeared at the boundary of the darkness. The center figure stepped into the light, revealing himself as a Black Shirt with a set of sergeant's stripes on his left arm. "Process them," he said.

Four more emerged from the darkness and descended upon the prisoners, rousing them to their feet. They formed the prisoners into a line, kneeling them side by side. Austin was placed at the leftmost extreme of the line. At the other extreme was the crying man.

"Mr. Hung Nguyen," the sergeant said as he and two other Black Shirts moved behind the crying man. "You are found guilty of violating the Manpower Readiness Act by means of murdering a Mr. Quang Ngo."

"It wasn't me!"

"Quiet!" The butt of a rifle came crashing down on Mr. Nguyen's head, and he collapsed in a pile on the ground. "Pursuant to wartime protocols," the sergeant continued, "you will face summary execution."

The two Black Shirts propped Mr. Nguyen back up onto his knees. Despite the blow, he was still conscious, his eyes glassy as one of the Black Shirts put a black hood over his head. Without any ceremony, a shot rang out, the burst echoing off the unseen warehouse walls. Mr. Nguyen fell to the ground, blood leaking from the new hole in the hood.

A dizziness overcame Austin, as if reality itself were slipping from his grasp. It had been so quick, so unremarkable. No time to process the impending darkness before the bullet did its job.

The sergeant moved to the next person in line. "Mr. Trent Samuels. You are found guilty of violating the Manpower Readiness Act by means of murdering Ms. Olivia Hernandez."

"I called it off!" Mr. Samuels protested. "I told the guy not to kill that cheating whore!"

"Pursuant to wartime protocols," the sergeant continued as though the man hadn't spoken, "you will face summary execution." Another Black Shirt shoved a hood over Mr. Samuels's head.

Austin saw the flash, and a ringing filled his ears. This was it: the comeuppance that only a few hours ago he was sure he'd never have to face.

"Mr. Albert Lawson. You are found guilty of—"

Before the sergeant could finish, the well-dressed prisoner leapt to his feet from a spot in the center of the line and made a break for the darkness.

"Stop him!" the sergeant yelled.

The Black Shirts leveled their rifles, but before they could get off a round, the man was lost in the murk. The Black Shirts held their fire, seemingly unwilling to shoot without their target in sight.

The idea spread among the condemned men like a wildfire. Mr. Lawson was the first to try and follow the well-dressed man's lead, but his knees failed him as he tried to stand, and he fell face-first onto the concrete floor—a hail of lead from the now-alert Black Shirts there to greet him. His death was not enough to stop the rest of the line, however, and the men scattered like a flock of pigeons chased by a dog.

Austin shut his eyes as the fleeing bodies fell around him, the ring of the rifle bursts assaulting his ears. By instinct, he made himself small, falling forward onto the ground rather than trying to make a break for it. He lay there till silence overcame the room and only opened his eyes when a Black Shirt hoisted him back up onto his knees. The floor was covered in bodies, blood trickling toward Austin and pooling against his knees.

"Mr. Kelly," the sergeant said, standing behind the only other prisoner who hadn't made a break for it. "You are found guilty of violating the Manpower Readiness Act by means of murdering Mr. Marshal Reynolds."

Not wanting to see any more bloodshed, Austin kept his gaze forward into the darkness. He frowned slightly as he saw new figures standing there, their silhouettes motionless right at the boundary of the light.

"Pursuant to wartime protocols, you will face summary execution."

The single shot rang out, well-mannered and orderly compared to the barrage moments before. Its effect was just as reliable, though, and the prisoner flopped forward, the black hood still over his head.

This was it. Austin's turn.

Fear gripped him like a vice as the Black Shirt moved behind him. He held his breath, awaiting the sentencing—his last opportunity to learn the name of the kind old man whose death had led him to this place.

"Mr. Austin DeSantis," the sergeant said. "You are found guilty of violating the Manpower Readiness Act by means of murdering—"

"Stop," a voice said from the darkness.

Austin exhaled the breath he'd been holding, feeling a mixture of relief and lingering dread. With a frown, he realized he still didn't know the kind old man's name.

An officer emerged into the light, looking a man apart in his olive green uniform and balaclava-free face. He marched forward and held up a computer tablet in front of Austin. "Translate," he ordered.

On the screen was a paused video of a woman standing at a podium with the White House seal emblazoned on the front.

"Translate?" Austin's voice was as worn as a stripped screw.

"Into Latin." The officer hit play.

The president has issued a statement concerning the reports of an alien superweapon coming out of China.

Not understanding what was happening, Austin looked on dumbly.

"Let's go!" the officer snapped. "Simultaneous!"

Base instinct took over, and Austin's mind fumbled to find the Latin.

"'Princeps publice . . .'"

Austin struggled to conjure the words, the Latin knowledge he'd spent so many years cultivating buried underneath a thick layer of fear.

"Faster!" the officer barked.

"'De fama teli terribilissimi alienigenarum locutus est,' Austin spat. "Quod e Sinarum regno profectum esse dicitur.'"

US intelligence has detected no signals that indicate the alien mother ship orbiting Earth contains a planet-killing device.

He was messing up his declensions, confusing his vocab, but he had no choice but to speed on.

"'Speculatores Civitatum Foederatarum nulla signa reppererunt navis aeriae alienigenarum principalis Orbem Terrarum circumvolantis quae machinam continet ruinam planetae nostrae minitantem.'"

The president has reached out to the Chinese general secretary and implored him to stand down his nation's orbital nuclear launch platforms and return them to normal readiness, as failure to do so could compromise the Premise and launch humanity into an unwanted war.

A scream broke Austin's concentration. The well-dressed man was hurled back into the light by two Black Shirts, a foot-long gash carved across his belly, intestines protruding out. Austin's mind went blank as he watched blood sputter from the well-dressed man's mouth. By the time he looked back at the tablet, Austin could see the officer's eyes narrow.

"'Princeps ducem Sinarum,'" Austin strained, forcing himself to focus. "'Obsecravit ut omnes suggestus telis nuclearibus orbitantibus emittendis accommodatos pro tempore exarmet et in solita promptitudine retineat, quod nisi faciat periculum sit ne foedere fracto omne genus humanum invitum bellum capessat.'"

The video ended, and the officer peered toward the tall silhouette that had been looming in the darkness throughout the examination. A coldness welled up from deep inside Austin as he agonized over his translation. He knew he'd flubbed "orbital nuclear launch platforms" and that his syntax was second-rate, but all that disappeared in an instant.

Out from the shadow stepped General Fergusson, his coarse face unmistakable. Austin scanned the general's expression, searching for even the slightest hint of satisfaction.

But before he could discern anything, darkness overtook him. The Black Shirts had slammed a hood over his head—the rough face of the general the last thing he would ever see.

11

The harsh glare of fluorescent light flooded Austin's eyes. He'd been under the hood for hours, his captors giving him no explanation as they moved him about. With each passing second, he was sure a bullet would splatter his brains all over the inside of his veil.

But he was still alive, and as his vision came into focus, he realized he was sitting in a classroom, facing a chalkboard, a large crucifix attached to the wall. His arms were bound behind his back. The Black Shirts, who had duct-taped his ankles to the chair, stood at his side as he tried to get his bearings. To his right was a door that presumably led out to a hallway. To his left, on the opposite wall, were windows where weak daylight pushed against the closed blinds. The classroom was empty save for the solitary chair he'd been taped to and a small wooden teacher's desk at the front. On the desk was a crest that read "Saint John's College High School." He realized exactly where he was: Washington, DC.

His last visit had been a year before the Great Panic. The Saint John's principal had tried to recruit Austin to come teach Latin full-time, offering a sign-on bonus and counting his years in grad school toward seniority, making tenure only six months of work away. Austin had said no. He'd thought it was beneath him to teach high school; nothing less than a professorship would do.

He came crawling back when the Great Panic kicked off, only to find the position already filled. He spent the next five years scraping by, doing odd jobs here and there to keep himself from total destitution, not a day going by where he didn't wonder what his life would have been like if he'd said yes.

General Fergusson entered the room, and the Black Shirts snapped to attention.

With the amount of time the general spent on the news, his face was as familiar as Austin's own reflection, though much more imposing without a screen between them.

"Dismissed," the general ordered, and the Black Shirts hurriedly exited.

As General Fergusson pulled a knife from the sheath on his belt, the hairs on Austin's neck stood up. He watched warily as the general made his way closer, the knife held aloft in his hand.

Austin braced himself, sure he was about to be stabbed, but the general only stalked around him, cutting the zip around his wrists. Austin winced as he felt the cool metal of the knife against his skin.

"The Black Shirts are effective, but overcautious." General Fergusson severed the duct tape wrapped around Austin's right ankle. "There's no way to eliminate all risk, though." The general moved over to the left ankle now. "Take that humble shopkeeper, for instance. He was just opening his store—a low-risk proposition ordinarily—save for the presence of you and your gang."

The image of the old man's bloodied face flashed in Austin's mind, sending a wave of nausea up from his gut.

"You're lucky I got to you when I did, Mr. DeSantis," General Fergusson said after he'd finished cutting Austin free. "You were mere seconds from being processed."

"I didn't mean for it to happen," Austin said, his lips quivering.

"I know, Mr. DeSantis. We captured your confederates; we know the whole story. Even if you didn't deal the death blow, felony murder is still murder, and any blood drawn in the act of the robbery is also on your hands."

Cynthia's face appeared in his thoughts, her swollen belly heaving.

"What happened to them?" Austin asked.

"They've been processed."

"Even Cynthia?" he stammered. "She was due in a few weeks."

General Fergusson raised an eyebrow. "An unborn child has no rights, DeSantis. It shared its mother's fate."

Another surge of nausea hit him, and Austin thought he might vomit.

"I spoke to the attorney general," General Fergusson continued. "He knows you didn't land the killing blow. He's willing to give you immunity from prosecution. That was no small feat. The president ran on the Manpower Readiness Act, and his administration is loath to waive it." General Fergusson paced over to the window and took the drawstring of the blind in his hand. "But after watching you translate, I assured him you were worth it."

General Fergusson pulled the string on the blind.

The alien craft over DC filled up Austin's view. It was an awesome horror, TV having done the craft no justice, unable to capture the sheer magnitude of its enormous scale. It looked like a giant metal teardrop hanging from the sky, held aloft by a tether—like a cruise ship held up by a fishing line. Coming down from the craft like a metallic beanstalk was a cylinder, touching down on the ground somewhere in the park next to the high school a little over a mile away.

"Did you see what happened in Rome," General Fergusson asked, gazing out the window, "or had the Black Shirts got to you by then?"

"I saw," Austin replied.

"First contact between aliens and humanity," General Fergusson mused. "The most seminal moment in human history—hijacked by some cassock-wearing nobodies. Men so irrelevant that even their own adherents don't bother to show up to their sermons on Sunday." General Fergusson turned to face Austin. "The aliens asked the pope to send a delegation of priests up to the mother ship. No world leaders, no government officials, just *priests*."

Austin stared back at the general, not daring to open his mouth.

"The president went ballistic," General Fergusson said, shaking his head. "He thought it'd be suicide if at least one representative of Earth's governments didn't go along. He begged the pope to include an American representative—practically got down on his knees. Lucky for us, Pope Stephen relented and told the aliens they had to agree to include an American or no one from the Vatican would go at all."

"Suicide?" The question leaked out of Austin, despite his best efforts to stay silent.

"The Chinese think the aliens have a superweapon aboard the mother ship," General Fergusson replied. "Unless they can be convinced otherwise, they're going to launch their nukes and drag humanity into an all-out war."

Austin tilted his head, wondering why the general was telling him all this. "So, the president is sending you to join the delegation? Up on the alien ship?"

General Fergusson smiled. "Who better than the Face of Earth's Defense?"

Austin rubbed his aching wrists, his muscles still tense.

"What does this have to do with me?"

"The DIA has language capacity in two hundred thirty-seven languages. Urdu, Pashtun, Minangkabau, hell, they can even translate Xhosa in the event we ever find ourselves in a South African battle space. But when the aliens came down here and started yelling a dead language at us, we were stumped. That's why we need you."

Austin furrowed his brow. "Me?"

"I read your file. You started a whole verbal Latin program at UVA, got the department to teach spoken and not just written Latin for the first time."

"That was a long time ago."

"Not that long." General Fergusson moved closer. "I saw you in that warehouse, how you handled yourself under pressure, you were made for this."

The smell of the bodies, the crack of the rifle rounds—it all rushed back in an instant. "There has to be someone better."

General Fergusson's face softened, the sharpness of his features easing. "There isn't, DeSantis. Fluent Latin speakers don't grow on trees." He pointed out the window at the alien craft in the distance. "And my ride to orbit leaves in an hour. We don't have time for an exhaustive search."

Austin's mind conjured the hideous giant alien on TV, and he could feel himself starting to panic again.

"I know you're scared," General Fergusson said, empathy seeping into his tone. "But I'm giving you the chance at a fresh start. This is an opportunity to see that your mother is comfortable in her old age."

"Comfortable?" Austin couldn't hide the hope in his voice.

The corners of General Fergusson's mouth curled up with a feline subtlety. "We'd be sure to top up her Fedcoin account with a generous deposit. Yours, too. She'd finally be able to move out of that dingy apartment. It's the least we could do in light of the vital service you'd be providing to your nation."

Austin pictured his mother's threadbare nightgown, the long list of things she'd put off buying. He'd left her with nothing, not even enough money for food.

"And you'll drop the charges?"

"A clean record," General Fergusson said, taking a few steps back to lean on the teacher's desk. "Provided, of course, that you cooperate fully. Do everything I say."

As Austin looked out the window at the alien craft, all he could see was a million ways in which he could die. But when he turned back to General Fergusson, he focused on the high school seal. If only he'd said yes all those years ago.

"When do we start?"

The smile spread wider across the general's face. "We roll out to the cylinder in half an hour. In the meantime, I'll have one of my attendants get you some water and a change of clothes."

Heading for the door, General Fergusson paused. "One more thing: there will be a Catholic priest accompanying us.

He's the director of the Vatican Observatory. The pope wanted him to join the delegation from Rome. We flew him in from Arizona so he can hitch a ride up with us."

Austin tilted his head, unsure what General Fergusson wanted him to do with this information.

"Whatever you do," General Fergusson continued, the crucifix on the wall framed above his head, "don't trust him."

12

DeSantis," General Fergusson said, pointing down the fairway, "go wait with the priest." Before Austin could say anything, the general was walking away with a colonel, engrossed in a briefing on fortifications.

The priest was about a hundred yards ahead, in front of the cylinder. He was dressed all in black, save for his white clerical collar, and he had a mop of salt-and-pepper hair that clung to his head in undulating waves, only becoming tame where his sideburns met his well-trimmed beard. His gaze was fixed on the cylinder, the silver hue of the structure reflecting off his glasses, making it look like his eyes glowed with excitement. He stood with a slight hunch, exuding a confident casualness, as if he were perfectly at home next to an alien ship. The priest's pose contrasted sharply to the nearby Regulars who moved about with a ramrod energy.

The cylinder had touched down in Rock Creek Park just east of the high school, turning what was once DC's largest public park into an armed camp. The military had moved in in force. On the drive there, Austin's vehicle had passed a column of Abrams tanks so long he thought the army must have emptied out Fort Knox.

The cylinder had come down on the tenth-hole green of a public golf course, making it the heart of this new armed camp. The Regulars had already constructed a barricade of sandbags around the cylinder, ringing it for three hundred yards in every direction. Now they busied themselves setting up additional fortifications under the watchful eye of hundreds of Black Shirts, their covered faces scanning the scene for disobedience and sloth.

The throng of soldiers, however, felt minuscule next to the cylinder. It towered over them like an iron skyscraper, pushing down on the earth with such force that it leveled the putting green into a flat plane. Austin couldn't look away from its mirror-smooth exterior. It reflected nothing—not the still-green grass of the fairway nor the moist brown dirt of the sand trap it had bisected.

Austin craned his neck back in an effort to see the top. He was just barely able to make it out. The craft above made the cylinder look small as it hung there like a pristine anvil, ready to drop down at any second to make quick work of the tiny beings below.

The sound of a sergeant shouting commands stirred Austin from his trance, and he made his way down the fairway toward the priest.

"You sure don't look like a soldier," the priest said as Austin approached.

"I'm not," Austin replied curtly.

"Then what brings you around these parts? Trying to get in a quick nine before lunch?"

Suppressing the urge to grin, Austin said, "Are you the Vatican astronomer?"

"I am." The priest extended his hand toward Austin. "Francis Ambrose."

Austin instinctively went to take it, but stopped himself. "I didn't know the Vatican had an observatory."

Father Ambrose held his hand up for a second longer before putting it down. "You're not alone," he said with undiminished enthusiasm. "But the Vatican Observatory has been operating continuously since 1891. We have one of the most extensive meteorite collections in the world. All part of the Church's mission to promote the sciences."

"Promote the sciences?" Austin scoffed. "Tell that to Galileo."

Father Ambrose's smile grew wider. "Ah, yes, how can we forget the infamous and often misreported case of Galileo? I will admit we could have handled that better. But creating the university system, proposing the theory that supports modern cosmology, and discovering genetic heritability have to count for something in the Church's favor, right?"

Father Ambrose's gaze lingered on Austin, as if expecting him to smile back, but Austin was resolved not to give him the satisfaction.

"Let me get this straight," he replied. "The Vatican has an observatory, but it's in Arizona, and it's filled with a bunch of priest astronomers. And the pope asked you—its director—to join a delegation up to an alien mother ship?"

"That just about sums it up," Father Ambrose said, still cracking a mischievous smile. "I'm not sure how useful my PhD in astrophysics will be for dealing with alien first contact, but—as my dear mother used to say—if you don't want to be told by the pope to go up to an alien spaceship, then don't join the priesthood."

It was all Austin could do not to laugh. Despite the general's warnings, it was hard not to like the priest.

"Aliens landed on Earth, but that still might be the strangest thing I've heard all day," he said.

"If you think that's weird," Father Ambrose shot back with a twinkle, "I'll tell you about the time the Creator of the universe became a human, was executed, and then rose from the dead."

This time Austin couldn't contain himself, and he chuckled aloud.

"Quite an elaborate way to kill us." Austin looked back to see General Fergusson approaching. His laughter evaporated in an instant. "Wouldn't you say, Father?"

"Ah, General Fergusson." Father Ambrose peered toward the approaching general. "The illustrious Face of Earth's Defense. It's a pleasure to meet you in person after all these years of watching you on television."

Father Ambrose extended his hand to General Fergusson, who, like Austin, let it hang there.

"I suppose they'd like to watch us suffer," General Fergusson continued. "Seems like the only reason to get up close like this."

Father Ambrose tilted his head. "They're pilgrims, General, not butchers."

"Of course you would say that," General Fergusson coolly replied. "Gullibility is a prerequisite for someone in your line of work."

"Oh?" Father Ambrose said, unperturbed. "Have I been crazy to believe in the Premise? The very argument you've been proclaiming to the world these past five years?"

"Yes." General Fergusson crossed his hands behind his back and craned his neck up at the craft above. "A noble lie meant to keep society from ripping itself apart. That's something you and your Church know all about. Don't you, Father?"

The hairs on Austin's neck stood up.

"You're right, General. I know all about lies." Father Ambrose put his hands behind his back, mirroring the general's pose. "I also know devious men have a tendency to see lies wherever they look, all the more so when the truth is smacking them right upside the face."

General Fergusson lowered his head to look the priest in the eyes. "You think their faith is sincere?"

"I do."

"Why?"

"Because they profess it to be so, and I see no reason for them to lie."

"No reason to lie?" General Fergusson laughed. "The reason is staring us right in the face."

Father Ambrose scrunched up his nose in confusion. "Enlighten me."

"It's power, Father. Pure power." General Fergusson narrowed his eyes. "Power is the reason the cat plays with the mouse before devouring it, why the pharaoh builds the pyramids, and why the alien drops a pillar of steel down from the sky."

"Said like a man who only sees power." Father Ambrose took off his glasses and began cleaning them on his shirt. "One who is blind to compassion and mercy."

"Compassion and mercy?" General Fergusson scoffed. "Those are mere luxuries for those at the top of the food chain." The general motioned toward the barricades. "Look around. America's first contact with an alien species. Are there any dignitaries here? Crowds of curious people at the cordon around the park? No. The politicians are off in a secure bunker and the highways are choked with residents trying to flee.

People know that power is what rules the day. That's why your churches have been empty these past years. That's why there's no one here to welcome our visitors. They're all waiting for the moment of truth when the aliens' power is unleashed."

Austin began to feel dizzy as General Fergusson's ominous words sank in.

"If you're so pessimistic, why are you here?" Father Ambrose asked, casually putting his glasses back on.

"Duty, Father," General Fergusson said flatly. "The Chinese think there's a superweapon up there in the center of the mother ship. The president wants me to check it out."

"*Is* there a superweapon?" A hint of curiosity threaded through the priest's tone.

"That's what I'm here to find out. But so long as the Commies think there's a superweapon, they're liable to start a war."

"If there isn't one, does the president think you can persuade the Chinese otherwise?"

"He does," General Fergusson said, glancing up at the craft. "But it really doesn't matter. Weapon or not, we're only prolonging the inevitable. Whether China fires the first shot or the aliens do, war *is* coming."

Austin thought of his mother. What good would his fresh start be if war still came in the end? His mind raced as he tried to decipher whether General Fergusson was telling the truth or just trying to wrong-foot the priest.

The sound of hundreds of rifles cocking all at once broke his trance. "It's opening!" a soldier shouted from behind them.

A crack appeared on the perfectly silver wall, a dark slit thirty feet high. As Austin watched, the gap widened, the metal soundlessly folding to the side like the opening of a stage curtain.

"I'd sure like to know your name," Father Ambrose whispered to Austin, "before we step into the unknown together."

Austin looked at Father Ambrose, a welcoming smile spread across his bearded face, and then at General Fergusson standing in a warrior's pose, his eyes narrow.

Without a word, Austin turned back to the cylinder, bracing himself for whatever was about to come through that door. From the corner of his eye, he saw the smile fade from Father Ambrose's face.

13

A dark hallway stretched out before them, a canyon of midnight on an otherwise sunny October day. Silence hung heavy in the air; the only sound Austin could hear was the whisper of a faint breeze in his ears, as if every soldier gathered behind him was collectively holding their breath.

The color of the hallway began to change, a faint blue filling up the darkness just as a robot appeared at the threshold. It looked just like the ones Austin had seen on TV in Rome: an ovoidal torso made from the same silver metal as the cylinder and tubular arms and legs without any noticeable joints. But unlike those robots on TV, whose domed heads glowed a deep crimson, this robot's head glowed a pale blue.

"Get ready, DeSantis," General Fergusson grunted. "I don't want to miss a single word."

"DeSantis?" Father Ambrose chuckled. "What a splendid name. Thank goodness you're here. I nearly flunked Latin in seminary."

Austin stayed silent, his gaze fixed on the robot, the glow of its head eerily hypnotic.

"Sequere me."

The voice filled Austin's ears, almost as if the robot were standing right next to him. Its voice was higher than the seismic bass of the robots in Rome—more like a tenor, and much more pleasant.

"It says to follow him," Austin translated.

The robot withdrew back into the cylinder.

"Let's go, then." General Fergusson strode toward the opening. Father Ambrose and Austin followed close behind. Reaching the threshold, Austin hesitated, but the general marched through as if stepping onto an alien ship were an everyday occurrence.

Austin, however, was not so brave.

"Where are my manners?" Father Ambrose said, stopping to wait for Austin. "Brains before beauty."

Austin's legs still wouldn't move.

"It's okay," Father Ambrose insisted. "You can do this."

The pale blue glow of the robot's head was fading as it got farther and farther away. They didn't have much time before it would disappear completely into the dark.

"I'll be right here with you," Father Ambrose said.

Closing his eyes, Austin took a deep breath and stepped forward, his foot landing on a firm surface.

"There you go!" Father Ambrose said encouragingly. "Just

another walk in the park."

Austin concentrated on his breathing, doing his best to compose himself as he hurried to catch up. Soon he was right behind General Fergusson and the robot, its steely legs moving with such grace that its footfalls made no sound on the metal floor. They walked only a little bit farther before they came upon a brightly lit silver wall—a dead end. But as the robot approached, the wall folded away like a drape.

It felt surreal—like stepping into a dream. Austin found himself in what looked like the drawing room of a Victorian mansion. Mahogany walls drenched with gold inlay surrounded him, their textured facade sucking the colors out of the Persian rug beneath his feet. The air carried the familiar scent of a wood-burning fire, the source of which was a marble hearth on the far side of the room. Around the fireplace were three plush sofas, their overstuffed cushions practically begging the three of them to partake in the fire's soothing glow.

On another wall, Austin saw a door leading to a washroom, with polished travertine tiles in front of a crystal-handled sink and a gold commode.

To his left stood the pièce de résistance, though: an ivory table covered in an abundance of food, its delicacies piled so high that Austin thought he might be smothered by a tidal wave of honey ham and caviar.

He hadn't seen food like this in five years.

"Genio quaeso indulgeas," the robot said in its sonorous

voice. "Iter paulo minus quam duas horas durabit."

"'Please make yourselves comfortable,'" Austin translated. "'The journey will take just under two hours.'"

"Comfortable?" Father Ambrose chuckled. "I'm worried I'll be so comfortable I won't want to leave."

The floor beneath them shifted, and all three of them flinched, reaching out for something to steady themselves.

"Noli timere," the robot said. "Ascendere coepimus. Maiorem quam viginti quinque centesimis variationem gravitatis non experieris."

"'Don't be alarmed,'" Austin said once he was sure that his footing was sound. "'We have started our ascent. You will not experience'"—Austin paused, wondering if he'd heard correctly—"'gravitational variance greater than twenty-five percent.'"

"I think he means we're only going to pull between .75 and 1.25 G's," General Fergusson said. "We don't have to worry about floating up to the ceiling."

Father Ambrose wasted no time, making his way over to the food table and generously drowning a shrimp in some cocktail sauce. "That's good to hear," he said between chews. "I get indigestion when I eat upside down."

"You're braver than me, Padre," General Fergusson sneered. "Two minutes in, and you're shoveling your mouth full of alien food."

"Would you like some?" Father Ambrose offered a prawn to General Fergusson. "We don't want to be rude to our hosts."

"Rude?" General Fergusson stretched out the word as if he were torturing it on the rack. "I'll tell you what's rude. For the last five years, we've sent hails at every frequency, in every language, trying to open a line of communication to the alien ship as it careened toward Earth. And what do we hear? Nothing!" General Fergusson stalked up to the robot. "I'd like to know why they thought it was okay to invade our airspace and drop down from the sky without so much as a hello first?"

General Fergusson glared at Austin.

"Me?" Austin asked sheepishly.

"Do I look like I speak Latin?" General Fergusson growled.

"Why did you not respond to our messages?" Austin asked once he'd regained his composure.

"Quia Summus Pontifex numquam nos salutavit."

"What did it say?" General Fergusson demanded.

"It said, 'Because the Supreme Pontiff never hailed us.'"

Father Ambrose erupted into laughter, causing cracker crumbs to cascade onto his shirt. "If only you'd asked Pope Stephen for a hand, General. We could have cleared everything up five years ago."

General Fergusson shot Father Ambrose a stern glance before redirecting his attention back to the robot. "Now you listen," he said, his finger just inches from the robot's pale blue head, "the United States of America—"

"Austin DeSantis," the robot interrupted. "Quid tu hic?"

Austin's mouth became dry at the sound of his name

coming from the robot.

"Austin? What a great first name," Father Ambrose said, oblivious to the fact that the robot was asking Austin why he was there, insinuating he was an unwelcome addition.

"Pope Stephen said there would be only one other—a military commander—yet you are here as well, attending the inspection."

"What's it saying, DeSantis?" General Fergusson demanded.

Austin's legs wobbled as he imagined himself being chucked out into space like unwanted cargo.

"You are not a soldier, though. No . . . you speak the language of the holy Church."

"DeSantis?" General Fergusson repeated.

"Ah, yes. You are a teacher; one who transmits knowledge to the young. But a few days ago, your master released you, sent you away without recompense."

Sweat began to pour from Austin's brow. How did the robot know so much?

"Are you okay, Austin?" Father Ambrose asked.

"There is more, Austin DeSantis, more that you hide."

Austin's breath caught in his throat as shame mixed with terror.

"You seek the one they call Aurelia. Spending hours gaping at her image. As if when you espouse her when you are alone, your flesh is actually made one."

"DeSantis! Answer me!"

"You are tortured by this fiction. It has caused you and the ones you love great pain."

Austin felt himself getting lightheaded, his body doing everything it could to avoid passing out.

"Unburden yourself, Austin. For you will only be free when you follow the Way, the Truth, and the Life."

"DeSantis, so help me!"

Austin had to cooperate fully; that was the deal. He opened his mouth, about to translate and speak his secrets into the world, but he closed it again before any words came out.

"If you don't tell me right now, I'll—"

"Hello, robot, sir," Father Ambrose interjected, stepping into the space between Austin and General Fergusson. "We haven't been properly introduced. What do we call you? Do you have a name?"

Austin's eyes went wide as the robot bowed deeply in Father Ambrose's direction.

"My apologies, Father. Please forgive my ill manners. My name is Virgil. It is my great honor to be your host."

The room fell silent, the revelation leaving them all stunned.

"You can speak English?" Father Ambrose asked, nearly dropping the Gruyère-covered cracker still in his hand.

"Yes, Father," Virgil said in his melodious voice. "For you, our most honored guest, I am happy to speak in whatever language you prefer."

"That's very kind of you," Father Ambrose replied. "Perhaps we can speak in English and give poor Austin a break."

"As you wish, Father."

General Fergusson glared at Austin, his eyes narrow on his craggy face.

"Please take a seat and rest," Virgil said. "There will be much to see during your inspection, and I must get back to my prayers." Virgil glided to the corner of the living room, got down on his knees, and made the sign of the cross.

Austin looked back at General Fergusson to register his reaction to a robot praying off in the corner, but he found that Fergusson's gaze hadn't moved; his narrow eyes were still trained on Austin.

Austin's throat tightened. He realized the one thing he'd brought to the table—the thing that had saved his head from a bullet—had evaporated the instant the robot spoke English. Now there was no telling what the general would do.

14

The room was quiet save for the crack of the fire and the sporadic hum of Father Ambrose's snores. They'd been in the Victorian living room for over ninety minutes, each on his own sofa. The alien robot was still on its knees in the corner, hands clasped in prayer.

The general sat unmoving on his couch, his thoughts impenetrable to anyone but himself. Austin still hadn't translated what Virgil had said earlier, and the revelation that he was totally redundant still occupied his mind. Even if he did reveal what Virgil had said to him, how would he explain Aurelia? Maybe the general already knew. If he didn't, though, Austin would only sink lower in his eyes, going from utterly useless to a major liability.

Austin's mother strayed into his thoughts again. Wherever she was, he knew she was broken, her worst fear—that her son would be taken from her—having come to pass. Not only that, but she'd have to beg Mr. Washington and the Armstrongs for food. He could have made that right, given her a gift that made all her suffering worth it, but he'd blown it with the general, ruined another opportunity for success, just like he had his whole life.

"DeSantis?" General Fergusson materialized next to Austin's couch with a feline silence, catching Austin off guard.

"I'm sorry, sir," Austin pleaded. "I didn't mean to freeze, but it knew things about me, things no one else knows, and—"

"It's all right, DeSantis."

Austin paused, searching General Fergusson's face for signs of irony, but finding none. "Sir?"

"What is the First Assumption of Alien Capability?"

Austin winced, his mind filling with the image of the kind old man's bloody back, the cold gaze of Lieutenant Wu as she wielded her whip.

"Cyber dominance?"

"That's right," General Fergusson said. "This is what complete dominance of the digital domain looks like. Any time you've touched a keyboard or used a phone, they have it, and they can call it up in an instant, giving them a signals intelligence advantage beyond anything we've ever dreamed of."

All of it.

They could see *all* of it.

Austin cringed at the idea of the aliens knowing all that about him.

"We have to stick together, DeSantis. We're on enemy

territory. They have the advantage, and there's no telling what they might throw our way."

"But, sir," Austin muttered, "the robot speaks English. You don't need me anymore."

General Fergusson furrowed his brow. "Don't be ridiculous, DeSantis. We're going to be linking up with the rest of the Vatican delegation up there. I wouldn't put it past those clerics to switch back to Latin just to keep me out of the loop. I need you, more than ever, to make sure they don't pull any dirty tricks."

A sigh of relief escaped Austin's lips as he felt a weight lift from his shoulders.

"Remember what I told you: the Catholics can't be trusted." General Fergusson gestured to Father Ambrose. "Even if he seems harmless, he's not on our side."

Father Ambrose looked serene snoring on his couch, but General Fergusson's warning took purchase in Austin's head. The priest's slumber transformed, suddenly seeming sinister; he was far too comfortable here.

General Fergusson slipped back to his sofa, resuming his emotionless stare as the orange glow of the fire washed over him. Austin hadn't blown it—although he'd come close. He'd redouble his efforts to make the general proud and prove he was worthy of the largesse he would receive on the other end.

"Father?" Virgil's voice filled the room, his tone soothing, like he was waking a sleeping babe.

"Was I asleep?" Father Ambrose rubbed his eyes.

"It seems so, Father." Virgil glided to the fireplace. "We will be arriving at the ship momentarily. I kindly ask that you remain seated. As we change our angular momentum, you will experience microgravity. But do not be alarmed, it will pass quickly."

For a moment, Austin's legs became light, but as quick as it began, it ended, his feet depressing back into the plush Persian rug.

"We have arrived," Virgil said.

A vivid light filled the dark room as the mahogany wall behind Virgil folded open. Austin strained to see, but the light coming in was so bright he couldn't see anything on the other side.

Following Virgil through this new door, he could hardly believe the sight before his eyes. They had stepped into a pastoral landscape. Not a ship with metal hallways or row upon row of alien technology, but a grassy plain, a verdant forest rising up on either side.

"It's Edenic," Father Ambrose said, his voice full of awe.

"Not Eden, Father," Virgil said as he walked into the shin-high grass. "We are all east of there."

Austin looked up, trying to find the ceiling, but all he could see was a bright blue sky.

"Virgil?" Father Ambrose asked, pointing to the tree line off to their left. "The forest curves up toward the sky over in that direction." Father Ambrose did an about-face and pointed again. "Over in that direction, too. Why is that?"

Virgil paused in his stride, the blades of grass curling up over his feet. "We are on a rotating habitat, Father. One of three similarly sized ones contained within the asteroid that encapsulates our ship." Virgil then pointed to the forest on the left. "When you look toward the rotational horizon, you can see the curve. The rotation allows us to experience .79 G's at ground level. While this is lower gravity than humans are used to, it is the gravity in which we are most comfortable."

Austin tried to detect whether stepping into a sylvan paradise orbiting high above Earth was surprising to General Fergusson, but if he felt anything, Austin couldn't tell.

"Is that the gravity on your home world, Virgil?"

"Yes, Father."

"Fascinating." Father Ambrose ran a hand over his beard. "Virgil, I've been wondering—what do we call you? Or, to say it another way, what do your people call themselves?"

"Our people communicate using visual means, Father." Virgil began walking again. "By changing their skin pigmentation to form symbols. As such, we lack an auditory word for our people. What do you humans call us?"

Father Ambrose stroked his beard again. "I don't know if there's a consensus, but since your arrival, many humans have taken to calling your people 'Pilgrims,' and we have been referring to machines like you as 'Diplomats.'"

"You humans surprise me," Virgil said, speaking slowly as if he was considering each word. "That nomenclature is incredibly apt. Please feel comfortable referring to us as such going forward."

Father Ambrose shot Austin a jubilant look, seemingly proud of having established the official taxonomy of an alien race, but Austin was careful not to meet his eyes.

"Now we must hurry to the chapel," Virgil said as a sled appeared, a slab of shiny silver metal that hovered half a foot off the ground with three seats on top. "The delegation from the Vatican has already arrived."

"Is it in the chapel that you would like to do the perpetual adoration?" Father Ambrose asked, climbing into a seat atop the sled.

Virgil positioned himself at the helm. "Yes, Father."

Taking a seat next to General Fergusson, Austin scanned his face to see if he knew what a perpetual adoration was, or that their destination was a chapel, but he appeared as surprised as Austin. As the sled began to move, Austin wondered what other details Father Ambrose was hiding from them.

The sled gained speed quickly, soon whipping over the grassy plain so fast the forests on either side blurred. The ground undulated slightly, the sled going up and down gentle grades, which made Austin realize that the terrain was not uniform but instead textured. At one point, Austin saw a bird that looked very much like a hawk circling above, soaring upward on thermal currents.

"Is that the chapel?" Father Ambrose shouted over the rushing air as the sled made its way to the top of a hill.

"Yes, Father."

"My God, it's huge," the priest said as the edifice unfolded before them. "It makes Saint Peter's look like a dollhouse."

The sled crested the hill, and the full scale of the chapel came into view. It was constructed of the same silver metal as Virgil, but so large it made the crafts that hovered over cities back on Earth seem insignificant. It stretched out so wide that Austin could see the curvature of the structure as it spread itself across the horizon. Its twelve spires rose up into the air for what seemed like miles, the center spire the tallest of them all. In front of the chapel was a crystal clear body of water that reflected the majesty of the structure back at itself like a liquid mirror. Austin absorbed it all, transfixed by its beauty.

As they drew closer, he spotted the delegation from Rome standing next to another sled parked beside the chapel wall. Austin couldn't get over the strangeness of traveling all the way from Earth to find a group of humans milling around, waiting like they'd made plans to meet up at the local park.

"Cardinal Benedetto!" Father Ambrose exclaimed as their sled came to a halt.

"Francis!" the cardinal replied in a thick Italian accent.

The Vatican delegation consisted of four members: the cardinal with his red skullcap, and three other priests. Accompanying them was another robot identical to Virgil, save for its domed head glowing a soft violet.

"Sorry to take you from your lens, Francis, but His Holiness insisted that you join us."

"It's my pleasure, Your Eminence." Jumping down off the sled, Father Ambrose took the cardinal's hand and kissed his ring.

Austin met General Fergusson's eyes. He seemed to be just as discomfited as Austin at having to witness the antiquated display.

"When I became an astronomer," Father Ambrose said, "I never thought I'd end up through the looking glass and up here in space."

"It is the mystery of divine providence," the cardinal replied.

"Your Eminence." Father Ambrose turned around and faced Austin and General Fergusson. "I'd like to introduce you to my—"

"Look!" one of the priests in the cardinal's delegation shouted.

A slit had appeared in the chapel wall, hundreds of feet high. Silently, the walls on either side began folding apart. Peering through the giant door, Austin at first saw nothing but a hazy white mist, but then the dot of a silhouette materialized. It grew larger by the second, until suddenly, a giant Diplomat stood over them, its domed head glowing a deep crimson.

"Pontifex honoratissime," the giant Diplomat's voice boomed, a deep bass that Austin could feel in his gut. "Eo ipso quod tu hic ades ecclesiam nostram illuminas sicut Dominus Deus noster omnem creaturam amore Suo illuminat."

Austin leaned over to General Fergusson and translated. "'Honored Bishop, your presence here illuminates our humble church as the Lord our God illuminates all of creation with His love.'"

"Humble . . ." General Fergusson snickered.

"In narthex investigationem tuam incipiamus, ut iudicemus num haec ecclesia sit habitaculum Domino Deo nostro dignum."

"'Let us begin your inspection in the . . . narthex,'" Austin said, tripping on the new word.

"That's right, Austin," Father Ambrose said encouragingly. "The narthex is the front room of a church. It's like an antechamber."

Austin shot Father Ambrose a sharp look and leaned even closer to General Fergusson, whispering the rest of the translation. "'To see if this church is a worthy dwelling place for the Lord our God.'"

"Accede propius. Nam narthex ingens est, et a via deerrare periculosum est."

"'But stay close,'" Austin translated, the hairs on the back of his neck becoming stiff, "'for the narthex is vast, and to get lost inside risks peril.'"

The giant Diplomat turned around and walked back inside. The violet-headed Diplomat followed, as well as the cardinal and his accompanying priests.

"They're leaving without you, Father." General Fergusson pointed at the group up ahead.

"Oh, I see." For the first time, Austin heard Father Ambrose sound deflated. "I just figured since we all rode up together, the three of us would proceed as a group."

Father Ambrose looked at Austin. He knew the father was searching for an ally, and he couldn't help but think of how kind the man had been to him so far. But after a moment, Austin looked up, meeting Father Ambrose's eyes.

"No," Austin said, trying to ignore the guilt that sat like a rock in his stomach. "You're not in our group."

A flash of distress streaked across Father Ambrose's face, a reaction he tried to hide, yet Austin saw it. Saying nothing, Father Ambrose walked into the church alone, leaving Austin and General Fergusson to face the peril of the narthex together.

15

The narthex sprawled endlessly in white obscurity, with no discernible walls, ceiling, or floor. Filled with a thick haze, it was like walking into a cloud. Austin could barely see Virgil as he led them farther inside. If it weren't for his pale blue head shining in the mist, he and the general wouldn't be able to see him at all.

"DeSantis," General Fergusson whispered. "Follow my lead."

Even two yards away, the general was nearly invisible. He gestured downward with his hand, signaling Austin to slow. Austin complied, and the blue light of Virgil's head faded until it was replaced by a milky nothing.

"Sir?" Austin said, trying to locate General Fergusson's silhouette. "How do we know which way to go?"

"This way, DeSantis."

General Fergusson's voice seemed to come from everywhere and nowhere all at once.

Disoriented, Austin stumbled around, groping for the general. "I can't see you, sir."

"This way," the voice said from some unseen place.

Squinting his eyes, he walked a few more steps. "I still can't—"

A surge of pain shot up Austin's spine. He fell forward, landing nose-first on the floor. A gush of blood rushed from his nostrils. He spun onto his back as fast as he could, covering his face with his hands. Before he could sit up, he felt skinny hands wrap around his neck and squeeze. He tried to call out, but thumbs pressed down hard on his larynx, stifling his vocal cords.

"I'm sorry, DeSantis, but you were always going to die." The bottom of General Fergusson's arms were all Austin could see, his face obscured in the dense mist. "War is coming, and we couldn't let China fire the first shot."

Austin pulled wildly at the hands around his neck, but they wouldn't budge.

"We'll claim that the aliens killed you unprovoked—their species the one to draw first blood. It will give us the moral high ground. And we need every advantage we can get in the coming war."

He felt a sharp pain behind his eye. The airless blood pooling in his brain, the whiteness fading to black.

"Just be glad that you died for a noble cause. That it didn't all end in the warehouse."

Flailing his arms, Austin tried to find something to grab. Just as his vision began to dot, his right hand landed on the general's weathered face. He found the eye socket and pressed his thumb as hard as he could, feeling the soft tissue compress.

The grip around his neck loosened, and he felt a trickle of blood returning to his head, the light getting brighter. He heard the general moan in pain, and Austin pushed the man to the side and twisted his body, freeing himself from the hands around his neck.

He sucked in air, desperately trying to reoxygenate his blood, as he rolled as far away as he could from his attacker. Luckily, the mist concealed him. When he thought he was clear, he got to his feet and ran, charging through the fog like a man possessed.

He ran until his breath ran out.

Panting, he looked around frantically, but all he saw was whiteness, an endless nothing in every direction. He remembered the giant Diplomat's words, "The narthex is vast, and to get lost inside risks peril." Panic gripped him as he realized there was no exit in sight. He could wander around for days, weeks, years, and never find a way out.

"Help me!" he screamed. "Help me, someone, please!"

It felt like his words stopped in midair, bricked in by the heavy vapor.

Falling to his knees, he thought of all the pain he'd caused his mother. He'd intended to make it right, undo the wrongs he'd committed, but that had been an illusion, a fiction fed to him by the government. As the general had said, he was always going to die for what he had done; it was just a matter of how. Not only would his mother live out the rest of her life thinking her son was nothing more than a thief and a murderer, but she'd also do it without any money to her name.

All because of him.

Unable to keep staring at the vacant landscape, he shut his eyes. When he did, all he could see was the kind old man with Cynthia standing over him, the Fedcoin machine in her hands. For the first time since it had happened, he looked straight at what he'd done: he'd killed that man, even if it was Cynthia who'd struck the fatal blow. Liam and Cynthia couldn't have robbed that store without him, they would have had to figure something else out, but Austin couldn't help himself. He'd wanted Aurelia so bad—damn the consequences.

He sat back and clutched his knees to his chest. He was forsaken, doomed to be tormented by his past until thirst took him in this cloudlike tomb.

When he had given up all hope, the mist began to change.

The white emptiness slowly gave way to a faded blue. As Austin looked on, it grew brighter, the nothing succumbing to its brilliance. Soon, Virgil was standing above him, his pale blue head shining, bathing Austin in a tender glow.

"Do not be afraid, Austin," Virgil said in his sweet voice. "I am with you."

"I—I was lost," Austin stammered.

"I know." Virgil reached out his hand. "But now you are found."

Austin took Virgil's hand—it was like nothing he had ever touched before. The metal felt warm, as though blood flowed underneath it, and it gave off a haptic sensation that made Austin's whole body feel as though it were wrapped in an embrace. The ache of his regret immediately subsided.

"General Fergusson attacked me," he said, his voice cracking a little.

"I know, Austin." Virgil's tone was soothing. "He will be punished."

"How?"

"Pilgrim justice is harsh and swift. It is how we maintain harmony. And this church is a place of peace, meant to be a dwelling space for the Lord our God. General Fergusson has violated that peace by his violence against you—a transgression of the most serious kind. Only by forfeiting his life will the scales of justice be level."

Austin's eyes widened. "You're going to kill General Fergusson?"

"No. Our leader has decided to show him mercy, for he is kind and gentle."

Austin furrowed his brow. "So he gets off scot-free?"

"No. General Fergusson has been banished. He is being escorted back down to Earth. You shall take his place as the representative from the United States, so as to honor our word to His Holiness Pope Stephen, that a non-Vatican representative should be present for the inspection of this church."

"Me?" Austin felt his heartbeat accelerate. "But I'm nobody . . . just a translator."

"Do not say such things." Despite the chide, Virgil's voice was consoling. "You are a child of God. Worthy of dignity and respect by dint of your creation."

Austin squeezed Virgil's hand, the robot's words like a healing tonic. "I meant I don't have the right qualifications."

Virgil pulled Austin forward, getting him to walk. "You are as qualified as any human, for there is not one of you that does not suffer from a limited intellect and a short lifespan."

Austin smiled, just another short-lived human grateful to be rescued from oblivion by this glorious AI.

"Austin!"

They both stopped at the distant sound.

"Virgil, do you hear that?"

"I do."

"Austin!" the voice shouted again.

They proceeded toward the sound until a figure emerged from the fog.

"Father?" Austin said.

"Oh, thank God." Father Ambrose grabbed Austin's shoulder. "You're okay."

"Were you looking for me?" Austin quivered.

"Of course!" Father Ambrose tilted his head as if Austin had asked the craziest question in the world. "I heard you shout for help so I ran to find you."

Austin grimaced, berating himself for his poor behavior earlier. He hadn't even had the decency to shake the man's hand. "You left your group to find me?"

"You sounded like you were in trouble." Austin saw Father Ambrose looking at his neck. He could already feel the swelling where General Fergusson's hands had been. "Are you sure you're okay?"

"Yes, Father. I'm better now," Austin assured him. "I'm sorry . . . about earlier."

"All's forgiven, Austin. I'm just glad you're safe."

The kindness in Father Ambrose's eyes sent a pain through his heart.

"Come," Virgil said. "Or we will miss the choir."

Taking Father Ambrose's hand as well, Virgil led them both forward to a large clearing, the mist gradually giving way to reveal a night sky above them, every star in the Milky Way visible before their eyes. In the center of the clearing stood the giant Diplomat, the smaller violet-headed Diplomat next to him, and the cardinal and his priests by their sides.

"What is this?" Austin asked, his curiosity piqued.

Before Virgil could answer, the room erupted in music, a transcendent melody that resonated within Austin's every fiber. It felt as though each cell in his body were singing, harmonizing with the ethereal song that scored the night sky.

The stars themselves seemed to move with the music, coming closer, so that they went from little dots in the distance to large orbs, dancing around all those gathered there as they poured out music and light.

"It's glorious!" Father Ambrose exclaimed as the music swelled, the view of the night sky shifting to focus on a nebula, a rampage of color and swirling gas.

Austin felt transported, the despair he'd felt earlier evaporating, replaced by a glory inside him like none he'd ever known. Turning to Virgil, he stared at his blue head. "I want to see more. Please let me."

Virgil's hand still lay sweetly in Austin's own. "As you wish."

The globes of light disappeared, and in their place were Pilgrims, surrounding Austin in every direction, including above him, their tentacle skirts wriggling. The ones above looked as if they were propped up on air, ready to fall down and smother him, writhing appendages and all.

Austin understood, in a flash of realization: the beautiful music was coming from this Pilgrim choir. His heart swelled in gratitude for Virgil for making sure that he hadn't missed this extraordinary experience. But then, in the middle of a note, when Austin was sure the choir was rising to a crescendo, the music stopped. It was as jarring as a car crash, the night sky disappearing to be replaced by an empty expanse of white as the Pilgrims swiftly retreated into the mist.

"What happened?" Austin asked.

Virgil pulled his hand away. His head was no longer blue, the soft glow replaced by a foreboding crimson.

"Necesse est investigationem differre," the giant Diplomat bellowed, its deep bass voice grating after the sublimity of the choir. "Michael mortuus est."

"Austin?" Father Ambrose said. "What did the big Diplomat say?"

Austin's mouth went dry. "He said, 'We must postpone the inspection.'"

Father Ambrose tilted his head. "Did he say why?"

"Yes," Austin gulped. "Because Michael is dead."

16

W ho is Michael?"

"For the hundredth time. I don't know!"

"Does the priest know?"

"The priest has a name."

"I'm sure he does, kid." The captain leaned forward.

"Where is he?" Austin demanded, returning the gesture in kind.

"He's fine."

"I'm not answering any more questions until I see him." Austin held his pose, inches from the captain's face. The captain stared back into Austin's eyes for a moment before relenting and sitting back in his chair.

Austin had been taken back to the high school, this time the boys' locker room, and was sitting at a folding table across from his interrogator, the smell of puberty hanging in the air. They had brought him here as soon as he had arrived back on Earth, while Father Ambrose was spirited off to some place unknown. In addition to the captain questioning him, two Black Shirts guarded the exit, black balaclavas covering their faces.

"What makes you think you can make demands?"

"Because of this." Austin gestured to the bruises on his neck. "Thanks to General Fergusson, I'm now the United States of America's representative to the Pilgrims." Leaning back in his seat, he added, "So you can either let me see Father Ambrose, or I can just sit here quietly and make sure the US government doesn't have any relationship with the Pilgrims at all. Your call."

The captain sat wordlessly for a breath before picking up his manila folder and walking out of the locker room.

Austin smiled, glad to have the upper hand for once. "Excuse me," he said to the Black Shirts. "Is there any chance you could get me a glass of water? I'm thirsty."

The taller of the Black Shirts shouldered his rifle and lumbered toward him. By pure instinct, Austin slid back into his chair.

"What?" The Black Shirt leaned his sizable frame on the table, his voice as comforting as a sandblaster.

"I just . . ." Austin faltered. "I didn't know who else to ask."

The Black Shirt leaned in further, pulling down the front of his balaclava to reveal a scar that cut across his face from his left temple all the way down to his upper lip.

"Do I look like a waiter?" The man's low growl sent a sliver of fear through Austin, and his legs began to tremble.

"Leave him alone, Sarge," the other Black Shirt said, the feminine voice thick with a Mississippi twang. "Not worth the trouble with the brass."

Grumbling, Sarge walked away, pulling up his balaclava as he did so.

The other Black Shirt approached. "Tell me something," she said, tugging down the front of her balaclava.

Austin was dumbstruck by the sight of her. It had never occurred to him that there could be women underneath those black uniforms. It was true that the Black Shirts had stringent size requirements, but they weren't so extreme that an above-average-sized woman couldn't qualify—obedience was prized more than stature, after all.

"What was it like up there?" she asked.

"Where?" Austin asked, mesmerized by her green eyes that shone against her wine-dark skin.

"You know," she said, her twang drawing out the words as she nodded up at the ceiling. "Up *there*."

"You mean on the ship?"

She shot him an exasperated look.

He blushed. "It was ..." he managed to eventually say, the whole experience eluding summary as he got lost in her gaze. "It was the opposite of everything I expected."

She smiled, a crooked smile that twisted her dimple. "I always wanted to go to space," she said, her voice somewhere distant. "Ever since I was a little girl."

Austin stared back at her, wishing he could have met her all those years ago.

"Come with me."

Austin snapped out of it at the sound of the captain's voice. He was standing in the locker room entrance with two new Black Shirts by his side.

"Are you taking me to see Father Ambrose?" Austin replied as the most beautiful Black Shirt he'd ever seen yanked the balaclava back over her face.

"You'll see." The captain made his way over and lifted Austin to his feet with a tight grip around Austin's forearm, and then led him out of the locker room and into the school gymnasium.

The gym was covered in equipment, banks of monitors and comms panels lined up in rows. A dozen Regulars ran back and forth, manning the machines.

The captain led him through a door on the far side of the gym, and as Austin stepped through, he realized he was in the wrestling room. The floor was covered wall to wall in mats, the ceiling so low it felt like a cave.

The captain guided Austin to a chair in the center of the room, positioned in front of a long table lined with military brass. On the left side of the table sat General Fergusson, looking smug in his dress A's, one eye bloodshot and not a hint of regret on his face.

"You!" Austin seethed. "What are *you* doing here?"

The captain forcefully shoved Austin into the seat.

"Is this him?"

The military brass all stood bolt upright as the Black Shirts pulled Austin up onto his feet.

Secretary of Defense Ramirez strode into the room, her unmistakable presence commanding attention. She took her seat at the center of the table, a head shorter than all the generals gathered there but somehow looming larger. The normally soft expression she had when talking to reporters or giving a speech from her homey office in the Pentagon was nowhere to be found, replaced by a stern sharpness. But Austin felt a flicker of relief nonetheless. She would make sure General Fergusson got what was coming to him.

"It is, Madam Secretary," General Fergusson replied as he and the other generals sat back down.

"He doesn't inspire much confidence," she said, raising an eyebrow.

"I'm glad you're here, Madam Secretary." Austin pointed at General Fergusson. "When I was on the ship, General Fergusson—"

"Max?" Secretary Ramirez looked in General Fergusson's direction. "Why is he speaking?"

"He's stupid, Madam Secretary."

"Stupid?"

"Yes, ma'am."

"How stupid?"

"The perfect amount, ma'am. Thinks he knows everything already."

"I see." Secretary Ramirez stroked her chin. "A know-it-all."

"He's a madman!" Austin protested. "He tried to kill me. He strangled me up on the ship!"

Secretary Ramirez's eyes narrowed as she focused on General Fergusson. "Max, is that true?"

Austin leaned forward, savoring the moment. The truth was finally coming out.

General Fergusson grinned. "Every single word."

"Max." Secretary Ramirez shook her head. "This is extremely troubling."

It was all Austin could do to contain himself, glad he could be there to witness General Fergusson's fall.

Secretary Ramirez pointed at Austin. "You didn't say anything to POTUS and me about strangling."

"It just felt right, ma'am. The kid looked like he needed a good strangle."

She chuckled, a smile bursting forth on her face. "You always did know how to lay it on thick, Max. Well done."

Austin felt the hope that had risen immediately drain away. He wanted to lie down on the wrestling mat and disappear. It was like he was in some sort of waking nightmare, everything he thought he knew reversed. "The president ordered me beat up?" he whispered, his internal monologue leaking out into the room.

"It was a matter of national security," Secretary Ramirez snapped.

"But why?" It was less of a question and more of a plea, a desperate incantation meant to ward off complete insanity.

"It's all part of your cover, Mr. DeSantis." Secretary Ramirez turned to General Fergusson. "Let's get him briefed on the next phase."

"What do you mean a 'cover'?"

Secretary Ramirez let out an exasperated huff. "Max, I don't have the patience for this kind of dumb."

"I understand, Madam Secretary." General Fergusson patted the air in front of him in an "easy now" motion. "Let me see if I can spell it out for him." General Fergusson turned back toward Austin. "You're old enough to remember the war in Afghanistan, right, DeSantis?"

Austin stared back, his face only able to convey a mixture of shell shock and rage.

"How about green-on-blue attacks? Does that ring a bell?" General Fergusson let the silence persist for a moment before continuing. "That's okay. You were a bit young at the time. A green-on-blue attack was when Afghan soldiers—soldiers *we* trained and equipped—would turn on their coalition counterparts and attack them."

None of this rang a bell. By the time Austin had been old enough to pay attention to the war in Afghanistan, it was basically over.

"Imagine it. Someone you've worked with, someone you trusted, suddenly turning their gun on you when you least expect it. Words can't describe the horror." A look of sorrow flashed across General Fergusson's face. For a second, he wasn't in the room; he was in his past, and it occurred to Austin this was not an abstraction for him.

"The Taliban were weak. No match for us. But they found *our* weakness: our trust. And by exploiting it, they were able to win the war." General Fergusson paused again, as if he'd lost his train of thought. After a second, he cleared his throat and started again. "That's why it's essential the aliens trust you, DeSantis. They're too powerful. Their trust is the only vulnerability we'll ever be able to exploit. That's how you fight asymmetric war."

Austin tried to figure out how General Fergusson could have mistaken that diatribe for an explanation.

"So . . ." Austin gritted his teeth. "You want to use their trust against them. That's why you tried to kill me?"

"Yes."

"But why? That doesn't make any sense!"

The general shrugged. "I had to make them hate me."

"How in the world does that get them to trust you?" Austin yelled.

"It doesn't. It's how I get them to trust *you*."

Austin opened his mouth, ready to hurl an insult, but paused momentarily. "I'm your translator," he eventually said.

"If they don't trust you, they won't trust me."

"No." General Fergusson leaned forward on the table, putting his weight on his elbows. "I deliberately drove a wedge between you and me, making it seem like we aren't on the same team."

"We *aren't* on the same team!" Austin shouted. "You tried to kill me, you psychopath!"

"Oh, come on," Secretary Ramirez moaned. "Not this again."

Austin could feel the mist, the cold chill encircling him. It was like he was back there in the oblivion. General Fergusson had done that to him, and he wouldn't forget it. He could say it was an act, but he'd felt the man's rage, his lust for blood.

"DeSantis," General Fergusson insisted. "I'm trying to tell you that was all part of your cover. You weren't in any real danger. I wasn't going to let anything bad happen to you."

"Liar! You did it when no one was looking—out of sight! You did it because you wanted to!"

"DeSantis . . ." General Fergusson said with a sigh, as though he thought Austin were the biggest idiot he'd ever met. "I had to do it 'out of sight' to make them believe I was trying to hide it. It was all meant to sell the act. That way I could make it appear as if you're against me, the sort of person who'd make a trustworthy friend to the aliens. But there is no out of sight up there. They were always looking. And we knew that."

Austin again opened his mouth to yell but hesitated, the

general's words sinking in.

"They traveled across the galaxy. You think they don't have cameras and microphones literally everywhere? That ship is a panopticon. They saw every breath we took, every word I whispered, every blow I landed while you were down there in the fog."

Austin searched his memory. "I didn't see any cameras."

"Come on, DeSantis, you know it's true." General Fergusson's face softened like he was trying to soothe a child.

A sick feeling settled in Austin's stomach. He was being used this whole time, and he'd been too thick to notice.

"Why not just be nice to them?" Austin's voice was barely above a whisper. "Get them to trust you that way."

"Don't be ridiculous, DeSantis," General Fergusson said dismissively. "I'm a general in the US military—a warrior. They could never fully trust me. We needed a nobody, a person who might have a plausible grudge against the government and everything it stood for, a condemned man with nothing left to lose. Someone the aliens felt could be recruited to their side."

Austin scanned the faces of the other generals, desperately trying to determine whether this revelation was true.

Secretary Ramirez shook her head. "You didn't really think you were the only person we could find who speaks Latin, did you?"

Austin felt his ego pouring out from his feet and pooling on the floor. He was everything they said he was: a nobody, a fool. And he'd actually managed to let himself think that, as the sole representative of his country to an alien race, he mattered in this world.

"Charlie," Secretary Ramirez said. "Let Mr. DeSantis know about China."

A general all the way on the right end of the table with wings pinned to his chest cleared his throat. "At approximately 0600 hours Beijing time, the politburo standing committee met in an emergency session to authorize a preemptive strike against the alien mother ship. The attack will begin in approximately thirty hours, when the Chinese orbital launch platforms are at the optimal place in their orbit relative to the ship. Orbital launch will be followed by launch of land-based ICBMs fired in an anti-rotational orbit. The Commies are trying to come at the aliens from both directions to see if they can overwhelm their defenses."

"And how will that work out for them, Charlie?"

"Like shit, ma'am," the general replied. "But they feel like they have no choice. We calculate a .07 percent chance of a successful strike. Even fired at the moment of optimum orbit, missile transit time will still be six hours. Ample time for aliens to intercept the warheads."

"And the alien response?"

"We expect a full-scale retaliatory strike across the planet, Madam Secretary. No human survivors expected."

Secretary Ramirez leaned forward. "That's what we're up

against, Mr. DeSantis. Unless, of course, we can get China to stand down."

"That's where you come in." General Fergusson looked Austin in the eye. "If we can get video of the center of that church and prove to the Chinese that it isn't a superweapon, we might be able to convince them not to attack."

Only a few minutes ago, Austin knew exactly how to feel about the man, a boiling hatred coursing through him. But now the general spoke to Austin as if he were his leader—his savior. Austin could feel the pull of the strings, the tug of the puppet master.

"You want me to take a video from inside the alien ship . . . like a spy?"

"Yes."

"To prove that it's just a church?"

"Yes."

"And you knew whoever Michael was was going to die so that you could send me on this mission?"

"Of course not." General Fergusson shook his head. "I'm not clairvoyant. My goal on that last trip was simply to set up your cover. We didn't know exactly how we'd use you, only that we would. And now we're using you to stop a war."

Austin wanted to scream at his would-be killer, but the explanation was so plausible. "But what if it *is* a superweapon?"

"Then we're all dead anyway."

Austin searched General Fergusson's face, looking for signs

of sarcasm. There were none. But then Austin's mind moved to Virgil and Father Ambrose. How little he had to work to see where he stood with them, how Virgil had saved him from that prison of regrets. Now General Fergusson wanted him to work against them, to turn on his newfound friends.

"What if I refuse?" Austin asked.

"The immunity deal you negotiated with General Fergusson will be off," Secretary Ramirez said without a flicker of emotion. "You will be processed for murder, and everyone you know and love—including your mother—will die in a global apocalypse." Secretary Ramirez stood up, all the generals doing likewise in her wake. "So, what's it going to be? Are you in, or are you out?"

17

Austin pawed the cold metal hunk in his pocket, careful not to engage the switch. The techs had been clear enough: there was only one minute of film in the camera—no way to shut it off once it started—and it would start recording only after the hundredth turn. Just one crank less and it wouldn't work at all. One extra, and he'd waste all the film recording the inside of his pocket.

"The aliens have cyber dominance," they had kept repeating. "There's nothing digital, nothing electronic. That's why you need to crank it. That's how the camera gets its power."

When he'd asked them if he could just pre-crank the camera up to ninety-nine, they'd jumped down his throat, telling him that the static electric charge would show up on the aliens' sensors. He'd have to charge the camera right before he got to the center of the church—not a moment sooner—all while remaining unseen.

This is what he'd agreed to do.

This was his only way out.

"You don't believe me, do you, DeSantis?" General Fergusson said as their Humvee turned a corner and the cylinder came into view.

Austin kept his eyes forward, trying to will away the dull ache of the bruises on his neck. "No," he finally said.

"That's smart," General Fergusson said without a hint of irony.

"Is it?" Austin faced the general. "Or is it just 'the perfect amount' of stupid?"

A feline smile crept across General Fergusson's face. "Words, DeSantis, just words. Ramirez is a politician—her whole persona is a lie. And politicians are afraid of smart people. They're worried you'll pierce the veneer and see them for what they truly are. I said that to protect you and make sure she didn't change her mind."

"Right." Austin's eyes narrowed. "You tried to kill me for my protection, too, I take it?"

"I *pretended* to try and kill you, DeSantis." The feline smile was replaced by a scowl. "You should be thanking me for making it look so good. The fate of humanity hangs in the balance."

Austin looked away, focusing on the back of the driver's seat. He could still feel the terror he'd felt lying there on the ground, the fingers curled around his neck, the thick and life-less fog pressing in on him as his vision began to darken. He would never thank General Fergusson for *that*.

"You think the robot is your friend, don't you?"

"I have no friends."

"You lie, DeSantis." General Fergusson's voice was higher, like he was on the verge of laughing. "I didn't get where I am without being able to read people. You like that robot. The priest, too. You think you can trust them."

Austin turned to look out the window, as if by pointing the back of his head at the general, he could stop him from so easily reading his thoughts.

"The aliens are a military force, DeSantis. Of that, I'm sure. And the robot was probably custom-built to befriend you and make you feel seen." General Fergusson waited, baiting him to respond, but Austin stayed quiet. "Don't believe me? That's okay. But ask yourself this: Why has your newfound robot friend kept the most important thing secret from you?"

Austin knew what the general was doing, but he caved in anyway. "What's that?"

"Catholic aliens." General Fergusson stretched out the words. "Does that make any sense to you?"

A chill ran up Austin's spine. "No," he admitted.

"It's a ruse, DeSantis, an enigma. All meant to keep us off-balance while the aliens enact their plan. The priest, the pope—all the Catholics—they're so intoxicated with the idea of aliens sharing in their delusion that they'll put up with anything to keep the lunacy chugging along."

With everything Austin had been through since the aliens arrived, this most obvious of questions had slipped from his mind, but now it slammed back to the forefront.

How can aliens be Catholic?

"Why didn't you ask Virgil on the ride up?" Austin asked.

"The mission is to see what's at the center of that ship. We're trying to stop China from starting a war." General Fergusson snorted. "Not call out the aliens as liars."

Austin's mind went back to the narthex. He felt Virgil's hand in his own, the haptic embrace, the sense of security and peace. It hadn't felt like a lie.

"Whatever you do, don't bring it up. Your mission is to film the center of their church. We can't risk you getting banished from the ship like me."

The Humvee came to a stop at a newly erected gate at the tenth-hole tee box. With each of Austin's visits, the barricades around the cylinder seemed to grow ever wider and more elaborate. Down the fairway, amid the thousands of bustling Regulars, Austin could make out Father Ambrose, standing alone outside the cylinder, like a man about to be sacrificed to the volcano.

Austin stepped out of the Humvee. "What if the aliens find the camera on me?"

"They'll probably kill you." General Fergusson exited the Humvee and straightened out his tunic. "But don't worry, they didn't find it on me."

The general walked over to the nearby guard shack, while Austin headed down the fairway to Father Ambrose.

"He's still in uniform after what he did to you?" Father Ambrose said, looking past Austin at General Fergusson in the distance. "Didn't you tell them what happened?"

"I did," Austin said.

"And they did nothing?"

A twinge of pain ran up Austin's arm. "Politics," Austin said, regretting that he couldn't just tell Father Ambrose the truth. "Apparently, you can't just fire 'the Face of Earth's Defense.'"

Father Ambrose put his hand on Austin's shoulder. "I'm sorry, Austin," he said. "Are you going to be all right?"

"I'm fine, Father," Austin assured him.

"Where have you been since we got back?"

The memory of the school wrestling room flashed through his head. "Debriefings," he lied. "Endless debriefings. They wanted to know every detail. What about you?"

"They tortured me."

"What?" Austin's eyes frantically scanned Father Ambrose's body, looking for signs of injury.

"It was rough, Austin. They took me to some barren FEMA trailer, nothing but saltines to eat. I had to sit there quietly without so much as an instruction manual to read." Father Ambrose's smile spilled out from underneath his beard.

Austin laughed, relieved. "I'm sure Virgil will have a nice

spread waiting for you, Father."

"I'll be happy enough just to see him again. When his head turned crimson, it was like he disappeared—taken over by some unseen controller."

"I know what you mean," Austin said. "The whole way back to Earth, I was hoping he'd return to us, tell us what was going on, but no luck. He didn't even say goodbye when we landed."

"I sure hope we get the old Virgil back; I have a million questions."

Austin nodded. He had only one question, though, one that—thanks to General Fergusson—he couldn't get out of his mind.

"It's opening!" a soldier yelled, the sound of hundreds of guns being cocked filling the air. The metal of the cylinder folded away to reveal Virgil, his head glowing pale blue in the late-morning light.

"I think we have our friend back," Father Ambrose said excitedly as he made his way toward the opening.

Austin felt a tightness in his chest as he followed close behind, the camera like a lead weight in his pocket. When he approached the cylinder threshold, he paused and turned around, taking in Earth one more time. In the distance, beyond the sandbags and long rows of soldiers, he noticed General Fergusson, his eyes trained on him, giving Austin the slightest of nods.

Turning around, he followed Virgil and Father Ambrose

down the cylinder's dark hallway until they reached the Victorian sitting room, the aroma of the feast laid out on the table welcoming them back.

"It is good to see you again, Father," Virgil said as Father Ambrose went straight for the food. "Are you well?"

"I'm starving, Virgil." Father Ambrose grabbed a slice of roasted red pepper pizza that looked like it had come straight out of a brick oven. "The US Army could sure take some hosting lessons from you."

"It gratifies me to see you comfortable, Father."

Austin considered food, but the thought of eating while betraying his friends made him queasy. Instead, he walked over to the closest sofa and sat down, letting the warmth of the fire lick his shoulders.

"You're truly a wonderful host, Virgil." Father Ambrose put down the pizza slice. "But to be honest, my mind is far hungrier than my body. I have a million questions for you."

"'Ask and it will be given to you, seek and you will find, knock and the door will be opened,'" Virgil said.

"Amen." Father Ambrose straightened himself up. "Who was Michael?"

"Michael was our leader, Father. He was kind and gentle." Virgil's voice was laced with melancholy. "Unfortunately, he succumbed to his wounds during your inspection."

Austin and Father Ambrose exchanged a look. "Wounds?" Austin asked.

"Earth's higher gravity is taxing on Pilgrim biology. Michael was very old. It was too much for him to bear."

"Michael . . . he was the Pilgrim who emerged at the Vatican two days ago?"

"Yes, Father."

Austin was transported back to his mother's apartment, watching the replay of the Arrival. He recalled the Pilgrim had been carried back into the cylinder by the Diplomats, looking unwell.

"Did he know going down to Earth would be so dangerous?"

"He was over five thousand years old; he was aware of the risks."

"Earth years or Pilgrim years?"

"Earth years, of course, Father."

"Oh, I didn't know it was so obvious."

"The Pilgrims keep Earth time so as to be coordinated with the liturgical calendar."

Father Ambrose's eyes widened. "I see. What devotion."

"Indeed, Father."

"But why would he . . ." The words had slipped out before Austin could stop himself.

"Why would he what, Austin?" Virgil asked.

Sweat pooled in Austin's armpits. Why would a five-thousand-year-old alien knowingly risk his life, just to stand in front of the pope? He desperately wanted to know the answer, but he reminded himself of General Fergusson's admonition.

"Nothing. Forget about it," Austin said, hoping that Virgil would not press him.

"There's something else that has been bugging me," Father Ambrose said, jumping in. "Where does the food come from?"

"The same place all food comes from, Father."

"Which is . . . ?"

"A farm."

Father Ambrose shattered into laughter.

Austin tilted his head. Of all the things to wonder about—who cared about the food?

"Fair enough," Father Ambrose replied once he caught his breath. "On a more serious note."

Austin leaned in, hoping Father Ambrose was finally going to address the elephant in the room.

"Here's one I've been wondering about ever since I was a little boy: Can one travel faster than the speed of light?"

Austin let out an exasperated breath.

"According to known physics," Virgil said, "the speed of light is a fundamental and immutable constraint."

"I knew it! You can't get past the cosmic speed limit?"

"Correct, Father."

"And how about us humans?" Father Ambrose grabbed a terrine of escargot. "How is our understanding of physics compared to the Pilgrims?"

"Elementary, Father. Your theoreticians seem stuck

proposing scientific theories that, by definition, cannot be tested by the scientific method. These include the many-worlds interpretation, the multiverse, and string theory. Until your leading minds realize this unscientific approach is foolhardy, your knowledge of physics is unlikely to advance."

"Thanks for the blunt assessment." Father Ambrose laughed, trying to cover his mouth. "I can't wait to drop that bomb at the next American Astronomical Society meeting."

Austin felt a headache coming on, each question that avoided the true mystery increasing the pain. He rubbed his temples in frustration.

"What about the narthex, Virgil?" Father Ambrose asked, his tone becoming more serious. "It was like nothing I'd ever seen."

"Did you like it, Father?"

"Very much so. But what was the meaning of it?"

"The narthex is a liminal space, Father, a place for the congregants to transition their perspective from the everyday to the heavenly and, in so doing, better prepare themselves for the sacrifice of the Mass."

Father Ambrose nearly dropped the terrine he looked so in awe. "How perfect. To behold the galaxy, the glory of God's creation—to take us away from the trivial things that distract us from the divine."

"That is the intention, Father."

"And the music, it was transcendent. I can't get it out of

my head."

"Thank you, Father. The choir has been practicing for centuries."

"Centuries!" Father Ambrose exclaimed. "It shows."

"Yes, Father. The choirmaster's standards are very high, and, despite my love of singing, I do not possess what is necessary to join."

Austin winced. The difference between a robot singing rather than just playing a song on its speakers was a fascinating riddle that Austin had never contemplated before. But right now, he couldn't care less, the trillion-dollar question still loomed, driving him mad. He rubbed his temples in frustration.

"What about your telescopy? You must have arrays that dwarf anything humanity has even dreamed of."

"Yes, Father. Our largest observatory—"

"Why did Michael *do* it?" Austin blurted out, unable to restrain himself anymore. "If he knew he could die, why did he leave the ship?"

Virgil turned his torso toward Austin, his pale blue head shining down on him. "Michael was nearing death, Austin. His greatest wish was to be physically close to our Lord and Savior. He had to act fast before his senescence overtook him, so when he saw the pope performing a Mass, he appeared in person, the risk notwithstanding."

Austin looked at Father Ambrose, puzzled. "The Eucharist, Austin," Father Ambrose said. "He wanted to be near the Eucharist."

"But that makes no sense," Austin protested.

"What does not make sense?" Virgil asked.

Austin could feel the camera in his pocket, burning his thigh. He'd done it, kicked the hornet's nest, risked his mission, but he couldn't stop himself. He had to know what these two were concealing. "It doesn't make sense he'd risk his life for"—Austin looked at Father Ambrose and then back at Virgil—"for some silly religious ritual."

The room fell silent, only the crack of the fire filling the air.

"It was not for some silly religious ritual." Virgil's voice was firm. "It was to be close to God—the Creator and Sustainer of the universe—who was present there in substantial form."

"But Michael's an alien," Austin said, exasperated. "Aliens aren't supposed to believe in God."

He glanced over at Father Ambrose. He had gone to eat another snail but stopped mid-bite. Austin wished he hadn't gone straight after his newfound friend's worldview, but he just couldn't keep silent any longer.

"Why not?" Virgil asked, sounding genuinely confused.

"Because it's a human superstition. You have science. Advanced technology. You don't need superstition and myth to explain things."

Virgil was quiet, nothing but silence from his domed head. Austin looked over to Father Ambrose, wondering if he would still protect him should Virgil decide to throw him out an air lock for his insolence.

"I do not understand, Father." Virgil turned his torso toward Father Ambrose. "Has Austin not studied the proofs of God's existence?"

"Probably not," Father Ambrose replied as he went back to eating his escargot. "Most people don't."

"How could that be?" Virgil asked, sounding astonished. "The proofs are not hidden. They are right there on your internet."

"Most people don't think to look," Father Ambrose said as he chewed. "And the ones who do assume, because many of the proofs are so old, that they've been rebutted."

"They have not been rebutted," Virgil replied indignantly. "And truth is ageless, Father. The passage of years does not make a true thing less so." Virgil turned his torso back toward Austin. "The Pilgrims do not believe in God out of superstition. Belief in Him is derived via reason and logic."

Austin studied Virgil, examining his head, looking for some way to detect what he was feeling, but his head glowed steady and his metal frame was still, his feelings impenetrable to Austin.

"Virgil," Father Ambrose said after washing down the escargot with a flute of sparkling water. "How many proofs of God's existence do the Pilgrims have?"

"There are four thousand seven hundred twenty-seven

arguments that are generally accepted as proofs of God's existence in Pilgrim society. There are ten thousand eight hundred seventy-two others that have been proffered but are at different stages of consensus. Some of the proofs rely on premises one can only support if they possess our knowledge of physics."

"Fascinating," Father Ambrose replied. "Which one of the proofs is the most popular?"

"The Argument from Contingency, Father."

"From Thomas Aquinas?"

"Yes, Father. Although Pilgrim philosophers had independently formulated the argument hundreds of millennia before Saint Thomas elucidated it in the *Summa Theologica*."

Father Ambrose laughed. "Oh, the poor 'angelic doctor,' if only he'd known back in the thirteenth century that the Pilgrims had beaten him to the punch by a few hundred thousand years." Father Ambrose took a sip of water. "I, for one, am a fan of the Kalam Cosmological Argument. Anything that begins to exist has a cause; the universe began to exist, ergo the universe has a cause. It's just so pithy."

"It is pithy indeed, Father, and consistent with our latest findings regarding the cosmological origin."

Austin's palms began to dry as he realized his question was not provocative enough to get him ejected from the ship. All the same, something nagged at him.

"What's your favorite proof, Virgil?" Father Ambrose asked.

"Mine is not a logical demonstration akin to Saint Thomas's five ways, but I find it persuasive nonetheless. It is the Argument from Love. There are compelling reasons to think that love exists in a way that transcends its physical manifestations. Which, if true, refutes reductive materialism."

"Ah, yes—love," Father Ambrose said with a nod. "Often a far swifter path to God than even the purest of reason."

"But that still doesn't answer my question," Austin finally said, realizing what was bugging him. "Even if Michael believed in God, why would he risk his life for a Christian ritual? How can the Pilgrims be Christian? Christianity is a human invention."

The room again went silent, save for the pop of the burning logs. This time he'd done it, pushed the issue too far.

"This is a question I cannot answer," Virgil replied, his voice firm.

"Why not?" Austin pressed, his heart pounding in his chest.

"Because," Virgil said, "you're about to find out."

18

Virgil stood at the front of the sled like a blue-headed Charon, ferrying them through the fog of the narthex while the mist lapped gently against the sides. He'd been silent since Austin had pressed him on why the Pilgrims were Catholic, retiring to the corner of the Victorian living room to pray. Austin desperately wished he could detect where he stood with the robot, but his steely body gave nothing away.

Father Ambrose put a hand to his forehead, trying to peer through the fog. "I don't see Cardinal Benedetto."

"The cardinal and his entourage have already entered the nave, Father." A wave of relief crested through Austin at the sound of Virgil's voice. "We must catch up with them."

The sled came to a stop in front of a massive silver wall.

"What's a nave?" Austin asked as he and Father Ambrose stepped off.

"It's the part of a church where the congregation sits," Father Ambrose said. "Where all the pews are."

"Does that count as the center?"

"That depends. Virgil, does the church have a transept?"

"Yes, Father." Virgil approached the silver wall.

"In that case, the transept would be the cent—" A riot of color exploded onto Father Ambrose's face.

The wall had opened to reveal a room that looked like a kaleidoscope, the walls and ceiling covered in a countless number of hues. It was like walking into a shattered rainbow, one that burned your eyes with its radiance, making the empty white of the narthex seem like a bad dream.

"It's magnificent," Father Ambrose marveled as the three of them walked inside.

With no mist hindering his line of sight, Austin could finally appreciate the scale of the rooms in the church. They were more like landscapes rather than chambers: the walls a horizon, the ceiling a sky.

They had walked only a short distance when the floor abruptly stopped, nothing but empty air in front of them, a black abyss below.

Father Ambrose backed away, but Austin leaned over the side, trying to see if he could perceive anything at the bottom. "Why is there a cliff in a church?"

"There is no cliff, Austin," Virgil replied.

"What am I looking at, then?"

"A dynamic floor."

Virgil stretched out his leg, extending it over the side of the cliff as if he were going to throw himself over, but then he took a step forward and stopped, seemingly suspended in midair.

Austin's eyes widened. "How are you not falling?"

"The floor is preventing me from doing so."

"But you're not standing on the floor. You're floating."

Virgil took a few more steps farther out from the edge. "I see the issue, Austin. You believe that because you cannot see the floor, it is not there."

Austin looked to Father Ambrose, who was now standing almost ten yards back, avoiding Austin's eyes. "But it is there?"

Virgil walked onward, floating higher as he did. "Yes, Austin. In order to make full use of the volume of a room, one must employ a dynamic floor—a floor that will automatically raise and lower for each of the individuals within the room. And in order not to impede lines of sight, the floor is transparent."

It took Austin a second to understand what Virgil was talking about, but when he pictured it, it made sense. No matter how large the building, humans were always limited to being on the floor, not utilizing the full volume of the space.

The scene in the narthex suddenly made sense to him, the way the Pilgrim choir seemed to be floating in the air. He realized now they must have been using a dynamic floor.

"But," Austin said, "if someone is higher than me and I walk under them, won't I just walk into the floor?"

"The computer that operates the floor is extremely sophisticated. It will make rapid adjustments to prevent that from happening."

Austin looked around at the massive space. It was bigger than any stadium he'd ever visited. In fact, the nave probably could have fit dozens of stadiums inside it with room to spare. "How many people can be on the floor at one time?" he asked.

"Approximately fifteen million humans or fourteen million two hundred fifty-seven thousand Pilgrims."

"Now that would be one well-attended Mass." Despite his quip, Father Ambrose had a pained look on his face.

"Please, let us continue," Virgil said. "The cardinal and his delegation are approaching the transept. We cannot let them get too far ahead."

Austin looked back down. The darkness seemed to go on forever, but if he didn't continue onward, his mission would be lost before it started. He lifted a leg, stretched it out, and fell forward. His stomach dropped, expecting to continue plummeting down, but, instead, he landed firmly, his foot resting on air as if it were stone. He took a few more steps, venturing farther out, and started to fill with a childlike delight.

"Take a look at this, Father. I'm floating!" Austin turned around and noticed Father Ambrose conspicuously looking away. "Don't tell me you're afraid of heights," he said as he made his way back to the priest.

Father Ambrose sighed. "Maybe it's better if you and Virgil just go on ahead without me."

"I'm sorry, Father," Virgil said, gliding back toward them. "As your host, I am responsible for you. I must stay by your side."

"Come on, Father," Austin said, trying to sound encouraging. "You can do it."

Father Ambrose gave him a pathetic look. "No, I really can't, Austin."

"You saw me out there. I know it looks like you'll fall, but that's just an illusion. It's kind of fun, actually."

"My mind knows you're right, but . . ." Father Ambrose grimaced. "I just can't."

"I am sorry, Father. I have failed you as a host," Virgil said. "Soon the cardinal will be too far ahead for you to be part of the inspection, and I will have to take you back to Earth."

The camera became heavier in Austin's pocket. "Why?"

"It was Michael's decree, Austin," Virgil replied.

"Come on, Father," Austin said, a bit pushier this time. "We've come so far."

"Austin, if Father Ambrose is uncomfortable—"

"Father, please." Austin tugged on his shirt, trying to coax him. "You need to get over yourself."

"Austin, unhand Father Ambrose."

"Come on, it's just a few steps, you'll be fine."

"Austin!" Virgil's voice boomed.

Austin froze, but his grip did not loosen.

"I was eight," Father Ambrose said, breaking the tension.

"I went up on the roof to get a Frisbee. I fell off. Dropped two stories. I was in a coma for three days. Missed two months of school."

"I'm sorry, Father." Austin let go of Father Ambrose's shirt. "I had no idea."

"It's okay, Austin. It's just . . ." Father Ambrose's lips quivered. "My mom was sick. Glioblastoma." Austin saw a tear leak from Father Ambrose's eye onto his beard. "And while I was in a coma . . ." Father Ambrose shook his head. "I never got to say goodbye."

Austin's heart started to throb.

"That's probably why I started looking up at the sky. That way, I could keep my feet firmly planted on the ground, looking up into the beyond. You can't fall when you're on the ground. I couldn't hurt her again."

The nave became small. Just the three of them with Father Ambrose's loss. Yet Austin could still feel the camera in his pocket, urging him forward.

"Perhaps you should look up now, Father." Virgil's voice was sweet.

Austin shot Virgil a severe look. To his surprise, though, Father Ambrose peered up at the ceiling, his bespectacled eyes straining as if focusing on something that wasn't there.

"Saint Kolbe?" Father Ambrose said, astonished. "The SS—they're injecting the carbolic acid. He's giving his arm to them freely."

"What's going on?" Austin asked, following the priest's gaze up, but he didn't see anything.

"Saint Francis, my namesake!" Father Ambrose continued. "He's preaching to the birds. They're listening! How marvelous!"

"Virgil?"

"It's all right, Austin," Father Ambrose said. "I'm fine."

"What are you looking at?"

"The saints, Austin. I'm looking at the saints."

"Virgil." Austin crossed his arms. "What's going on here?"

"The saints are exemplars, Austin," Virgil said. "They show us the way to a life in Christ. Each of the colors on the ceiling and the wall represents one of their stories."

Austin scanned the wall and the ceiling. "All I see are random blobs of color."

"You have to focus." Father Ambrose pointed at a dot off in the distance directly over their heads. "Take a look at that red shape and don't look away."

Austin followed Father Ambrose's finger, making sure he was focusing on the right one. At first nothing happened, but as he stared, the red spot grew larger, drowning out all the other colors until it filled his whole view. The red then began to have texture, and he realized he was looking at a cloak.

"What's happening?" Austin asked.

"Keep watching," Father Ambrose said.

His view zoomed out to reveal a bearded man wearing a crimson cloak. He was old and gray, standing in the middle of a stadium—the Colosseum in Rome, no less. But it wasn't the ruin Austin was familiar with; it was alive, throngs of people cheering as legionaries held a pair of lions by chains.

"It's Saint Ignatius of Antioch," Austin heard Father Ambrose say over the din of the crowd, the visage of the Colosseum still filling up his view. "He is one of the Apostolic Fathers. One of the most important theologians of the early Church."

"You're seeing this, too?"

"I am," Father Ambrose replied.

Austin was marveling at the re-creation of the Colosseum, how real the Roman crowd appeared, when suddenly the audience, in unison, let out a collective cry. The legionaries had dropped their chains, setting the lions free. The first of the beasts sunk its teeth into the man's shoulder, knocking him over, while the second went straight for the man's ankle, ripping it apart with his fangs. But the man did not scream. With his free arm, he made the sign of the cross, praying as the lions ripped him to pieces—the crowd hushed at the majesty of his end.

Austin blinked, and the image was gone.

"What just happened?" Austin rubbed his eyes.

"When you focus on a color, the nave computer directs a beam of light on your retina," Virgil explained. "Sound is then transmitted using sonic waves that vibrate the jawbone, inducing bone conduction."

Austin nodded, only partly understanding.

"It's like the stained glass windows in a church," Father Ambrose said. "They're there to tell stories, teach people about the saints and Scripture."

"Yes, Father," Virgil confirmed. "That was the inspiration."

Austin's head darted around. There must have been hundreds of thousands of colored shapes covering the ceiling and the walls. One could stand here for a lifetime and not examine them all.

"The computer can do all that and operate the floor, too?" Austin marveled as his head kept darting around. He noticed a green shape on the far wall. It was the same color as the eyes of the Black Shirt he'd met in the boys' locker room—the one with the Mississippi twang. The memory of her made his cheeks flush. "The computing power must be incredible."

"Yes. At least, compared to human computers."

"Does the computer have a personality like you, Virgil?"

"No, Austin. The nave computer does not have a mind. Humans often believe that computational power alone is enough to generate a mind. It is not. The nature of a mind is far more mysterious and complex."

His curiosity running amok, Austin was about to follow up, but he noticed that Father Ambrose was no longer next to him. "Father?"

"The saints, Austin," Father Ambrose replied, now standing at the edge of the dynamic floor. "They trusted in God's will, even to the very end. It's time I followed their example."

Father Ambrose was shivering, at the brink of all he could take, yet he leapt forward, as if jumping into a swimming pool, and landed on the dynamic floor with a thump.

"Well done!" Austin shouted as Father Ambrose marched ahead.

As Austin went to catch up, a feeling of relief coursing through his veins, his gaze landed on a shape the color of Virgil's domed head, one that was conspicuously larger than the rest of the colors. Before he knew it, the pale blue was filling his vision, becoming textured, revealing itself as a shawl. The image pulled back further until he saw a face—a woman's face, her eyes the same color as her shawl. She was smiling at Austin, looking right into his gaze.

Austin felt an intense wave of love, like the woman knew him completely, his mere existence filling her with joy.

He kept waiting for a scene, some sort of event like the previous image, but none appeared. It was only this woman and her loving stare.

A sharp pain shot through Austin's heart. How many hours had he spent leering at Aurelia, drooling over her body, without the slightest hint of tenderness in his heart? He felt gross, the folly of his past actions so obvious as he beheld this blessed woman. And yet this woman smiled at him, letting him know he was no less loved.

Even without Father Ambrose there to explain, he knew

instinctually who this was. It was Mary, mother of Jesus, and Austin could not bring himself to look away.

"Austin," Virgil said as the image faded. "We must proceed."

"I'm sorry." Austin began to walk, trying to catch up to Father Ambrose, who was already a great deal farther ahead. "I couldn't take my eyes off her. She was so . . . pure."

"Many come to behold the Blessed Mother as they pray. They find she helps direct us toward her son, our Lord and Savior."

Despite the majesty of the nave and its visions, Virgil's comment caused the nagging question to return to the fore of Austin's mind. Why were the Pilgrims Catholic? Virgil still hadn't answered.

"Michael himself," Virgil continued, "will come to pray in the presence of the Blessed Mother later today."

"Michael?" Austin asked, confused. "Didn't he die?"

"He did, Austin. May God rest his soul."

Austin slowed down. "Then how could he come here tonight to pray? Do you mean he'll come in spirit?"

"No, Austin."

"Then how?"

"We have chosen a new Michael. He is firm, but true of heart."

Austin puzzled over this answer for a few steps. "Michael isn't a name. It's a title?"

"Yes, Austin."

"What kind of title?"

"It comes from Scripture. Michael the Archangel, lord of the heavenly host."

General Fergusson flashed into Austin's mind. "Michael's a military commander?" he said, the hairs on the back of his neck standing up. "Like a general?"

"Yes."

The word hit Austin like a hammer. General Fergusson was right. The Pilgrims were a military force. And the giant contradiction—the reason why an alien race would be Catholic—remained hidden as he walked deeper into their fortress, an instrument of betrayal in his pocket, the fate of humanity on his back.

19

The transept had none of the nave's cheer. Gone was the frenzy of color, replaced by a gray ceiling and gray walls. Plumes of dust curled up behind their feet as they walked, the dynamic floor having given way to a chalky desert soil. Austin looked around, trying to identify features that he might find in a church, but all he saw before him was an empty desert, with a craggy rock face breaking up the monotony of the landscape.

"This road takes us by the stations of the cross," Virgil said. "It leads to the center of the transept. But we must take a short-cut after the second station to catch up with the delegation. I'm sorry I cannot show you all the stations, Father, but we were delayed too long in the nave."

Father Ambrose nodded, and the three of them pressed on. Unlike before, why the Pilgrims were Catholic no longer troubled Austin. General Fergusson had been right all along, and this strange church, the Pilgrims' religious affectations, none of it mattered; the only thing that mattered was the mission.

As they approached the rock face, it began unfolding to the side, revealing a Roman palace. Ionic columns stretched out before them in rows, with marble statues filling in the gaps in between. It was dim, lit only by a handful of torches, making it feel as if they were entering a tomb.

A whisper echoed in Austin's ear: *"Liar!"*

It felt as if a malign spirit were following him.

"Who said that?" Father Ambrose's voice faltered.

"The Sanhedrin, Father," Virgil said calmly, continuing to glide forward. "Please keep up."

"Traitor! Betrayer!"

Austin shrunk down as he walked forward, desperately trying to find out where the voice was coming from.

"Kill him! He must die!"

They turned a corner, and the source of the voices revealed itself. Before him was a crowd of humans clad in ancient garb. They wore simple robes that ended above their sandaled feet. Atop their heads were flat-topped turbans. They didn't so much stand as billow, like kelp under the sea. No one turned to look at the three of them.

"There are people here?" Father Ambrose asked.

"No, Father. These are only projections," Virgil replied.

"Blasphemer!"

Virgil plunged into the crowd, the projections floating to the side when he came near.

"King of the Jews!"

Entering the crowd, Austin noticed the people's expressions were as empty as a corpse at a wake. When they arrived at the front, Austin's breath escaped him.

Before him was Jesus, hands bound behind his back, cast down on his knees in front of a Roman prefect whose gold-lined toga shimmered in the torchlight.

Seeing Jesus on his knees, Austin felt a tightness in his chest. It had been only a few days since he'd been in the same position: kneeling in a dark warehouse, the end of his life close at hand. General Fergusson had saved him from the Black Shirts and given him a second chance. At that thought, Austin reached into his pocket and flicked the camera's armed switch to "on." With his forefinger, he began furiously turning the crank, counting to himself as he did.

"This is the first station." Virgil knelt down in front of Christ. "Jesus is condemned to death by Pilate."

Without hesitation, Father Ambrose knelt as well.

"My beloved Jesus," Virgil began, making the sign of the cross, "it was not Pilate; no, it was my sins that condemned You to die. I beseech You, by the merits of this sorrowful journey, to assist my soul on its journey to eternity. I love You, beloved Jesus; I love You, more than I love myself. With all my heart, I repent of ever having offended You. Grant that I may love You always; and then do with me as You will." His prayer finished, Virgil bent down lower and began to vibrate, his mechanical body, up until now so graceful, rattling like a shaky windowpane.

Questions flooded into Austin's mind. Why would a robot pray to the point of near seizure? Why would the Pilgrims build this place?

"Let us continue to the second station," Virgil said a few moments later.

Austin removed his hand from his pocket, congratulating himself for making it all the way to thirty-seven unnoticed.

They exited the palace, and Virgil led them back onto a dirt road that traveled through a narrow valley, scrubby hills covered in thistle on either side. The sky-like ceiling of the ship's interior was darker now, as if dusk were setting upon them. Austin used the time to turn the crank more.

"Austin, I've been meaning to thank—" Father Ambrose turned around too quickly for Austin to take his hand out of his pocket. "What are you doing?" he asked, gesturing toward Austin's hand.

"What do you mean?"

Frowning at him, the priest waved a hand at him. "What's in your pocket?"

Virgil stopped and peered back at the humans.

"Nothing," Austin said, trying to sound innocent.

Father Ambrose's face sharpened. "Austin, what's in your—"

"Come, Father," Virgil interrupted. "We cannot be late."

Searching Father Ambrose's face, Austin silently begged him to relent, but he held his ground. This was it: his betrayal had been discovered not by one of the aliens but by a member of his own species. Virgil, however, was already walking away. It was enough to get Father Ambrose moving again, though the sour taste of the unanswered question lingered in the air.

Cursing himself for almost being discovered, and cursing himself some more for forgetting if he'd stopped on fifty-one or fifty-two, Austin followed.

Not long after, they found themselves amid another crowd. *"Look at his crown!"*

The projections swayed before them, blocking their path, but Virgil went on, the crowd parting around him as he strode. *"King of kings, indeed!"*

They arrived at the front of the crowd to find Jesus slumped over, blood leaking from his head where a crown of thorns had been pressed into his skull.

When a Roman soldier came over with a large beam of wood, prepared to throw it on Christ's back, Austin reminded himself it was only a projection. Before the wood struck down, Jesus stopped him and hoisted the heaving beam onto his own shoulders, bowing under its immense weight.

Father Ambrose knelt. "The second station: Jesus accepts his cross."

Virgil followed suit, his metal body once again quaking as he prayed.

Before Austin realized it, he was back in the warehouse once again. The crack of the rifles, the men straining for the shadow, the bodies bleeding on the floor. Austin would have done anything, betrayed anyone, to be free of that horror. Yet here before him was Jesus, willingly taking on that burden. The contradiction was too much, and a searing pain shot through his heart.

Thoughts of General Fergusson stalked back into his mind, though, offering freedom and comfort for him and his mother. Austin's hand reached for his pocket. He pawed the camera for a moment before his forefinger found the divot and began turning the crank.

"Come," Virgil said. "We must proceed to Golgotha via the shortcut."

Without waiting, Virgil started down the road, walking so fast that Austin and Father Ambrose nearly had to jog to keep up.

As Austin debated whether he was on turn eighty-eight or eighty-nine, Virgil led them down a narrower path, a crevice only about six yards wide.

Their journey continued until they saw a crowd in the distance, gathered at the bottom of what looked like a long-abandoned quarry. In the center was a small promontory with three crucifixes atop it, a man affixed to each one.

"We have caught up with the rest of the delegation, Father."

Guiding them toward the crowd, Virgil directed their attention to the right. Austin turned his head to see a giant Diplomat approaching from a wider path that entered the quarry from another side, trailed by the cardinal and his entourage, the violet-headed Diplomat bringing up the rear.

This time, as they moved through the crowd, the projections barely moved for them. Austin found himself hemmed in by the lifeless specters, their silence somehow more unsettling than the whispers or the cackling that had come before.

Virgil stopped a few rows from the front, apparently content to watch the execution amid the throng. From here, they were close enough that Austin could read the Latin on the sign nailed to the top of the center crucifix: "Iēsus Nazarēnus, Rēx Iūdaeōrum—Jesus of Nazareth, King of the Jews."

This was the center of the whole church, the transept, and there was no superweapon as far as he could see—just a lifelike re-creation of the crucifixion. Relief washed over him at the realization that all he had to do was to record the scene and get back home, a war averted, his freedom attained. The projections, however, blocked his way. He'd have to find another vantage point to do what he'd been sent here to do.

Pressing further into the crowd, Austin made his way toward the very front. He tried to push the spectral figures out of the way, but when he pressed against them, all he felt was a hollow sensation that caused the hair on his arms to stiffen.

Eventually, he reached a spot at the front where there were no projections to obscure the camera's line of sight. Virgil and Father Ambrose remained a few rows back. He hoped they were distant enough that they wouldn't notice him sticking his hand into his pocket and cranking the camera once again.

Eighty-eight. Eighty-nine. Ninety.

The techs had shown him how to hold the camera—low down by his side, cupped in his palm, lens pointed at the subject. He'd then count to sixty, the total length of time before the camera exhausted its film. Then all he had to do was put it back into his pocket and return to Earth with his prize.

Ninety-three. Ninety-four. Ninety-five.

As he turned the crank, his attention was drawn to Jesus on the cross. Each breath seemed like agony. The weight of his body pulled him down, compressing his chest. He had to put all his weight on his brutalized arms just to take in air. His naked body was covered in lash marks, the skin torn apart like the kind old man at the muster.

Ninety-six. Ninety-seven. Ninety-eight.

Austin was gripping the camera, having taken it out of his pocket, when Jesus's eyes locked onto his. It was just a projection, but Austin could feel the gaze—judging his betrayal, calling him to love. His heart wrenched at the sight of it.

"Virgil?"

Austin flinched so violently that he nearly dropped the camera.

Father Ambrose was next to him, he and Virgil having approached unnoticed.

"Do congregants need to pass through here on their way to Communion?"

"Yes, Father. The congregants take Communion at the altar

rail in the chancel, but they must pass the crucified Christ on their way there."

"Chancel?" Austin asked, sweat dripping from his brow.

"The chancel is where the altar is located," Father Ambrose explained. "It's the heart of the church, its spiritual center, where Christ's sacrifice is re-presented at every Mass."

Austin's stomach twisted. He'd misunderstood. He'd found the physical center of the church, but not the heart. And he'd charged the camera prematurely, precisely what the techs had warned him not to do.

Austin trembled as he looked to his right and saw the giant Diplomat striding toward him, bathing the area in its crimson glow. His grip on the camera tightened involuntarily as he felt it looking at him, sensing the static electric charge in his hand, ready to reveal him as a traitor.

He felt exposed. His eyes darted around as he wondered what to do, but a loud crack and a bloodcurdling scream cut through his racing thoughts.

Startled, Austin jumped back, his gaze shooting to the Roman soldier with a giant wooden mallet in his hand. The man being crucified to Jesus's right had had his shins broken open, the tibia jutting out in a splintered mess. Another soldier was lining up his mallet on the man to Jesus's left, about to swing it down. A moment later, he did so and the transept again filled with a scream.

Austin fell backward, the projections closing in around

him. He could still see the promontory, though, his line of sight still unblocked. A third soldier appeared, thrusting a spear into Jesus's side.

The sound of tearing flesh echoed, unnaturally amplified. Blood poured from the wound, followed by water as the last drops of life hit the ground.

Austin watched in horrified awe as the giant Diplomat leaned over him, its crimson head filling up his view. He knew he was done for, the object of betrayal right there in his hand. But before he could cry out for mercy, the transept went dark, and the air filled with a resounding wail.

20

Qui peccata nostra ipse pertulit in corpore suo super lignum!"

The crimson glow of the giant Diplomat washed over Austin as he cowered in the dirt.

"Ut peccatis mortui iustitiae vivamus: cuis livore sanatis estis."

The light returned to the transept, the darkness vanishing in an instant. The giant Diplomat was still looming over Austin like a colossus, but now the crowd had vanished. Only the delegation was still there, save for two men on a ladder carefully taking Jesus down from the cross, and Mary sitting at the foot of the cross, cloaked in her pale blue shawl.

"Austin?" Father Ambrose asked. "What did the Diplomat say?"

Trying to compose himself, Austin got back up on his feet, the camera like a hot coal in his clenched fist. "He said, 'He Himself bore our sins in His body upon the cross, so that, free from sin, we might live for righteousness. By His wounds, you have been healed.'"

"Amen," Father Ambrose said, making the sign of the cross.

Austin looked to the cardinal, hoping that the elderly bishop would do something to distract the giant Diplomat, if only for a moment, but Cardinal Benedetto was on his knees in prayer, and the priests who accompanied him were doing the same.

Austin looked for Virgil, but his eyes came upon the violet-headed Diplomat first. He looked away as soon as he could, not wanting to let it be known he was staring, but the Diplomat had already noticed him and began walking toward Austin with a graceful stride.

"Come," Virgil said, appearing in Austin's line of sight. "We must proceed to the chancel."

Austin's heart raced as he imagined the other Diplomats' sensors blaring in alarm at the statically charged camera in Austin's hand.

Virgil steered them toward the back wall of the quarry, the rock face having been recently cut open to add new tombs to the site. Virgil ducked inside one of the tomb entrances, vanishing into the darkness within.

Following closely behind, Austin discovered Jesus's body on a small stone slab. The two men from the ladder were cleaning him, removing the dried blood from his wounds. He heard a sound and then noticed Mary off to the side of the tomb, her face streaked with tears.

"The fourteenth station," Father Ambrose said as the three of them walked by the scene, so close they could have reached out and touched the projections. "Jesus is placed in the tomb."

"Yes, Father," Virgil said, leading them deeper into the shadows.

"Our faith is so strange," Father Ambrose mused. "Our chief symbol is a man executed in the most brutal and humiliating way. But now we barely notice the cross. It's just a part of the scenery. These stations help remind us what the cross truly is."

"Indeed, Father," Virgil said, proceeding ever deeper into the dark tomb. "Lest we ever forget the true ugliness of sin."

Austin glanced behind him, searching for the glow of the giant Diplomat, but all he saw was darkness. Perhaps the military techs had been wrong and the Diplomats couldn't detect the camera's static charge. Then a thought occurred to him: perhaps the Pilgrims hadn't detected the charge because he'd miscounted the cranks, discharging the camera in his pocket. If so, his mission had already failed. He shuddered, trying to repress the thought.

As he walked on, the walls and ceiling became bright, the cramped grave yawning into a wide-open space, its walls now gold.

A hum coursed through the air like an electric heartbeat, filling the place with energy that made Austin's skin tingle all over. For the first time since they'd arrived, he entertained the possibility that there might actually be a superweapon; perhaps this energy was what the Chinese had detected. He looked around, trying to find a distinguishing feature, but the room was the same in all directions: gold so encompassing he couldn't tell where the floor ended and the walls began. Up ahead, he noticed a splash of pink, the only spot of color in the otherwise monotone room. As they got closer, he realized it was a table sitting atop an altar two golden steps up from the floor.

Separating the altar from the rest of the space was a waist-high railing. It looked like a molten metal waterfall, appearing in midair and then flowing down to disappear into the altar floor.

"Behold the altar, where the sacrifice of the Mass may be presented."

"It's like nothing I've ever seen." Father Ambrose approached the railing. "How does the priest enter?"

"The altar rail moves aside automatically for a priest, deacon, or bishop, Father."

Father Ambrose rubbed his beard. "What about an ambo? I don't see one."

"We did not anticipate you would need one, Father," Virgil replied. "The celebrants will be perfectly visible to all the congregants in the nave by means of the directed light beams, the same mechanism that allowed you to see the stories of the saints. And the celebrant will be able to access the missal in the same way, eliminating the need to carry a book."

Making sure Virgil and Father Ambrose were behind him, Austin walked up close to the altar rail. This was it, the end of the line, no spot to hide, no crowd of projections to camouflage himself with. He put his forefinger on the crank, about to make the final turn, when the giant Diplomat glided up next to him, his approach completely unheard.

"Ecce!" the large Diplomat bellowed. "Testimonium nostrum Christi qui resuurexit!"

The Latin passed through Austin's skull untranslated as he braced himself for the attack, his comeuppance finally at hand. Instead, the gold wall behind the altar burst into a scene filled with color.

Austin found himself looking at three men on crucifixes. It was the scene they had just walked through, except the point of view was elevated and further back in the crowd. Unlike in the transept, the people in the crowd were animated, moving about and shouting jeers. He watched again as the Roman soldier drove the spear into Jesus's side.

The walls went dark for a few seconds, until they filled up again with the image of a rock with ropes around it, the Roman imperial seal affixed to the knot. The image had a greenish tint like an infrared camera recording in low light, and alien writing scrolled across the screen.

With everyone distracted by the display, Austin realized this was his best chance to record the center of the church. He turned the crank one last time and opened his palm, aiming the lens at the altar, hoping the camera hadn't already been discharged.

Then it dawned on him that he recognized the tomb.

There was a flash of white light, and he was blinded.

He held the camera steady as he covered his eyes with his other hand. In a few moments, his vision returned. The alien writing flashed red across the screen. The rock was gone, the ropes in a heap on the ground. Two Roman soldiers approached the tomb. An instant later, they were running away, a man bathed in white light at the cave's center.

"Virgil, is this what I think it is?" Father Ambrose's voice trembled.

"Yes, Father," Virgil said. "Behold, our witness to the risen Christ."

Austin tried to hold the camera steady, but his hand had begun to shake. Those were the words the giant Diplomat had said, the words he'd been too overwhelmed to translate.

"This isn't a re-creation . . . is it?" Father Ambrose gasped. "This is a *recording.*"

"Yes, Father."

"How can this be?"

"The Pilgrims have been observing Earth for millennia. It is still the only other planet in the galaxy we have found with life."

As the image on the screen shifted, Austin held his breath.

Jesus stood by a lake, surrounded by a crowd. Austin could see the wounds on his wrists. He pulled his robe aside to show a curious person the hole in his torso, and the crowd gasped and called his name.

The image changed again.

Jesus on a hilltop, his followers gathered around. Then he started floating in the air. The alien writing on the screen flashed red, scrolling across as if lit on fire.

The image cut again to Earth from the vantage point of a satellite in orbit. A small ball of light came up from the planet, growing into an immense flame. It passed by the camera and disappeared into the emptiness of space.

Austin gasped, his body hungry for the air he'd been too stunned to take in. He held the camera steady, uncertain if sixty seconds had passed.

The image changed again, starting over, an instant replay.

As the fire passed by the camera, it went frame by frame until the image froze. The camera then zoomed in. In the center of the fire was a man: the unmistakable face of Jesus.

"Glory to God!" Father Ambrose exclaimed, his eyes wide. "You witnessed the Ascension!"

"Yes, Father."

"I don't know what to say." Father Ambrose looked as though he might fall over. "You've been watching us all this time? Is that what UFOs are?"

"No, Father. Our surveillance has remained undetected—

except for one incident in 1587."

"Did this conflict with Pilgrim religion?"

"No, Father. Pilgrims are not like humans, prone to mythic and legendary beliefs. Our philosophers had long ago concluded that the universe had a creator, but we believed the Creator did not care about His creation, devoting His entire divine being to contemplating Himself—until we witnessed this. The evidence of divine intervention was incontrovertible. We knew then the Creator cared for His creation—that He loved it. This meant the only reasonable course of action was to devote ourselves entirely to Him."

Austin couldn't believe what he was hearing. He had his answer now about why the Pilgrims were Catholic, but the answer made him feel dizzy, like his entire conception of reality had been turned upside down.

Then he noticed the violet-headed Diplomat coming toward him. He closed his hand, concealing the camera in his fist.

"When the data of what happened to Jesus finally reached the Pilgrim home system," Virgil continued, "a crewed mission was prepared with all due haste. But the preparation took time and the distance of space is vast, the speed of light an immutable constraint. It took us many centuries to arrive."

"How far did you travel?"

"The Pilgrim home system is over one hundred light-years away."

"At light speed?"

"No, Father, we could only proceed at a fraction thereof."

"Good thing Pilgrims live so long."

"Yes, Father. Even though Pilgrims live long, the journey has taken over a thousand years, a sacrifice without equal in Pilgrim history. But God's Church is on Earth, the only known place in the universe where one can be in the presence of the Creator in His substantial form. For that we would travel any distance, endure any hardship, just to be close to Him."

Father Ambrose met Austin's gaze, his face drained of color. "Austin, do you know what this means?"

Austin shivered. The Diplomats were closing in. Not knowing where to hide the camera, he shoved it back into his pocket.

"This changes *everything*."

PART III

21

Austin was alone—Cynthia and Liam nowhere to be seen. The old man stood behind the counter, arranging the lottery tickets. Austin went to him, elated, the deathly blow undone.

Seeing him approach, the old man said, "Why, Austin?"

Austin's heart began to race. It was happening again. He tried to run, but he couldn't.

"Why didn't you stop her?" The old man's empty, lifeless eyes bore into him.

Austin looked down. Liam's gun was in his hand. He leveled it.

"Do it," the old man demanded.

The gun grew heavier.

A woman came at the old man from the side, her belly swollen, a Fedcoin machine in her hands. Austin pointed the gun at her, his finger on the trigger, but he couldn't squeeze.

She mocked him with a smile as the machine came down. The old man's skull broke open, drowning the store in a river of blood.

Austin's eyes shot open.

The old man had found him once more, tormenting him in his sleep, just like he had every night since Austin had returned to Earth and been stuffed in this cell.

Austin touched his face. For the millionth time, he wondered how long he'd been here. There were no windows, no distinction between night and day. Time was marked solely by the two flavorless meals that slid through the slot in the metal door and the growing length of his haggard beard—haggard like his sanity.

"DeSantis?"

The muffled voice came from the other side of the steel door. Austin braced himself, preparing for another hallucination.

"I have some good news."

The voice was clearer now, louder, and Austin began to fear this would be the worst one yet. But then he heard the bolts releasing, and the door slid open for the first time since he'd been placed there.

General Fergusson stood in the doorway, a towel over his shoulder and a wooden box in his hand. Austin blinked, unsure if he could believe what he was seeing. "I convinced them not to kill you."

"Are you real?" Austin's voice cracked—a casualty of extreme underuse.

A faint smile curled the corners of General Fergusson's mouth. He took the towel from his shoulder and began to roll it up, carefully and deliberately, like it was origami. When he was done, he snapped it at Austin.

Austin cried out in pain as the towel stung his cheek.

"Does that answer your question?" Without waiting for an answer, General Fergusson took a seat on the foot of Austin's cot.

Austin sat up, removing his legs from the woolen blanket and putting his bare feet onto the cold floor. "How long have I been here?"

"Five weeks and five days."

Austin touched his beard. Forty days, and yet it seemed he'd been there one hundred times as long. "Did it work?" he asked.

"Did what work?" General Fergusson placed the wooden box on the cot, arranging it so that it rested perfectly flat on the blanket.

"The video I took," Austin said, exasperated. "Did you use it to show China it wasn't a superweapon? That it was just a church?"

"Oh, that." General Fergusson opened the box. "A lot has happened, DeSantis."

Despite the ever-present chill of the cell, sweat had pooled under Austin's armpits. "What do you mean 'Oh, that'? What's happened?" Austin's voice was stronger now, finding its old rhythm.

General Fergusson took a piece of soap out of the box and reached over to the metal commode, the cramped cell so small he barely needed to lean.

"I nearly died trying to get that video!" Austin's words echoed off the concrete walls, and his mind went to the chancel. The giant Diplomat looming over him, the violet-headed Diplomat coming his way. He'd thought they were going to kill him, but before he knew it, Virgil was putting him on a sled back to Earth. Virgil's head had turned from pale blue to crimson, and he hadn't spoken so much as a single word to Austin the whole ride back.

"It discharged in your pocket, DeSantis." General Fergusson ran the faucet atop the metal commode, wetting the bar of soap. "We couldn't use any of it."

Austin's stomach dropped. "I failed?"

"Yes." General Fergusson pulled a brush from the box and rubbed it on the soap, generating a milky lather.

"But what about China?" Austin's head became light, and he began to sag, the light fading from his eyes. "Why haven't they attacked?"

"There are riots in China." General Fergusson grabbed Austin's face with his hand and began to lather it up. "Christians are marching, demanding they be allowed to worship openly. The regime is afraid to attack them, lest the aliens intervene. We're on the verge of another Tiananmen. And this time it doesn't look like the CCP's going to make it to the other side."

Austin remained still despite the tickle of the soap.

"About fifteen minutes after you emerged in DC, the rest of the delegation arrived at the Vatican. They weren't back a few hours before Pope Stephen released the aliens' video. The whole world has seen it."

Austin's eyes widened. "Father Ambrose? Was he with them?"

"Yes." General Fergusson rinsed the brush in the sink, cleaning off the remaining lather. "The video sparked a global frenzy." General Fergusson placed the brush back into the wooden box and pulled out a straightedge razor. "The junta in Brazil swore allegiance to the pope, saying that as the largest Catholic nation, it was their duty to defend Christendom." General Fergusson turned Austin's head, bringing the blade to his right cheek. "The UK is about to vote to become a republic. People are thinking the monarch's role as head of the Church of England is a major liability."

General Fergusson moved the blade down Austin's cheek in one smooth motion, the hair giving way to the sharpened blade.

"Every day at noon the twelve alien crafts over world cities broadcast the Our Father." General Fergusson brought the blade down again, his dark eyes focused on Austin, like a sculptor perfecting a bust. "They play it so loud no one can even think for a three-hundred-mile radius. When the one over Medina goes off, Saudi Arabia descends into chaos, the apostasy of it all shoved right in their face." Finished shaving the whole right side of Austin's face, the general rinsed off the blade for the first time. "The hard-liners want King Salman to try and shoot the craft down even though they know an attack is suicide. But he refuses to destroy his nation and start a world war. And to thank him, he's met by one coup attempt after another. Won't be long before they finally take him out."

"If I failed . . ." Austin's mind returned to himself, the rest of the world nothing more than an abstraction in his cave. "Why am I still alive?"

General Fergusson stopped rinsing the blade and looked at Austin. "Because I saved you," he said as his mouth curled up at the sides. "Again."

The general let the revelation hang there, as if to elicit a reaction from Austin, but he was too exhausted to be upset.

"Ramirez wanted you dead," General Fergusson continued, "but I went over her head, straight to the president. Told him that we need you, that soon it would become clear. And now that day has come."

"Need me?" Austin's voice broke, ashamed that a part of him felt grateful.

"You're my weapon, DeSantis," the general said as he started on the left side of Austin's face. "Our only hope in the fight ahead."

This close to General Fergusson, Austin noticed how emaciated he was: the veins popping out of his hand, the outline of the bones in his legs. He realized he'd never seen the general eat, as if he didn't need calories but simply sustained himself on hate.

"Fight? There won't be a fight," Austin said. "You saw the video. They're Christians. They saw Jesus rise from the dead."

The general raised his eyebrows at him, continuing to move the blade deftly down his skin. "Did they?"

"Of course they did." Locked away in the cell, Austin had had a lot of time to think about it. "If you were there and saw how seriously they took the video—"

"I was there, DeSantis." General Fergusson flicked the razor and a chunk of Austin's mustache disappeared. "I saw the giant 'church,' the ornate pageant the aliens put on to impress you and a bunch of Catholic priests. It's all a parlor trick, a ruse meant to deceive the gullible and ensnare the overeager."

"A trick?" Austin's voice faltered.

General Fergusson smiled. "They have a video. Of what exactly? A man on a cross? A person coming out of a grave? They traveled across the galaxy, DeSantis. How hard could it be to fake a video?"

All this time he'd been so sure of what he'd seen, but what the general said . . . the way the old man came to visit him and made him question what was real . . . perhaps the general was right.

"Suppose they did fake the video. For five years, I watched you on TV," Austin said as General Fergusson carefully shaved the last bits of his mustache, "saying the Premise was true, that the Pilgrims could have blown the crust off our planet ages ago. If the Pilgrims intend to harm us, why haven't they blown us up already? Why go to such lengths to make something like this up?"

"You're right." General Fergusson moved the razor to Austin's chin, attacking the last remaining hair on his face. "I don't know what their endgame is, but I know this: power such as theirs doesn't remain sheathed for long."

He grabbed the towel and wiped Austin's face clean. Reaching up, Austin felt the results. It was smooth, like a newborn's cheek.

"The world is on the brink, DeSantis. Something is going to give. When it does, we'll be powerless to stop these aliens, save for you."

Not sure what to believe anymore, Austin only shook his head. "How?"

"The alien robot *trusts* you. That misplaced trust is our weapon, humanity's only hope against total annihilation."

He didn't want to be a weapon. He didn't want any of this. "Virgil doesn't care about me. The whole way back to Earth, he never said a word."

"He's calling for you now, DeSantis." General Fergusson folded up the soiled towel into a neat square. "He's standing outside the cylinder in DC."

Austin shot upright, hating the hope that filled him with that news. He didn't deserve it after his betrayal. "He is?"

"Yes." General Fergusson smiled smugly to himself. "And now Ramirez looks like a fool, having advised the president to kill our inside man."

"Are you taking me to Virgil?" Austin said, ignoring General Fergusson's machinations.

"Of course I'm taking you to him, DeSantis." General Fergusson stood up. "That's why we needed you clean. A soldier never goes into battle with an unclean weapon."

Austin felt his heart racing again, a blend of anticipation and unease coursing through him. "What do you want me to do?"

"Just what you've done before: ingratiate yourself. Make the robot trust you. When the time to strike is upon us, you'll know. Then we can fulfill the deal. Charges dropped, and a new life for you and your mother."

His mother. Austin hadn't forgotten about her. Thinking of her suffering, not knowing what happened to her son, weighed heavily on him.

"Can I talk to her, let her know I'm okay?"

"Of course not." General Fergusson was so close that Austin could feel his breath against his face. It was both the breath of his savior and of his tormentor. "America has many enemies, and if they found out the kind of access you have with the aliens, you'd only put her in danger."

Austin winced at the thought of doing his mother any more harm. "What if you're wrong?" he asked, unable to keep the doubt he felt from surfacing. He didn't know the Pilgrims, but he knew Virgil. And from everything he'd seen of the alien robot, he couldn't believe that Virgil's intentions weren't genuine. "What if the Pilgrims are sincere Christians and have no intention for war?"

The feline smile returned to General Fergusson's face. "You'll see, DeSantis. Soon the aliens will make their move, and when they do, you'll know why I'm the way that I am."

22

Habeas Corpus.

The Latin drowned out the helicopter's roar, so loud it was like the whole world was vibrating.

"What's it saying?" the Black Shirt sitting across from Austin asked.

"It's saying, 'Present the body.'" The words echoed back to Austin in his headset.

Instead of replying, the Black Shirt adjusted his rifle. Austin looked out the open door of the Blackhawk as the Washington Monument passed by. They were flying up the Potomac on their way to Rock Creek Park, Austin's first time on a helicopter, despite having been to space twice.

"Daniels?" the Black Shirt manning the mini-gun addressed the Black Shirt across from Austin. "You seen the God nuts yet?"

"Just from the ground."

"Take a look starboard in about thirty seconds."

As the helicopter passed the Lincoln Memorial, its entire chassis rolled ten degrees. They were heading north up Rock Creek, the tributary for which the park got its name. Looking to the left, Austin could see the brownstones of Georgetown passing by as they made their way to the Pilgrim craft that loomed over the city like a leviathan.

"Shit! It's like they're multiplying down there," Daniels said.

Tens of thousands of people pushed up against a steel wall around the perimeter of Rock Creek Park, the crowd so large it backed up into neighboring streets.

"Been four incursions already today," the Black Shirt manning the mini-gun said, training his gun down on the crowd. "Eight tangos KIA."

"We did those nuts a favor." Daniels laughed. "Sent them straight to God."

"I'd sure love to fire a few bursts," the Black Shirt manning the mini-gun grunted. "Thin 'em out a bit."

The helicopter descended over the park barricades. The leaves had fallen off the trees since Austin had been locked away, leaving just the barren branches to filter Austin's view of the ground. He caught sight of a group of Regulars standing in the creek, their uniforms laid on the side, one dunking another in the water.

"Was that Peterson?" Daniels asked, incredulous.

"Yup. This God stuff is spreading through the base like a

virus. Every time you turn around someone is getting baptized or stalking off the base to go to church."

Daniels snorted. "There's never been a shortage of morons in the army."

The helicopter slowed, landing on Military Road, the main boulevard that bisected the park. Daniels led Austin out and took him to a waiting Humvee, another Black Shirt standing in front.

"Welcome back," the Black Shirt said. "We missed you around here."

Austin recognized the Mississippi twang immediately. It was the Black Shirt he'd met in the locker room over a month ago. She was looking at him now, her green eyes glistening in the December sun.

"Missed me?" he asked, unable to keep the grin from his face.

"Sure," she replied, opening the Humvee door. "Base isn't the same without you."

He got in and she followed, sitting next to him in the back. The Humvee pulled away with a jolt, bound for the cylinder.

The barricades had grown substantially since Austin had been gone. There were now three lines of defense taking up the entirety of the golf course, the outermost laced with razor wire and guard towers, the inner two fortified with sandbags and machine-gun nests. Between each barricade was a sea of Regulars, so many that Austin wondered if the army hadn't shoved a whole brigade into this base within a base.

"I thought of you when I was up there," Austin finally admitted, having just worked up the courage as the Humvee made it through the last layer of defenses.

She squinted at him with her green eyes.

"You know, in space," he added.

"Oh, yeah?" she said.

"Yeah." He cleared his throat, feeling heat creep up his neck. "I hope you'll get to go up there, too, one day."

Holding his gaze, she brought her hand to touch his briefly. It was the best he'd felt in a long time.

Habeas Corpus.

The ear-piercing demand broke the moment as the Humvee stopped in the middle of the tenth-hole fairway. Austin saw Virgil standing outside the cylinder, his head glowing a pale blue.

"Virgil!" Austin gasped. He turned to his beautiful captor.

"Well?" she said, tilting her head. "What are you waiting for?"

He burst out the Humvee door and ran down the fairway.

"I am very glad to see you again, Austin," Virgil said in his sonorous voice as Austin closed the distance between them. "Please come with me."

Austin followed Virgil into the hallway, eager to put the chaos of the military camp behind him. He couldn't believe how familiar it felt to be here. If someone had told him a few months ago that he'd be a regular on board an alien spacecraft, he would've laughed in their face.

Within a few moments, he was approaching the silver wall, and it was folding away to reveal the Victorian living room.

"Austin!" Father Ambrose sprang up from the sofa and ran over to him, throwing his hand on Austin's shoulder. "I'm so glad to see you. We were so worried."

"Worried?" Austin asked as Virgil strode into the room. "Both of you?"

"Of course, Austin," Virgil said. "I am your host, and as such, I have a deep responsibility for you. An obligation of the highest importance in Pilgrim culture. I became worried when we could not locate you for quite some time."

"You didn't write, you didn't call," Father Ambrose joined in. "When Virgil told me even the Pilgrims didn't know where you were, I got scared. I know what that crazy general did to you up on the ship."

"You both came here looking for me?" he said, his voice trembling. Austin had awoken that day in his cell, sure the world had forgotten about him, but these two had kept him in their minds.

"All the way from Rome." Father Ambrose smiled. "I rode the Vatican space elevator up to the mother ship and then came down on this one to DC. I know that isn't a trip across the galaxy, but that's still a pretty big hop for an old man like me."

Austin laughed, the sound strange to him to his ears; he'd barely smiled since he'd returned to Earth.

"Come, you must be hungry." Father Ambrose ushered Austin over to the wall where the table of food was usually located. As they approached, the mahogany wall folded away and the ivory table appeared with two plates of pasta dowsed in an amber sauce, green herbs sprinkled atop.

"We were just in Rome, so I had Virgil prepare Bucatini all'Amatriciana, a local specialty. You'll love it, Austin. The tomatoes taste like they were freshly picked from the garden. Nothing like the garbage the army feeds you." Father Ambrose put the plate in Austin's hand.

As Austin dug into the meal, a robot no bigger than a deck of cards came out from the underside of the table. It gripped the surface of the table like a bug, retrieving a hunk of Parmigiano-Reggiano with two free legs and then approached their plates with a silent grace. Rapidly, but with great care, it shaved the cheese, dusting the pasta until the red sauce of the Bucatini was almost completely obscured.

"Amazing isn't it, Austin? These little guys are the ones preparing our wonderful meals."

Austin's eyes grew wet with gratitude. The past few weeks, the Black Shirts had only fed him slop through a slot in the door.

"Austin," Virgil said, his voice gentle but prodding, "where have you been these past forty days?"

Austin felt his stomach tense. These two had traveled around the globe to ensure he was safe. How could he tell them he was a murderer—locked in a cell while the authorities debated whether to execute him for his crimes?

Not wanting to see the looks on their faces when they found out, he instead said, "I thought you two had forgotten about me."

"Austin," Father Ambrose said, putting down the plate of food. "Of course not."

"After the chancel, you sent me back here *alone*." He turned his attention to Virgil. "And you didn't say anything to me the whole ride back. I thought I was being punished."

"I'm sorry, Austin," Virgil said, "but I was deep in prayer. Every time I look upon the risen Christ, I can't help it, I must immediately give thanks to our Lord."

Austin reminded himself he was talking to an advanced AI, one the Pilgrims probably programmed to react a specific way to that video, his whole existence controlled, no agency of his own.

"Come, Austin. Let's sit down." Father Ambrose gestured toward the sofas.

"I still do not understand, Austin," Virgil said as he approached the couch. "Why did you not reach out?"

"You never told me how to get a hold of you."

"There are many ways to reach me, Austin. You could have come to the elevator and simply spoken. I would have heard it.

Or you could have composed an email and sent it to yourself. I would have seen the digital footprint."

He would have never thought to reach Virgil by emailing himself, but he got the point. The aliens' reach really was as vast as General Fergusson said. They saw everything—as long as tech was involved. Austin had fallen off the grid, and considering the Pilgrims' awesome power, that had to be an extraordinary thing to do. He knew Virgil wanted an explanation, and Austin was desperate to give him a satisfactory one, but there was no way he could tell him the truth.

"The truth is . . . I've been avoiding you."

"What?" Father Ambrose's glasses nearly fell off his face. "Why?"

"I betrayed Virgil's trust, Father. I told the military the Pilgrims' secret."

Father Ambrose's head darted between Austin and Virgil, his forehead creasing. "What secret?"

"I told the military the Pilgrims are soldiers in my debriefing," Austin said, slumping his head. It was a partial truth, and he hoped it would be enough. He sniffed. "I'm sorry, Virgil. Please, forgive me."

"I cannot forgive you," Virgil said.

"I understand." The words seeped out of Austin like air from a balloon.

"No, Austin, you do not understand," Virgil said. "I cannot forgive you because you did not betray me. One cannot forgive someone for a wrong that did not occur."

Austin looked up, confused.

"Virgil?" Father Ambrose asked, still stuck on the revelation. "The Pilgrims are soldiers?"

"Yes, Father. Pilgrims may live much longer than humans, but the journey from the Pilgrim home world to Earth is a long one filled with many trials. The crew must be disciplined and able to work within a strict chain of command."

"That makes sense," Father Ambrose said, defused. "It's no different than a ship at sea."

"Yes, Father. That is an apt comparison."

"But, Austin," Father Ambrose asked, "why did you think that was such a big deal that you avoided us?"

Austin took a breath, trying to gather his thoughts. "I didn't want the military to think the Pilgrims are more of a threat than they really are. But after the umpteenth interrogation I just let it slip."

Father Ambrose scoffed. "The military is more than capable of being paranoid without your help. A few words from you aren't going to make a difference."

Austin's muscles relaxed. It seemed to have worked. "I can't believe I avoided you over that. I feel silly now."

Father Ambrose took off his glasses and started cleaning them on his shirt. "I suppose if we're confessing things, I came here to see you, Austin, and confirm that you're okay. And I'm thrilled to see that you are." Father Ambrose put his glasses back on, a pained look on his face. "But Virgil was also giving me a ride back to the United States. It's time for me to get back to my observatory."

"What?" Austin couldn't help his surprise. "You're the Vatican's chief astronomer. Shouldn't you be right here? Isn't this like your Super Bowl?"

Father Ambrose smiled but didn't laugh. "I observe the stars and collect meteorites. My involvement here was always a bit accidental, a quick decision by Pope Stephen to fill out a delegation. Now that we know why the Pilgrims are here, there isn't much use for an astronomer like me. And my absence has placed a considerable burden on my staff. It's time I relieved it."

Austin hadn't expected to find Father Ambrose waiting for him, but now that he was here, his sudden departure became that much harder to swallow. He'd missed the man. "That makes no sense. You're the expert on space."

"This isn't about space, Austin. It's about doctrine. Are the Pilgrims fallen? Can they participate in the sacraments? Do we add the video they provided to the Gospels? These are the questions being asked, and there are others in the Church better placed to answer them than me."

Austin stood up from the sofa, his brows knitted together. "I thought the whole point was to have an inspection so that you could have Mass in the ship. What's so hard about that?"

Virgil glided in front of Austin and stood next to Father Ambrose. "Yes, Austin, that is our deepest desire. To be close to our Lord, to have the Eucharistic presence up on our ship. But our Lord has invested His holy Church with the authority to decide on such matters, and we shall await her decision."

"How long will that take?"

"Years. Decades. Centuries." Father Ambrose shrugged. "The Church has a lot of doctrine it needs to develop. This isn't just some light switch you flip."

Austin grunted. "The Pilgrims traveled across the galaxy, and you ask them to wait?"

"We are prepared to wait as long as necessary, Austin."

The Church, the Pilgrims—they measured time in decades . . . centuries. But Austin didn't have that long.

"It's not like we can't all keep in touch." Father Ambrose walked back over to the plates of pasta. "Come on, let's at least enjoy a meal together before we part."

Austin considered protesting, the urge to convince Father Ambrose to stay tugging at him, but it didn't seem like it would do much good.

He could feel time slipping away as he nodded and took his food. It was an excellent meal. The tomatoes really did taste like they were fresh from the garden. Father Ambrose and Austin ate while Virgil watched, a few robotic comments intermixed. When they were done, they stood up and exited the Victorian living room. As they walked down the dark hallway toward the exit, Austin stole a glance back, wondering if this was the last time he'd ever see that comforting space.

"Father Ambrose," General Fergusson growled as the cylinder wall unfolded. He stood on the fairway with a platoon of Black Shirts by his side. "You are in violation of Nineteen US Code, Section Fourteen Fifty-Nine: failure to enter the United States at a designated border crossing."

"Ah, yes." Father Ambrose laughed. "It's good to be back in the good old US of A."

General Fergusson raised an eyebrow. "Arrest him," he commanded.

Three Black Shirts advanced. Before they could reach the priest, Virgil leapt in front of them.

"Nolite sacerdotem attingere!" Virgil's voice had changed, now a bass so low it was like a concussion grenade, and his head had turned a furious crimson. It felt like Austin's friend had disappeared, an angry Pilgrim automaton in his place.

"He said, 'Do not touch the priest,'" Austin shouted, afraid of what would happen if the Black Shirts didn't comply. "You need to leave Father Ambrose alone!"

"Father Ambrose is in violation of US law," General Fergusson said, undeterred. "He will be placed under arrest."

But the Black Shirts held still, seemingly unsure of what to do with the alien robot in front of them.

"Don't do this," Austin pleaded to General Fergusson. "You're going to start a war!"

"Please, I don't want there to be violence," Father Ambrose protested. "I'll cooperate."

General Fergusson raised his hands, signaling for the Black Shirts to stand down.

Virgil, however, kept his arms outstretched, ready to act.

"The priest will be confined to the base while we refer his case to Customs and Border Protection." General Fergusson addressed Virgil directly. "If he comes with us willingly, they won't put their hands on him. But I will not let him go, no matter what you say or do."

The fairway fell into an icy silence, every weapon trained on the machine. Virgil stood there unmoving; his body poised to strike. Austin fixed his gaze on Virgil's dome, desperate for a sign of what he was thinking. All their fates were tied to whatever he did next.

But Virgil's head just glowed steady, bathing the field in that dreaded crimson hue.

23

The morning sun glinted off the FLIR lens of a parked Abrams tank a little way ahead as Austin walked down Military Road. The debriefers had kept him up all night in that sweaty boys' locker room, not letting him rest until they went over every detail of what had happened in the cylinder. There was no sign of General Fergusson, no check-in to see how Austin fared, no feline smile to put him in his servile place. Instead, there were only lingering questions. Why had the general nearly started a war over a petty crime? Only Father Ambrose's pleading and Virgil's acquiescence had saved humanity from the brink.

The mystery nagged at Austin as he put one foot in front of the other. He'd been confined to Rock Creek Park Base and ordered to report to a FEMA trailer on Military Road where he could get some rest. But Father Ambrose was caged somewhere, and he couldn't sleep until he knew the priest was safe.

Rubbing his arms to coax some warmth back into them,

Austin spotted two Black Shirts standing guard in front of a FEMA trailer. The rest of the trailers were unattended. He remembered Father Ambrose mentioning they'd put him in a FEMA trailer before, and figured this was as likely a place as any for them to keep him.

"You hear about Jayden?" The shorter Black Shirt's voice carried down the road as Austin approached unnoticed.

"No, what?" the taller Black Shirt replied.

"He didn't make it. Bullet severed his carotid."

"Sheesh, killed by some God-crazy civvies," the taller Black Shirt said, pulling down the front of his balaclava to reveal his face. "I thought they were supposed to be peaceful?"

"Apparently not when you get between them and their god."

Austin eased into the gap between two trailers just a few dozen yards away from where the Black Shirts were standing.

"It's okay, though," the shorter Black Shirt continued. "I heard Sarge baptized him in the creek right before the incursion."

"He did?"

"Yup."

"That's insane." The taller one shook his head. "I can't believe the Jesus freaks got Sarge."

The shorter Black Shirt leaned against the trailer door. "This God shit is running through the base like a virus."

"If the aliens are on God's team, then I'm on the other one."

The taller Black Shirt adjusted the grip on his rifle. "I don't trust those three-legged freaks for a second."

"Amen to that, brother."

Austin wanted to stay there and listen to these two talking about the fissures running through the base—anything to avoid confronting them and risking the limited freedom he had at this moment—but there was only one way forward.

Taking a fortifying breath, he stepped into view.

"Who the hell are you?" The shorter Black Shirt leveled his rifle at Austin's face.

"I'm here to see the priest," Austin said, his mouth suddenly dry.

"On whose authority?" the taller Black Shirt asked.

The Black Shirt had basically confirmed Father Ambrose was inside. Austin fought the urge to pump his fist in the air. Instead, he said, "General Fergusson's."

The two Black Shirts laughed.

"My ass." The shorter one took a step forward. "Get the hell out of here."

Austin's heart raced. It was now or never.

"Inepti!" he yelled. "Nonne intelligitis me hic rem magni momenti suscepisse!"

The shorter Black Shirt straightened almost immediately.

"Sinite me introire, alioquin enim paenitebit! Nunc eamus!"

Austin paused.

Their guns were lowering, drooping down.

"Nunc amentes!" Austin pressed, letting his face flush with anger.

"I think that's General Fergusson's translator," the shorter Black Shirt said.

"Who the hell else would I be?" Austin took a step forward, pointing his finger at the shorter one's face. "And unless you want to be processed, you'd better let me in right now!"

Pulling his balaclava back over his face, the taller one gave the shorter one a nod. Once the door was open, Austin stepped inside.

They shut the door behind him, probably glad to see him gone.

Austin took in the austere nature of the place. There was a small bed with a thin sheet along the left wall, a phone booth–sized bathroom in the opposite corner, and a foldout table with two benches. Sitting at the table, still dressed in his clerical clothes, was Father Ambrose, an open sleeve of saltines in front of him and a mischievous grin on his face.

"What did you say to those two?"

Austin returned the grin. "Just that I was here on important business, and if they didn't let me in, there'd be hell to pay."

"Inepti?" Father Ambrose raised an eyebrow. "Was the name-calling really necessary?"

Austin sat down at the table and shrugged. "Sometimes it helps to get a little creative with your punctuation, Father."

Father Ambrose released a hearty laugh, one that lessened the sting of the December chill. Yet Austin noticed the twinkle in his eyes had dulled, like a shirt laundered too many times.

"I'm glad to see you, Austin."

Austin thought back to how Father Ambrose had come looking for him when the general had attacked him, how he'd traveled around the world to see that Austin was safe. This was the least Austin could do.

"Are you doing, okay?" Austin asked.

Father Ambrose played with a saltine in his hand. "To be honest . . . I've been better."

Austin recognized the priest's deflation, the pain of being under the government's thumb, powerless to do even the most basic things. "This is bullshit, Father. Just General Fergusson doing it because he can."

"Yes, it's unfortunate. But you know how governments are about their rules. It'll all get sorted out in the end."

Austin flashed back to the warehouse, its floor covered in bodies. That was one way the government sorted things out in the end. "You're not worried about being locked up here?"

Father Ambrose smiled and then took a small bite of the saltine. "The cuisine's a bit pedestrian, but I've been in Rome the past month and a half, so I've got no right to complain."

Austin studied Father Ambrose's expression, searching for any sign he might be putting on a brave face, but he appeared sincere. "What *is* bothering you, then?"

Father Ambrose took a deep breath. "You heard those two guarding the door. 'If the aliens are on God's team, then I'm on the other one.' What a terrible thing to say."

Austin shifted uncomfortably on the hard plastic bench.

"You can't blame them for thinking the video is fake," he said. "You know how advanced the Pilgrims are. Faking the video would be easy."

"That's true," Father Ambrose admitted. "The Pilgrims certainly have the means to fake a video. But they didn't just give the Vatican some film footage. They gave us petabytes of data, observations of Earth from that time. Things we can verify in the archaeological, geological, and astronomical record. So far, everything we've scrutinized checks out."

Austin flashed back to his cell, General Fergusson with a blade to his face. He'd made the Pilgrims' evidence sound so flimsy. "There you go, Father," he said, his shoulder lifting slightly. "As the evidence emerges, the holdouts will come around."

Father Ambrose's expression remained unchanged. "I'd agree with you if it was only ever about the evidence."

Austin tilted his head. "What do you mean?"

Father Ambrose took off his glasses and started cleaning them. "The evidence was always good, Austin, even before the Pilgrims showed up. Did you know that we have more evidence attesting to Jesus's existence than we do for Alexander the Great? Yet you don't hear people doubting whether

Alexander the Great existed. And as for the Resurrection itself, scholars have spilled oceans of ink trying to come up with a naturalistic explanation that conforms with the universally agreed upon historical facts, but they've basically come up dry."

Unsure what to say, Austin watched as Father Ambrose wiped his lenses with his shirtsleeve, noticing for the first time how worn his clothing was. When the priest carefully put his glasses back on, he looked Austin in the eye.

"The point is, this wasn't some legend we were asking people to believe. This was a historical event, one for which compelling evidence is readily available to anyone with an internet connection. But people don't bother to look, so why should a video of Christ literally walking out of his tomb make any difference?"

"Because it's a video, Father," Austin said, his tone sure. "Seeing is believing."

"Okay," Father Ambrose said calmly. His gaze bore into Austin's. "What about you? Do you believe?"

The question smacked Austin in the face. "I don't know," he said after a moment, admitting his true feelings.

Father Ambrose's eyebrows raised questioningly. "Why not? You've seen more than just about anybody else. What more would you need?"

An unsettling tightness gripped Austin's chest. He'd had forty days in a cell to think about the answer to this question, yet it eluded him still. "I'm not sure."

"That's my point." Father Ambrose leaned back, rubbing at the bags under his eyes. "It's rarely about the evidence. There's more at stake."

"Like what?"

"The central delusion."

Austin's brow furrowed; he didn't recognize the concept. "What's that?"

"It's the delusional belief we are all the centers of the universe, each one of us a god, worthy of all praise and all thanksgiving, the power to decide right and wrong our domain."

Father Ambrose gazed into the distance, as if confronting some long-fought adversary. Austin, however, was just more confused. "I don't think I'm a god," he replied.

Blinking his focus back to the present, Father Ambrose met Austin's eyes. "Perhaps . . ." he said, letting the word linger. "But here's the thing: the second you think that God is Lord, that He became man and died for our sins so that we may have everlasting life—when you truly believe that insane proposition—it changes everything, right down to the foundation of who you are. That's when the central delusion disappears." Father Ambrose pulled another saltine from the package and took another bite. "In my experience, people will move Heaven and Earth, go to any length, to preserve the central delusion— evidence to the contrary be damned."

"That's strange," Austin said as Father Ambrose sat there

chewing.

"What is?"

"You're a bit old to realize just now that not everyone believes in God."

Father Ambrose burst out in laughter, spraying a few pieces of saltine on the table. "Touché, Austin," he said after composing himself. "It's not exactly a new revelation. I suppose I just allowed myself to think this time it would be different."

Austin grabbed a saltine of his own and took a bite. "If I'm being honest, Father," he said between chews, "there's one thing that's hard for me to understand."

"What's that?"

"If the Pilgrims saw Jesus rise from the dead and believe he was God, why bother traveling across the galaxy to come here?"

"That's easy," Father Ambrose said, mouth full of saltine. "They came for the Eucharist, the source and summit of the Christian life."

Not sure if he was thinking of the right thing, Austin paused. Finally, he said, "You mean the cracker Catholics eat at church?" Father Ambrose's expression fell, and Austin immediately felt bad. "I'm sorry, Father. I didn't mean to—"

"No, it's all right. I realize you don't know any better." Father Ambrose took another saltine from the sleeve and held it in his hand. "Can I ask you a question, Austin?"

"Of course, Father."

"When you were ten, were you still you?"

Sitting back, Austin scrunched up his face. "Is this a trick question?"

"It's a sincere one, I promise."

Austin thought about it to see if there was something he was missing, but nothing came to mind. "Yes."

"How about when you were one?"

Austin shifted on the bench. "Yeah, I guess I was still me."

"How can that be so? According to the latest research, at your age, you've probably replaced all the cells in your body three or four times. Wouldn't it be more appropriate to think there have been three or four Austins?"

"That just seems weird."

"Exactly," Father Ambrose said. "That's because you understand intuitively there is something deeper going on than just the cells of your body, that there is an essential *you*, a *you* that persists over time, even as the various parts are replaced."

Austin pondered the explanation for a second. "Like a classic car that gets fixed over time? Or the Ship of Theseus?"

"Precisely! And we could call the *you* that persists over time something like your 'essence,' or to use Aristotelian terminology, your 'substance.' Your substance isn't something I could see under a microscope, it isn't a thing I can measure. But just as you are the same 'you' now as when you were then, it is something that's as real as this table."

Austin digested the explanation as Father Ambrose lifted the saltine he'd taken out of the sleeve. "So, during Mass, when

I pick up the host and say, 'This is my body, which will be given up for you,' echoing Jesus's words from the Last Supper, the substance of the host changes from simple bread to God—the Creator and Sustainer of the whole universe."

"But it looks the same," Austin said. Then, raising an eyebrow, he quipped, "And I assume it tastes the same."

"Yes, but you look different now than when you were ten, and yet you were still you. Substances aren't something we can see just from a thing's external appearance."

Austin shifted again as he thought it through. "What does this have to do with the Pilgrims coming here? Couldn't they just say the magic words on their own planet?"

Father Ambrose laughed. "It's not a spell, Austin. The only reason I can change the substance of the host during the Sacrament of the Mass is because I was given that power by a bishop at my ordination, who was given that power by another bishop at their ordination, and so on all the way back to the apostles themselves who were given that power by Jesus at Pentecost. This chain all the way back in time is something we call the 'apostolic succession.'"

The pieces were beginning to click into place in Austin's mind. "So, if the Pilgrims want the Eucharist, they need a priest like you, part of the succession. That's the only way to get it."

"Yes," Father Ambrose replied.

Austin rubbed his chin. "What about the Pilgrims? Can they become priests?"

Father Ambrose shook his head. "The apostles were all human. For reasons we'll never know, that's how Jesus—God Himself—organized things. It's not within the Church's power to change it."

"So the Pilgrims *need* us."

Taking off his glasses, Father Ambrose looked Austin in the eyes. "Very much so."

The gravity of what Father Ambrose was saying dawned on him, and Austin leaned back in shock. "If what you say is true, that means the Pilgrims will never leave."

Father Ambrose's expression became dour. "Yes."

Austin thought about the fissures already spreading through the base. The Pilgrims had arrived just over six weeks ago. What would the world look like in a year? In ten?

"Can we handle that?" he asked.

"I don't know," Father Ambrose said, looking to some unseen worry beyond Austin. "You saw how Virgil's head changed color yesterday when the Black Shirts wanted to arrest me. He looked like he was ready to fight. The Pilgrims don't realize I would do anything to avoid violence. They might be pious, but they're still aliens. No matter how advanced they are, I fear a grave miscalculation is inevitable."

Father Ambrose was starting to sound a lot more like General Fergusson.

"Meanwhile, humanity is as disunited as ever," Father Ambrose continued. "You would think, at a time like this, at least the Christians would come together, but the Protestants are upset that the Pilgrims are Catholic, and our Orthodox brothers are upset the Pilgrims want to be in full communion with Rome. Even as our churches are filling with people once again, many of the newcomers just want to know about the Pilgrims. They treat Sunday Mass like some sci-fi convention, making a mockery of the whole thing." Father Ambrose glanced down at the floor, his expression growing gloomier. "And the Middle East, Austin . . . I pray for the Middle East."

"Why would the Middle East be affected?"

"The Pilgrims' arrival has upset our Muslim brothers. They don't appreciate alien crafts broadcasting the Lord's Prayer over their holy places, shoving what they perceive as apostasy right in their faces."

He'd been so disconnected from the world, he hadn't seen it fraying like Father Ambrose had. He didn't know what to say to make it better.

"We must trust in God's providence, Austin, especially when it's hard. I just thought I'd be able to pray over this in my observatory, surrounded by my meteorites. Somewhere familiar where I could firm up my spiritual strength." Father Ambrose stretched out his arm, gesturing toward the drab interior of the trailer. "But it seems that the Lord has other plans for me."

Father Ambrose's mouth tried to curl up into a smile but failed. This place was crushing him, and it broke Austin's heart to see it. As much as he wanted Father Ambrose nearby, he knew what he had to do: use the one piece of leverage he had with General Fergusson to set Father Ambrose free.

"Father, what if there was a way—"

The trailer door burst open, and an enormous Black Shirt appeared in the threshold, the balaclava off his face. He beheld Austin with an icy stare, one made all the more sinister by the giant scar slicing across his face.

24

In the month and a half since Austin had been locked away, Sarge had found religion, yet he looked no less scary, the deep scar on his face giving him an air of always-brewing menace.

He'd burst into the trailer in a frenzy, but as it turned out, Sarge wasn't there for him. He was there for Father Ambrose. Having just learned there was a priest on the base, he was desperate to give his confession. That was just fine with Austin. He had to see General Fergusson anyway.

Contrary to their first meeting, Sarge had been kind enough to direct Austin to the Rock Creek Park offices where General Fergusson had set up his personal headquarters. It took a bit of searching, but he finally found them: a series of low-slung buildings built in the utilitarian style of the National Park Service located west of where Father Ambrose was being kept.

He made his way to the largest of the buildings and went inside, walking down a hall until he found a large room laid out like mission control.

Austin took it in. Six rows of computers faced a wall covered in screens, with one especially large one in the center. On the opposite end of the room, the wall was covered from floor to ceiling by a mirror, the outline of a small door visible in the glass. The room was eerily silent, the two-dozen Regulars staring at their computer screens, not making a sound. It was as if they were mannequins—not even the hum of breath disrupted the air.

Most of the screens displayed live feeds of the Pilgrim crafts over various cities. He recognized the craft over Paris right away, the Eiffel Tower a dead giveaway. He also quickly identified the craft over Washington, DC. There were other cities on the screens—Beijing, Johannesburg, Sao Paolo, Jerusalem— but it was the central monitor that caught Austin's attention.

It depicted smoke billowing from a city skyline, black plumes curling around the minarets of a giant mosque. The feed had a chyron at the bottom that said "Medina" and the three smaller screens to the right showed images of men rioting.

A stern-looking major approached him.

"What's happening?" Austin asked, hushing his voice as if in a library.

"Shhhh!" The major grabbed hold of Austin's arm and dragged him through the door in the mirrored wall.

"DeSantis," General Fergusson said, looking into the

command center through what Austin now realized was a two-way mirror. "Glad you could make it for the show." General Fergusson glanced over at the major, gesturing for him to go. As he did, he closed the door, leaving Austin alone with the general.

"I need to talk to you," Austin said.

"Medina has been like that for over three hours." General Fergusson nodded at the central monitor. "It usually takes the police six hours to restore order after the aliens' broadcast of the Our Father at noon. But today, it's much worse. The Saudi military is divided. King Salman has had so many attempts on his life that he doesn't dare leave his quarters." General Fergusson waved a hand toward the Regulars at the computers. "And here we are, condemned to watch Medina burn as the aliens break our encryption, drive us to silence behind our terminals, little more than voyeurs in uniform."

Austin beheld the footage, the carnage continuing to grow. "It's about Father Ambrose," he said.

General Fergusson faced Austin. "How was your visit?"

Austin opened his mouth, but words failed him.

"Don't be surprised, DeSantis." General Fergusson's lips curled. "I know *everything* that happens on my base."

A queasy feeling churned Austin's stomach. "Why did you arrest him?"

"I wanted the robot to see that you hate me, that we're at odds. That way, he's less likely to believe we're on the same side."

Austin clenched his fists, his knuckles turning white. "Release him," he said, barely able to keep his voice level.

A single, cold laugh escaped General Fergusson's lips. "He's more useful to me here, DeSantis. Besides, he's a criminal just like you."

"He isn't a criminal," Austin said, his voice rising. "If you don't let him go, I'll tell Virgil I'm your agent. I'll tell him you made me carry a camera onto the ship, and you're setting me up to be an infiltrator."

General Fergusson's eyes narrowed, a dangerous glint in them. "Are you threatening me, DeSantis?"

Sweat formed on Austin's back, but he steeled himself and said, "I am."

General Fergusson moved closer. "You would really tell the robot that you're a spy?"

Austin stood tall, even though his heart was racing. "If I have to."

Stepping even closer, the general leaned in until his mouth was so close Austin could feel the breath on his ear. "What makes you think that isn't *exactly* what I want you to do?"

Austin's skin went cold.

"Go ahead and confess." A feline smile crept across General Fergusson's face. "It will only endear you to the robot further, dig you in deeper."

Patting him once on the shoulder, the general pulled away, walking to the mirror with his hands clasped behind his back.

"The Pilgrims didn't just bring a video; they brought all sorts of supporting evidence." Austin tried to sound defiant. "They're not faking. They're Christians, and they come in peace."

"Peace?" General Fergusson pointed at the central monitor. "Does that look like peace to you?"

His eyes followed the general's finger, and Austin saw a building on fire. It certainly didn't look like peace, but he couldn't bring himself to say it.

"That's what I thought," General Fergusson said.

Austin fidgeted. Every shot he took against the general was batted back. He'd been cornered and defeated, and he didn't know what else to do.

The major burst into the observation room, breaking their tense silence.

"Sir," the major said, urgency in his voice. "Extension coming down from the craft over Jerusalem!"

Without hesitation, General Fergusson charged into the command center, and Austin followed.

"Get Jerusalem on the central monitor, now," General Fergusson snapped. "Quiet time is over."

The command center erupted in chatter as the central monitor changed to a live feed of Jerusalem, where Austin could see a cylinder coming down from the craft's underside like a car radio antenna.

"Sitrep," General Fergusson barked.

"Sir, the extension's expected to touch down in Zurich Garden," an officer yelled from the front of the room, "just outside the southwest corner of the Old City. Touchdown expected in seventy seconds."

"Where's the IDF? They need to get a cordon over there!"

"Our military attaché says they need half an hour to set one up."

"They don't have that long!" General Fergusson took up a position in the center of the command room. "What assets do we have in the air?"

"Three Predators with a full optics suite circling at six thousand feet. Four hours of uptime remaining."

"Do we have any more nearby?"

"Ninth squadron has two fueled and ready at Ben Gurion, sir."

"Get 'em up."

As General Fergusson issued commands, Austin watched the extension descend all the way to the ground.

"Sir, NSA is patching through CCTV footage from the Jerusalem Cinema on the western end of the park. It has a line of sight on the touchdown."

"On the central monitor now."

The image switched from the live feed of the Pilgrim craft to a city park, where the silver extension was landing; it was not on the ground for more than a few moments before the wall started folding away.

The room fell silent as a Pilgrim appeared at the threshold, stretching out one of its three legs to step out into the park.

Eight Diplomats followed the alien out and formed a circle around it, their heads glowing a deep crimson, the color contrasting with the Pilgrim's ashen skin.

Another set of Diplomats came out and formed an even wider concentric circle. Once the Diplomats were in formation, the whole group walked out of the camera's frame.

"Get me a visual on that thing!" General Fergusson yelled through the unease that had filled the room.

"Sir, we're receiving reports that the alien is heading eastbound on Ma'ale HaShalom Street. NSA is picking up live streams of bystanders recording with their phones."

"Get one of them up there, damn it!"

The central monitor switched to a man live streaming from his phone camera. He was saying something in Hebrew as the Pilgrim and his entourage walked toward him. Unlike the late Michael in Rome, who had looked sickly and needed to be carried back to the extension, this Pilgrim walked with vigor, taking large strides over the gridlocked cars.

The Pilgrim and his retinue came right at the man and then bypassed him in one giant step. As the live streamer pointed his camera upward, Austin caught sight of what was concealed by the tentacle skirt: a beak the color of blood and large enough to bite the door off a delivery van.

"Nolite, obsecro, viam impedire." The Diplomats spoke in unison, their deep bass voices like a siren, alerting all those nearby.

"They're saying, 'Please, get out of our way,'" Austin shouted into the chaotic command center. General Fergusson gave him a quick nod to let him know he'd heard.

The Pilgrim continued its march down the street, and Austin could see flashing blue lights, the sight of cops and soldiers trying to clear people out of its path. The live streamer pursued the Pilgrim, but he was soon grabbed by an Israeli policeman, and the Pilgrim disappeared out of frame.

"Goddamn IDF!" General Fergusson screamed. "How soon till they clear the area?"

"IDF says they are working on it, sir."

"Get me another visual *now*!"

"Sir, we've got a visual from one of our Predators. The Pilgrim just passed the Western Wall in the Old City. Putting it on the central monitor now."

The image cut to an aerial shot of the Pilgrim outside a mosque with a golden dome. The image zoomed in, and Austin could see the Pilgrim kneeling and making the sign of the cross with its long bony arm.

"Sir, IDF is saying the Al-Aqsa Mosque complex has been evacuated and is now secure."

"That bastard," General Fergusson seethed. "Praying at the Dome of the Rock, the third holiest site in Islam. These aliens are just begging for a jihad." General Fergusson pointed his hand at the screen where a man could be seen running across the plaza toward the Pilgrim. "Who's that inbound?"

"Sir, it looks like a Waqf. Religious police on the Temple Mount. Non-Muslims are not allowed to pray up there."

"Where the hell is the IDF?" General Fergusson yelled. "I thought they had this place secure!"

As the man got close to the group, one of the Diplomats rushed over and tackled him to the ground. The man wriggled in the Diplomat's clutches but was seemingly unhurt.

"Sir." A colonel, a briefcase handcuffed to his wrist, approached General Fergusson. "The president has declared DEFCON 1. Field commanders have nuclear authorization." The colonel opened the briefcase and handed General Fergusson a red laminate card.

"Where's POTUS?" General Fergusson asked.

"COG protocols have been activated," the colonel replied. "The president is en route to a secure location."

Nuclear authorization. The words hung heavy in Austin's mind.

The command center fell silent as every eye fixed on the Pilgrim praying on the plaza, possibly the last image they would ever see.

Time seemed to stretch as they all waited. Austin wasn't sure whether it took seconds or hours, but when the Pilgrim stood up and started walking back in the direction it had come, there was a breeze in the room as everyone exhaled at the same time.

"Sir, IDF says the alien has a clear path back to the extension. The cordon is secure."

General Fergusson handed the red laminate card back to the colonel. "Looks like I won't be needing this today."

The colonel took the card, a restrained smile on his face. Austin felt his heartbeat slow down as the apocalypse was averted.

An alarm blared at one of the computer terminals.

"Sir! Short-range rockets inbound from the West Bank! The Palestinians have fired on the Pilgrim craft over Jerusalem."

The room fell back into chaos.

"Time to impact?"

"One minute, sir."

"Can the Israelis shoot the rockets down?" General Fergusson demanded. "Where's their damn Iron Dome?"

"Standby, sir."

Austin's heart resumed its manic pace. There was nothing anyone could do except watch the monitors and hope the Israelis could prevent an interstellar war.

"Sir," the colonel said, still holding the briefcase, "the president has ordered a preemptive strike on the alien mother ship. Orbital launch platforms will fire in five minutes. All other commanders are instructed to hold back nuclear ordinance for a possible second strike."

"China?"

"Their orbital platform remains on standby, sir. The politburo is in hiding. We're not sure who's in charge over there now. They won't be assisting in the attack."

General Fergusson nodded stoically.

"Sir, we have detonations!"

Little explosions lit up the sky around the Pilgrim craft, bursts of yellow glowing against the smooth silver.

"Are those impacts?" General Fergusson demanded.

"No, sir. Rockets are detonating away from the Pilgrim craft. They were intercepted."

"Did the Israelis get them? Was it Iron Dome?"

"No." The Regular informing General Fergusson tilted his head at his monitor. "IDF says they couldn't launch in time."

General Fergusson furrowed his brow. "Then who intercepted them?"

"Sir." An officer spoke haltingly from the front of the room. "Infrared sensors showed extreme IR radiation emanating from the alien craft in directed beams. It seems the aliens intercepted the rockets."

A chilling silence filled the room.

"They're armed," General Fergusson said, dismayed. "Those goddamn alien crafts above major world cities are armed."

"Sir, the extension is retracting back into the craft. There are no Pilgrim casualties. The president has ordered the orbital launch sequence aborted. We have been stood back down to DEFCON 3. Nuclear launch authorization withdrawn."

A cheer filled up the room. Doomsday averted right before their eyes.

When the cheering subsided, General Fergusson turned to face Austin, his narrowed eyes slicing through Austin's relief. "You see, DeSantis?" he said, his voice cutting. "War is coming."

25

With a creaking whine, the Humvee pulled up alongside Father Ambrose's trailer. A queue of Regulars, dressed in full battle gear, waited patiently outside the trailer in a single file that went all the way out of Austin's field of view. At the head of the line was Sarge, his six-foot, four-inch frame perched outside the trailer door like a nightclub bouncer. Austin and the Black Shirt commander exited the Humvee and approached him.

"What is this?" The Black Shirt commander scowled.

"You know what it is, Matthews," Sarge replied.

"He's a prisoner," Matthews protested. "He can't be offering confession."

A second Humvee pulled up behind the first, and a squad of Black Shirts emerged. They took up a position behind Matthews.

"He's the only cleric on the base." Sarge folded his tree-trunk arms. "Until General Fergusson rescinds his ban on chaplains at frontline installations, this is the new chaplainry."

"All right, enough of this." Matthews made his way toward the trailer door, but Sarge stepped in front of him.

"He's busy." Sarge glowered. "What about that do you not understand?"

The Black Shirts behind Matthews raised their rifles, prompting the Regulars to abandon the line and surround the Black Shirts, their own rifles raised.

"What are you doing!" Matthews yelled.

Sarge glared back.

"I'll see that you Jesus freaks get court-martialed for this," Matthews spat. "Every single one of you!"

"What's going on?" Father Ambrose appeared at the trailer's threshold, his voice calm.

"You're coming with us," Matthews said to Father Ambrose as the Regulars kept their rifles leveled, their fingers perilously close to the triggers.

"Something happened, Father." Austin's voice shook. "You and I need to go see Virgil right now."

Realizing they were one sudden move away from a bloodbath, Austin met Father Ambrose's eyes, pleading with him to do something.

"'Blessed are the merciful,'" Father Ambrose began, his voice cutting through the air, "'for they will be shown mercy.'"

A hush fell over the Regulars.

"'Blessed are the clean of heart, for they will see God.'"

Austin peered at the closest Regular. His face was softening, but his rifle remained raised.

"'Blessed are the peacemakers. For they will be called children of God.'"

Father Ambrose's words hung in the air, a stillness coming over the people, one as taut as a piano wire. Austin gazed at the Regulars with their raised rifles, too scared to breathe.

After a few moments, a Regular lowered his rifle, then another, and soon they had all stood down.

Father Ambrose made his way toward Austin, but Sarge still stood in front of Matthews, blocking Father Ambrose's way.

"It's okay, John," Father Ambrose said to Sarge. "Tell everyone I'll hear each and every one of their confessions when I'm back, even if I have to go through the night."

Sarge's face went tight for a second, and then he reluctantly stepped aside.

Father Ambrose patted him on the shoulder and then got into the first Humvee with Austin, which wasted no time in pulling away.

On the way to the cylinder, Austin explained everything that had happened in Jerusalem.

"My goodness, was anyone hurt?"

Austin smiled amid the gloom. After that entire download of info, all Father Ambrose cared about was the well-being of others. "A Diplomat tackled a man, but he looked no worse for wear."

"Good."

The Humvee navigated through the numerous barricades and then stopped in the middle of the tenth-hole fairway. Stepping out of the vehicle, Austin and Father Ambrose made their way toward the cylinder.

"Do we just walk in?" Austin asked.

Father Ambrose shrugged. "Worth a shot." He walked right up to the cylinder, and as he did, the walls unfolded to reveal the dark hallway into Virgil's world. Austin took an anxious glance behind him at the hundreds of nervous troops lining the barricades. He braced himself for what lay ahead.

In the Victorian living room, they found Virgil on his knees, his head a deep crimson, his hands clasped in prayer.

"Virgil," Father Ambrose said. "We need to talk."

Virgil remained motionless, the color of his head unchanging.

"It's important, Virgil," Austin said.

Virgil still didn't move.

Austin shot Father Ambrose a frightened look, but instead of returning the look or offering words of reassurance, Father Ambrose went over and tapped Virgil on his dome as though he was knocking on a door.

"Virgil, wake up!"

The staccato thud of Father Ambrose's knuckles on Virgil's skull sent chills down Austin's spine. Just as Father Ambrose raised his fist again to give Virgil his biggest thwap yet, Virgil's head turned pale blue, and he rose to his feet in one graceful motion.

"Father," Virgil said, seemingly unperturbed by the knocks. "It is so wonderful to see you. How are you doing?"

"Not well, Virgil. Do you know about what happened in Jerusalem?"

"Of course, Father." Virgil glided over to the unlit fireplace. "Michael is quite pleased; he fulfilled his obligation."

Austin and Father Ambrose looked at each other in confusion.

"What obligation?" Austin asked.

"Michael's final wish."

"Which was what, exactly?" Austin pressed.

Virgil turned his torso to face Austin. "That Michael would pray for the repose of his soul at the place where Our Lord and Savior prayed to His father."

Frowning, Austin looked at Father Ambrose for clarification.

"The Temple Mount is where the Jewish temple was located during Jesus's time," Father Ambrose said. "It was the center of all Judaism, the dwelling place of God. Jesus spent a lot of time there."

Austin scrunched his nose. "Let me get this straight. Michael just risked *everything*—injury to himself, war, the fate of humanity—just to say a prayer?"

A blue flame erupted from the fireplace floor, the fire tight and compact, like a blowtorch.

"Pilgrims take final wishes very seriously, Austin," Virgil said. "They are a critical part of the social order. Michael is firm, but true of heart. He will stop at nothing to honor the dying requests made of him."

Before Austin could open his mouth and dress Virgil down, Father Ambrose jumped in. "The Temple Mount is the third holiest site in Islam—where Muhammad purportedly ascended into Heaven." Father Ambrose's voice was mild, like a patient teacher. "Michael needs to understand these human considerations before he acts."

Virgil grabbed a dried-out log from next to the fireplace and carefully placed it into the center of the blue flame, the inferno engulfing his hand. "Father, the Church considers Muhammad to be a false prophet, does it not?" Virgil held his hand steady in the flame.

"Yes, but—"

"Then why would God permit a false prophet to ascend into Heaven?"

"He wouldn't, Virgil, but that's not the point. There are *sensitivities* that need to be taken into consideration."

"All Michael did was pray," Virgil said. The blue flame disappeared, leaving only the burning log in Virgil's hand, which began casting an orange glow. "Spreading the Gospel by his example."

"We need to be careful how we spread the Gospel, Virgil."

"Careful, Father?" Virgil placed the burning log onto the fireplace grate. "Didn't our Lord say, 'Go ye into the whole world and preach the Gospel to every creature.'"

"Yes," Father Ambrose said. "But it also says in the First Letter of Saint Peter that we are called to spread our faith with 'gentleness and reverence.'"

"Does it not also say in First Peter that 'when you are maligned, those who defame your good conduct in Christ may themselves be put to shame,' Father?" Virgil's hand was glowing red, like steel fresh from the forge. "Michael offered his prayer in love and gentleness, but his prayer was met with violence. Isn't it those that opposed him who are shamed by their behavior?"

"Enough!" Austin snapped. "There could have been a war! The US was minutes, maybe *seconds*, from firing its nukes."

"Yes, we detected that. It was very strange, the attack was initiated and then called off."

"They called it off because you managed to blow up those rockets with your lasers. Thirty more seconds and—"

"Not lasers, Austin. Microwave beams."

"Don't you get it?" Austin barked. "It doesn't matter what kind of beam it was. What matters is that we all could have died. And unlike a machine like *you*, humans can't upload their minds to the cloud. When *we* die, that's it. We're gone, forever."

Virgil stood straight up, his hand still the color of flame. "I know death, Austin." Virgil spoke deliberately, his tone somber.

"And I fear it as much as any human."

Austin felt a pang of remorse; Virgil dying was the last thing he wanted to see.

"Let's all take a deep breath," Father Ambrose said. He looked back and forth between Austin and Virgil. "Virgil, you do whatever it is you do to relax."

"I pray, Father."

The priest smiled. "That's a good start," he said, and then cleared his throat. "We all want the same thing: harmony between the Pilgrims and humans. Isn't that right?"

"Of course, Father. Humans, like Pilgrims, are created in the image of God. We want nothing more than peace with our brothers and sisters in Christ."

"That's good, Virgil." Father Ambrose nodded approvingly. "Let's discuss what we can do to prevent any further misunderstandings."

"Like what, Father?"

"Pull the craft over Medina back up into space," Austin said, trying to sound levelheaded, though he knew his irritation was leaking through. "The one over Jerusalem, too."

"But, Austin." Virgil took a step forward from the fireplace toward the two of them. "We are called to spread the Gospel to all of creation."

"You said that already—"

Father Ambrose put his hand up to quiet Austin. "We know, Virgil," he said. "But perhaps, for the sake of comity, it would be best. At least for the time being."

"It does not seem wise to sacrifice eternal salvation at the altar of comity, Father. It seems more important that the inhabitants below our craft hear the Good News."

"Virgil, you must understand—"

"If you keep this up, they'll attack again," Austin interjected. "Is that what you want?"

"Of course not, Austin."

"But if they do, then what?"

"Then we will defend ourselves, just as we did in Jerusalem."

Austin could feel his cheeks flush. "And if people die?"

"No one died in Jerusalem."

With a huff of exasperation, Austin looked over to Father Ambrose.

"Virgil." Father Ambrose took a deep breath and stroked his beard, trying to re-center the conversation. "How can we convince the Pilgrims to pull those crafts back, that prudence dictates you take a gentler approach to your evangelization?"

Virgil's glowing hand had faded back to its original silver color. "There is one way, Father."

"What is it?" Father Ambrose asked.

"If His Holiness, Pope Stephen, were to make clear that our crafts over Jerusalem and Medina are not spreading the Gospel with the 'gentleness and reverence' that Saint Peter himself commanded, then we would have no choice but to remove them."

"Out of respect for the magisterium?"

"Yes, Father."

"Austin," Father Ambrose said, his tone threaded with urgency. "We've got to get a message to Rome before it's too late."

26

Excusing themselves from Virgil's presence, Austin and Father Ambrose hurried down the dark hallway.

When they reached the outside world, they saw two Humvees idling on the tenth-hole fairway, the Black Shirts who had brought them there still waiting. Austin bounded over to the closest Humvee, addressing the nearest Black Shirt. "We've got vital information for General Fergusson. You've got to take us to him now."

The Black Shirt's eyes narrowed. "The prisoner comes with us."

Austin turned to find three Black Shirts surrounding Father Ambrose. "We don't have time for this," Austin seethed.

"General's orders," the Black Shirt insisted. "Now back up."

Austin held his ground.

"Back up now," the Black Shirt growled, "or I'll have you in a cell so fast your head will spin."

Father Ambrose's calm presence did little to ease the tension.

"It's all right." The voice cut through the standoff. Austin turned to see two green eyes approaching, the most beautiful Black Shirt he'd ever seen filling up his view.

"What's going on?" she asked.

"Father Ambrose and I need to see General Fergusson." Austin's hands loosened, his tone instantly calm. "It's urgent."

She turned toward the Black Shirt that Austin had nearly gotten in a fight with. "What do you say, Miller?"

"Can't do it," he replied. "I've got direct orders to bring the priest back to his trailer."

The Black Shirt stroked her balaclava-covered chin as her green eyes looked upward. She was thinking, puzzling out her next move, and Austin wished he could watch her think like that all day.

"I'll take you to the general myself," she said to Austin. "You can speak to him and get this all sorted. Does that work?"

Austin looked at Father Ambrose, who nodded.

"Go," Father Ambrose said. "Convince General Fergusson to put me in touch with Cardinal Benedetto. It's the only way."

Austin nodded a goodbye to Father Ambrose and jumped into the Humvee. The female Black Shirt followed him into the back seat.

"Claire, by the way," she said as the Humvee started driving.

Claire. Her name echoed in his mind. It was beauty itself, the sound of it made more perfect by her sweet Mississippi twang.

"Austin," he sheepishly replied.

"I know," she said. "There aren't actually a lot of people around the base, or, you know, *the planet*, who have met aliens."

Even with the balaclava on, he could tell that she was smiling.

It took them a few minutes to clear all the checkpoints, the fortifications around the cylinder still growing by the day. When they finally exited, they took a hard right onto Military Road and began traveling at speed.

They had just crossed the bridge over Rock Creek when they began to slow. Austin leaned over, trying to see through the front windshield. They were nowhere near General Fergusson's headquarters. Fifty yards ahead, parked lengthwise across Military Road, a JLTV was blocking their path, and a Regular gestured for them to stop. Another Regular manned the .50 cal on the JLTV and two others sat atop parked ATVs.

The Humvee stopped, and Claire opened the rear passenger door as the Regular approached. "Can you move that thing?"

The Regular came right up to her, eyeing everyone in the vehicle. "Sorry. Road's closed."

"Closed?" she said, nonplussed. "We're heading to General Fergusson's HQ on an urgent matter. Just let us scoot by."

"No can do," the Regular said, glancing nervously down the road behind them.

"On whose orders?" Claire said.

"Captain . . ." the Regular paused, like he was thinking. "O'Malley," he finally said.

Claire shot Austin a skeptical look, her green eyes meeting his. Even Austin could tell something was wrong.

"Where's the captain?" Claire got out of the Humvee, leaving the door open behind her. "I want to speak with him."

"He's in the can," the Regular said, shifting uncomfortably.

"The can? Why don't one of those two privates on ATVs go get him?"

"I'm sorry, ma'am," the Regular replied, defiant now. "They can't."

Austin's heart began to race. This wasn't right.

"Why not?" Austin watched Claire's hand travel down to her rifle grip.

Her question lingered, unanswered, as a siren filled the air. She spun around, her green eyes going wide. Austin twisted to peer through the rear windshield of the Humvee.

Behind them, a crowd of people was marching down Military Road, banners in their hand and crosses held aloft, thousands of them, the throng stretching so far back he couldn't see the end of it. They were chanting something, but Austin couldn't tell what.

"My God," Claire said. "You let the civvies in?"

"This is bigger than the army," the Regular said. "These people deserve a chance to have their questions answered."

Claire got in the Regular's face. "You and your unit. Take up defensive positions now. We need to stop them. That's an order!"

"It doesn't have to go like that," the Regular replied. "I'm praying it doesn't. Just put your guns down."

The crowd was getting bigger, closing in on their position. Soon they would be surrounding the Humvee. Austin shifted uneasily at the thought.

"We took an oath," Claire said with a frown. "Doesn't that mean anything to you?"

"Sorry, ma'am," the Regular said, motionless. "The time of you Black Shirts telling us what to do is over."

For a moment, they all lived in that eternal nothing, Claire and the Regular, each with a hand on their guns. Her gaze shifted briefly to Austin, taking him in with her eyes.

Before he could plead with her to just lay down her gun, she raised hers up and opened fire.

There was a flash, the whiteness of the muzzle blast drowning out everything in the world. When he could see again, the Regular was falling over, a giant hole in the side of his neck. But Claire was falling, too, her helmet split, the Regular having got off a return volley before the darkness took him.

"Claire!" Austin screamed as her body slumped to the ground.

The motor roared to life, the tires screeching as the Humvee sped away. The driver jerked the wheel to the right, accelerating onto the off-ramp to Ross Drive.

Lead rained on them from the roadblock, the rear windshield's ballistic glass splintering into a spiderweb. Austin was too shocked to duck, the image of Claire getting shot playing repeatedly in his head.

The drumbeat of the .50 cal brought him back from his trance. More rounds collided with the grass around them, chunks of earth spraying into the air. They were milliseconds from the safety of the underpass out of their killers' line of sight. But it was a few milliseconds too many, the massive rounds of the .50 cal crashing into the doors and roof of the Humvee with a diabolical crack. Austin closed his eyes, bracing for the pain of death.

No pain came. When he opened his eyes again, he saw the sky, the .50 cal having punched several holes in the roof.

"Donnie!" the driver yelled as black smoke poured from a giant hole in the hood. The Black Shirt riding shotgun was dead, the anterior part of his head no longer attached.

"Donnie!" the driver kept yelling as he sped south down Ross Drive, swerving close to the oak trees on either side of the narrow road.

Austin opened his mouth to tell the driver to focus, when day suddenly turned to night, and a deafening wail, far louder than the base siren, filled up the darkness.

They didn't careen for long in the blackness before their motion was interrupted by an unseen object. Austin slammed into the door as the Humvee flipped onto its side. The vehicle scraped along Ross Drive on its driver's side, sparks spraying, only coming to a stop when it slammed into an oak tree.

When Austin came to, the sky had turned bright again. Donnie was on top of him, his corpse spilling warm blood onto Austin's shoulders. The scent of leaking diesel fouled the air. The driver was already trying to climb out of the passenger-side door. Austin moved his legs, testing that they still worked. A sharp pain spiked through his whole body, originating from his left foot. He grabbed his ankle, half expecting to feel an exposed bone, but felt only his boot.

"Let's go!" the Black Shirt driver yelled, opening the rear passenger door from atop the Humvee.

Putting his weight on his right foot, Austin threw Donnie's body off him and somehow managed to pull himself out of the smoldering Humvee. The Black Shirt had already taken a defensive position behind the overturned vehicle. Austin followed where his rifle was pointed: the two Regulars on ATVs had given chase.

"I'll hold them off," the Black Shirt said, taking a shot. "Now go!"

Austin sat atop the Humvee, frozen, Claire's perfect face still in his mind. Why had that happened? What was going on?

A round hit the back of the Humvee, narrowly missing Austin and snapping him back to attention. He hurriedly lowered himself down and limped into the woods. As the sound of gunfire raged behind him, he moved as fast as he could manage, ducking into a thicket of ponderosa pines, changing direction to confuse any pursuers. When he couldn't hear the gunshots anymore, he made his way up a ridge, using tree branches to help him ascend, the pain in his ankle searing.

When he got to the top, a faint roar reached his ears. Looking up, he saw three helicopters flying in a V formation, miniguns firing onto some unseen target below.

The sky went black again, a horn blaring so loud he thought he would puke. His hands went to his ears, but the sound disoriented him. He collapsed, and by the time the horn stopped, Austin was rolling down the ridge, desperately grabbing at dead leaves and tree branches in an effort to slow his descent.

He came to a stop as light returned, cuts and scrapes all over his body, everything bathed in a dull red glow. Above him, the Pilgrim craft pulsated red, like Virgil's hand when he'd taken it from the fire, bathing the whole park in a fiery aura. He saw the extension was gone, the physical connection with Earth severed.

Knowing he had to get to General Fergusson's HQ at the park offices, he raced down the hill, trying not to pass out from the pain. He'd already taken too long. After a while, though, the pain became too much and he plunked himself down onto a fallen log.

"Honey, it's me." The voice tiptoed through the forest, just loud enough to be heard over Austin's panting breaths. "Are the girls safe?"

He went toward it, hoping it was a Black Shirt with a vehicle, someone who could help him get to the general.

"Wait, what?"

As he got nearer, he saw a woman Regular leaning on a tree, a phone pressed to her ear and a rifle propped against a rock eight yards away.

"My God, who would do that?"

She didn't turn as Austin got closer, seemingly too engrossed to notice the sound of the rustling leaves.

"I don't know what happens now, Scott. Put Katie on."

Austin was close enough to see her service patches: a lieutenant—US Army, Twenty-Second Mechanized Battalion, her dark hair oddly familiar. Before he could convince himself not to, he reached out and tapped the lieutenant on the shoulder.

She twisted around in shock, her eyes turning cold when she saw him.

Austin recognized her instantly.

"Who are you?" she screeched, the phone still pressed to her ear.

Austin was too overwhelmed to reply. Her face had been seared into his mind. The memory of the old man's broken skin, the crack of the whip—it all came flooding back.

"No, not you, honey," Lieutenant Wu said into the phone, her eyes still locked on Austin. He searched her face to see if there was any recognition, but he saw none.

"Mommy has to go now. Oh don't cry hon', I love you," she said, putting the phone away.

"A phone?" Austin hit every syllable with disgust.

"I don't know how you made it this far into the base." Lieutenant Wu took a step back, her face nervously scanning Austin's civilian attire. "But if you let me turn you in, I can see that you aren't charged for coming through the park barricade."

Austin stepped to the side, conspicuously standing between the lieutenant and her gun. She was defenseless now—exposed. "You don't remember me, do you?" he said menacingly.

She tilted her head, terrified. "I can't seem to—"

"What is the First Assumption of Alien Capability?"

Her eyebrows slammed together in confusion.

"Can't remember?" he pressed.

"Cyber dominance," she meekly replied.

Austin nodded. "A phone like that is enough to get you twenty lashes at a militia muster. I wonder what it would get you at a frontline installation?"

He recalled how he had longed for her to know what it was like to feel powerless after what she'd done to the kind old man. But as she looked at him, a small wrinkle in her brow, he realized she still couldn't place who he was. There were too many old backs to choose from, too many poor saps ripped red for the sin of a cell phone.

"My youngest has Down syndrome," she pleaded. "She

doesn't understand why Mommy can't call her."

Austin laughed bitterly. "I'll be sure to tell General Fergusson that when I see him. I'm on my way now."

To Austin's surprise, her face didn't contort in fear; it merely fell. "I doubt he's here. Probably on his way to some bunker by now."

Austin eyed her suspiciously. "Nice try."

She shook her head. "It doesn't matter anyway. Rome's gone. Nuked. It won't be long before the Pilgrims attack."

Her words froze him. Austin searched her face, desperately looking for any sign of deceit. "What are you talking about?"

"A nuke went off near the Vatican. The whole thing is gone. So is the Pilgrim craft above the city. All of it vaporized."

Austin's breaths became labored. He was already too late. War was here. And Claire was dead. Poor sweet Claire.

"You're lying." Tears welled up in his eyes. "The Pilgrims would never—"

"It wasn't the Pilgrims . . ." Lieutenant Wu's voice shook. "It was us."

27

It was dark when Austin reached Father Ambrose's trailer. After he'd learned that Rome was gone—no cardinal to send a message to, no Pope or Vatican, either—he'd changed course. In its place was nuclear destruction, thousands of Romans dead in an instant, many thousands more soon to meet their doom as fires raged and fallout rained down. There'd be no peace between humans and Pilgrims now. Not after the place the Pilgrims had journeyed so long to get to—and the man they'd crawled across the galaxy to see—had been destroyed by man's savagery, a transgression that Austin figured they simply would not let stand.

Austin was certain the Pilgrims' vengeance would be swift, the stain of humanity rectified for good. That was why he decided to head to Father Ambrose's trailer, to wait out the end of the world with the closest thing he had to a friend.

The problem was Father Ambrose's trailer was overrun, hemmed in by hundreds of Regulars, each one with a white armband on, all eager to have their confession heard before the very end. Sarge stood at the front of the line like a sequoia—immense and immovable—the only thing between Father Ambrose and a stampede.

From the back of the crowd, Austin tried to peer through the mass of bodies, but a tall medic praying the rosary blocked his view. He was about to give up and walk away when the trailer door opened and a soldier who looked too young to shave walked out with Father Ambrose close behind.

Austin readied himself to shout at the priest, but as he watched Father Ambrose negotiate the steps of the trailer, he saw the movements of a man who had aged decades in a few hours, and decided to stay silent. He didn't want to burden his friend any further. As Austin turned to leave, though, their eyes met across the crowd. Gazes held, their silent exchange conveyed paragraphs. Father Ambrose's face turned apologetic, as though he felt he should be tending to Austin but couldn't. Austin shook his head, releasing the man, letting him know he'd done enough for him, that there were others who needed him more. With a nod, the priest called in the next penitent, taking them into the trailer and out of view.

Austin hobbled away from the crowd as a convoy of black MRAPs rolled by. He hadn't gone far when a dark silhouette emerged from the shadows, its skeletal form creeping toward him between the streetlights. Austin's eyes darted around him, looking for an escape if he needed one when General Fergusson's voice cut through the night.

"There you are."

Austin's muscles tensed. "You're still here?"

General Fergusson walked into the light. "Of course, DeSantis. Where else would I be?"

"I don't know," Austin said. "In a bunker somewhere with the rest of the brass, awaiting the onslaught."

"I don't run, DeSantis." The general's face was uncharacteristically flat—no feline smile to underline his bravado. "I'd like to show you something."

He waved his hand, and a Humvee down the road turned on its headlights and drove over. Opening the rear door, he gestured for Austin to get in.

Austin hesitated, his mind involuntarily flashing back to Claire and her green eyes.

"Your driver survived and made it to my HQ," the general said. "I know what happened, but you're safe now."

"The Regular killed her," he said, his voice quivering. "Why would he do that? She was—" Austin stopped himself, afraid that he wouldn't be able to hold back the tears.

"Did you see the protestors gathered outside the base on your helicopter ride in?" General Fergusson asked.

"Yes," Austin replied.

"Regular units sympathetic to the protestors let them in. As Black Shirts and loyal Regulars went to repel the crowd, sympathetic Regulars opened up on them." General Fergusson shook his head. "It was a bloodbath, a close combat melee where you couldn't tell friend from foe. They nearly overran the cylinder defenses, but they held—just."

A jet flew by overhead, the night sky lighting up as its ordinance hit its target on the far side of the park.

"We've nearly restored order now." The general pointed at a passing black MRAP. "I brought in the Three Hundred and Second Military Police Brigade to handle base security, and I've ordered all Regular units to stand down and leave the base. I trained these Black Shirts myself, DeSantis; there won't be any more surprises."

Gesturing toward the waiting Humvee, the general said, "It's time we get going."

Too exhausted to argue, Austin staggered into the Humvee, the pain in his ankle sharper than ever.

"It's a sprain," General Fergusson said, taking a seat next to Austin. "If it was broken, you wouldn't have been able to walk as far as you did."

"What are you going to show me?" Austin asked.

"The extension is back down." General Fergusson looked forward, every battle-scarred year on his face visible in the moonlight. "It descended about an hour ago."

"Is that where we're going?"

"Not yet." General Fergusson turned and looked Austin in the eye. "There's something you have to see first."

***

The command center was silent, a palpable heaviness in the air. The sergeant at the nearest terminal to Austin looked drained, his eyes so bloodshot little white could be seen.

On the large central monitor was a map of Saudi Arabia. The bottom half of the country was almost entirely colored red. The other monitors rotated between CCTV footage and videos from the internet. In every one of them, people were running away in a panic, pursued by small objects Austin could barely make out.

A colonel pushed past Austin and ran up to General Fergusson, brandishing a handful of notes and eagerly miming for the general to follow him to the observation room. The general, however, stayed exactly where he was. "I'm declaring OPSEC level Delta," he said. "There's no point in silence; the aliens already know we're watching them. Anyone here who needs a break is relieved. You've served your country with honor today, boys."

Two lieutenants got up from their terminals, saluted the general, and exited the room.

The colonel, still holding the notes, launched into his report. "Sir, the Saudi ICBM salvo has completed its orbit and is about to initiate its final burn on the way to the target."

"Noted," General Fergusson grunted. "And the swarm?"

"The main one is about to engulf the northeastern suburbs of Riyadh, sir."

As the general was debriefed, Austin turned his attention

to a monitor displaying what seemed like an airport terminal filled with bodies. In the center of the image was a woman in traditional Saudi garb—a long black gown—holding a child by the hand. They were both face down on the floor. Nearby a check-in agent was slumped over his computer like a discarded doll. The image was so still that Austin knew it was video only because of the digital clock that ticked away above the check-in counter, keeping perfect time down to the second of all of the life these people would never see.

"This is it?" Austin asked, horrified as realization set in. "The Pilgrim attack has begun?"

General Fergusson's focus stayed on the monitors, and Austin followed his gaze to the map. He realized that the red was the death zone, the tan the places not yet attacked; it wouldn't be long before the whole of Saudi Arabia would be covered in red.

"Sir, the Saudi ICBM salvo has completed its final burn. Time to target ten hours and forty-one minutes."

CCTV footage to the right of the central monitor caught Austin's attention. It showed an intersection transformed into chaos. Cars had smashed into one another, some on fire; in each one, there was a driver slumped over their steering wheel.

"How long until the attack gets here?" Austin asked.

General Fergusson turned to face Austin. "They're not coming here, DeSantis."

Austin searched General Fergusson's face, trying to tell if

he was being defiant. "What do you mean?"

"The alien attack is limited to Saudi Arabia."

"Saudi Arabia?" Austin asked, confused.

"Two hours, DeSantis. That's all it took. Two hours for the CIA and MI6 to both independently confirm that the attack on the Vatican was carried out by Prince Khalid, eighteenth in line for the Saudi throne, in retaliation for the alien praying at the Temple Mount. The prince smuggled a one-megaton nuclear device out of the Saudi arsenal and delivered it to Vatican City by sailing it up the Tiber River on his yacht. This was not a sanctioned attack. He acted alone."

General Fergusson's face contorted in a grimace.

"That information was to be treated as eyes-only, total digital embargo, transmission of reports by paper and hand delivery. No exceptions!" The general shook his head.

"Unfortunately, at 0511 UTC, the Italian ambassador to the UN, who'd earlier been briefed on these findings, broke the digital embargo by texting the substance of the intelligence assessment to his mistress in Bologna." Picking up a laser pointer, he flashed it on the map of Saudi Arabia. "The attack began at 0512 UTC when the aliens plunged Mecca in darkness, blotting out all light in the city, both natural and artificial. Shortly thereafter, small four-legged robots were seen emerging from the alien craft over Medina, falling to the ground and killing people on contact. Corporal, can you pull that up on a monitor, please?"

A video of the Pilgrim craft over Medina appeared on the screen. Small objects rained down from it like a silver hailstorm. The video then paused and zoomed in on one. It was a little machine with four legs and a tear-shaped body, the same machine that had grated Austin's Parmigiano-Reggiano back in the Victorian living room.

"At 0532 UTC, additional landings were detected thirty kilometers southwest of Riyadh, and twenty-five kilometers south of Ad Dammam. The swarms rapidly spread out in all directions, making contact with most Saudi major metros within thirty minutes. At the current rate, we expect that every square inch of the country will be infested with these killer machines in the next eighty-eight minutes."

Austin's breath escaped him as he thought of all the needless death. "How do you know they aren't coming here?"

"Captain Hammond," General Fergusson said to one of the Black Shirts behind a computer terminal. "Pull up the hospital footage."

The central monitor changed from the map to security footage of a hospital nursery. From where the camera was placed, they could see the entire area. The entrance had been shattered, and a baby was lying on the floor just before its threshold. It was wiggling on top of some bed linens as four little machines clung to the doorframe like bugs stopped by an invisible fence.

On the far side of the room was a priest holding an infant

next to a running faucet. A doctor was pushing another bassinet toward the priest while about a half-dozen school-age children huddled in the opposite corner.

"Captain, do we have audio?" General Fergusson asked.

"Yes, sir."

"Put it on."

"But, sir—"

"I know, son, but we have to."

The captain complied and the command center was filled with the voice of the priest speaking Italian, the sound coming from a set of speakers set up in the front of the room.

Austin's heart raced. "What is this?"

"This is security footage the NSA obtained from King Fahad Medical City Hospital in Riyadh," General Fergusson said.

"What's going on?"

"Keep watching."

The priest placed the head of the newborn underneath the running water three times as he continued to speak in Italian before putting the child into the bassinet next to him and taking another baby. Austin realized the priest was performing a baptism.

"We were able to identify the priest," General Fergusson said. "His name is Monsignor Vincenzo Innocenti. He was the chaplain assigned to the Italian embassy in Riyadh. We're still not sure how he made it from the embassy across town to the hospital amid the carnage."

The priest and the doctor began to wrestle, the doctor suddenly realizing that the priest was baptizing the children. As the doctor held the priest, the school-age children descended upon him, attempting to rip a baby he was trying to baptize from his arms. After a short struggle, a small girl ended up with the baby.

"We don't have much time. The Diplomats will be here soon."

Monsignor Innocenti was right; within moments, a Diplomat was standing in the nursery doorway, its arrival marked by the children's shrieks, their horrified voices echoing through the command center.

"No . . ." Austin's head became light. "Please, no."

Austin winced as the Diplomat went for the infant lying on the sheets, but to his surprise, the Diplomat picked it up gently, cradling the baby's head. But as soon as the Diplomat stepped away, the little machines behind it pounced, charging into the nursery with a ferocious speed.

It took only seconds for a machine to find its way to one of the children. The little girl vainly tried to push it off with her small hands but to no avail. Soon she was limp on the ground, her eyes wide open.

Austin's heart slammed against the walls of his chest as he watched. He distrusted his own eyes; the Pilgrims couldn't really be capable of such evil.

"Permission to be relieved, sir," a Black Shirt from behind

a computer terminal said between tears as the sound of children's screaming filled the command center.

"Granted," General Fergusson replied.

Austin watched as the doctor and the children were killed one by one. The priest made a futile attempt to shield a young child with his body, but the boy went limp, the whole exercise in vain.

"This can't be happening." Austin's voice was so broken it was unrecognizable to himself.

"It is happening, DeSantis."

Austin noticed that the infant by the door, the infant the priest had baptized, and the priest himself were being spared.

"The machines…" Austin sputtered. "They're only killing Muslims?"

"Yes," General Fergusson coldly replied. "The machine swarm stopped at the Yemeni border and is avoiding migrant workers. That tells us that the killing is selective, the genocide limited to Arabia—only people of Saudi nationality and Islamic faith."

"But how…"

"Cyber dominance, DeSantis. In addition to the humans they directly witness being baptized like these infants, the aliens likely have a file on every living human, updated every second. They know who's a baptized Christian and who isn't. There's no collateral damage. Every kill desired."

Austin felt so queasy he thought he would pass out. As

revenge for the Vatican, the Pilgrims weren't throwing a nuclear tantrum, destroying cities in emotional fits like a drunkard breaking plates. They were attacking with a scalpel, deciding who lived and who died down to the very man.

Austin looked up as the sound of sobs filled the command center. A little girl with a baby in her arms knelt on the ground in front of the Diplomat—the last two unbaptized survivors. She knelt there almost as if she was begging the Diplomat for mercy. But the little machines did not stop; they only made their way to her more slowly, as if they knew the need for rushing was done.

"No, please," Austin said, his voice trembling. "Not her. Please."

The priest rushed toward her, trying to intervene, but the machines struck too soon.

When she fell, she fell backward, her eyes wide open, her dead stare looking directly into the security camera lens.

"The aliens have revealed their true colors, DeSantis," General Fergusson said. "Now you can see why I am the way I am."

The world became hazy, the dead eyes of the girl all Austin could see. He reached out, trying to steady himself, but his legs felt like jelly. He thought he saw the priest take the baby from the girl and run off in the direction of the sink, but he couldn't be sure. The darkness overcame him, his body going to meet the ground.

As he passed out, the girl's face was still with him—her dead eyes, her sweet visage—like a tattoo on his mind, haunting him as his consciousness faded, tormenting him as Arabia burned.

28

DeSantis, wake up."

Light dripped into Austin's eyes, his head shooting with pain.

"Get up, DeSantis. We're running out of time."

Austin blinked, finding General Fergusson leaning over him. He lay on the floor of the observation room. He could see the command center through the two-way mirror behind the general. "What happened? How did I get in here?"

"You fainted. I brought you in. Can you stand?"

Austin wobbled as he got to his feet, General Fergusson helping him up. He inadvertently put his weight on his sprained ankle but was surprised to feel no pain.

"I had the medic inject it with cortisone while you were unconscious. You should be able to stand on it."

Austin stepped back, putting equal weight on both feet. "How long was I out?"

"Too long."

It was just General Fergusson and him in the room. He could see through the two-way mirror that the map was back up on the central monitor, the red having filled in most of the archipelagoes of tan in the southern half of Saudi Arabia.

"The Saudi counterattack failed," General Fergusson said. "The aliens were able to divert the Saudi ICBMs. Sent them drifting off harmlessly into space. They never stood a chance."

Taking a few steps forward, Austin noticed the taste of bile in his mouth. "Why did you bring me here?"

"I couldn't have an unconscious man in my command center."

"No." Austin dusted off his pants. "Why did you show me all of this?"

Walking over to the two-way mirror, General Fergusson gazed into the command center with his hands behind his back.

"Those five years leading up to the alien arrival, we were closer to the brink than you'll ever know. It was every country for itself." General Fergusson turned to face Austin. "But there was one mantra that everyone paid lip service to: an attack on one is an attack on all. The minute the aliens started firing—no matter whom they targeted—we would all fire back, humanity's last stand."

General Fergusson's head fell. "Empty words, DeSantis—that's all they ever were. And after Jerusalem, when the aliens didn't destroy a dozen cities after the Palestinian Authority launched rockets at them, it became official US policy. We would wait to see if the alien response was limited before fighting back. No matter how many of our species were butchered, so long as it wasn't us, we'd simply watch, watch as Arabia bleeds."

Austin looked at the map, the nation stained red. "That's why you showed me this?" Austin said. "To remind me that we never stood a chance?"

Turning from the mirror, General Fergusson put his hands on Austin's shoulders. "You needed to see what unfettered power looks like. The power to kill millions but still choose down to the single solitary individual who lives and who dies. It's the power of God."

General Fergusson was only a few inches from Austin's face, his narrow eyes peering into his core, and Austin felt like he finally understood the man, finally saw why he was the way that he was.

"You were right," he said, removing General Fergusson's hands from his shoulders. "I was just too blind to see it."

Austin waited for the general's lips to curl up into his feline smile, but his face was still, lips unmoving. "I didn't bring you here to tell me I'm right. I never had any doubt that I was. I brought you here to remind you that only you can balance the scales of power and put an end to this madness."

All the memories of General Fergusson calling him "his weapon" flooded back into his mind. He'd never wanted it, never really believed it, but his ears were beginning to open.

"How?" Austin asked.

"The robot."

Austin could see the pale blue light of Virgil in his mind's eye, its glare cutting through the mist. "Virgil?"

"Yes. We need you to make the aliens feel vulnerable, just like us humans."

Austin looked at him like he was insane. "By killing?"

"If necessary."

Austin imagined it. The sands of Arabia scattered with Pilgrims, their blood a down payment on the infinite debt they had to pay. As he did, the kind old man crept into his head, looking up at Austin, pleading, before his brains were scattered all over his immaculate floor. "I don't want to kill. I can't be party to that again," he said, his voice trailing off.

General Fergusson took a deliberate step toward him. "Power only understands power, DeSantis. Sometimes there is no other way."

Austin thought about the power of the Pilgrims, their massive spaceship, the mysteries of their church. There was no power humanity could bring that could match it. "What about talking?" Austin asked, the memory of Virgil rescuing him, his haptic embrace, still lingering despite the carnage.

"Look at the screens, DeSantis." General Fergusson pointed back into the command center. "Do they look like a race that responds to talking?"

Through the two-way mirror Austin saw a live stream of a Bedouin camp. Lifeless bodies of men, women, and children all lay on the ground, tents fluttering in the breeze.

"Virgil said they would listen to the pope."

"There is no Pope," General Fergusson replied. "He's dead."

"I know . . ." Austin said, desperate to find another way. "But Father Ambrose isn't. Maybe he can convince them."

General Fergusson shook his head. "You and the priest already tried talking to the robot; look what good that did."

Austin gaze shifted to the map. The red was still spreading relentlessly. "I have to try."

General Fergusson walked back to the two-way mirror, looking out at the command center. "This base is still a tinder-box. If I try to clear out the Regulars waiting for confession outside the priest's trailer, there'll be a shoot-out. We don't have time for that. In less than forty-five minutes, Saudi Arabia will be totally consumed."

Austin walked over to stand next to General Fergusson. "Then I'll do it," he said. "Alone."

General Fergusson looked at him, sizing him up and down. "It's a noble thought, DeSantis, but it's no use."

"Maybe," Austin said as he focused on the Bedouin camp on the monitor, a little boy in the foreground, his eyes wide open to the sky. "But I have to try."

29

Austin stood amid the devastation of the fairway, the barricades broken, bodies strewn about. Even with the help of the rebellious Regulars, the crowd had been no match for the power of the Black Shirts, their fruitless incursion brought to an ignominious end.

They were trying to get to the cylinder.

Trying to see God.

Little did they know there was no God inside that steel pillar, just cruel aliens who rained down death from on high.

"If anything so much as twitches from that cylinder, we're opening fire," the Black Shirt commander said.

Austin nodded and then walked forward without a word.

Its walls folded away as he approached, and the sound of a thousand guns cocking filled the air around him. He left them behind as he stepped inside the dark hall and walked to the Victorian living room. Virgil was kneeling in the center, his hands clasped in prayer.

"Virgil," Austin said, "I need to talk to you."

The robot was silent, his head casting crimson rays off the gold-inlaid ceiling.

"Virgil!" Austin shouted.

When Virgil didn't respond, Austin moved closer, reaching out his hand to rap his head like Father Ambrose had done, but before his hand connected, one of Virgil's metal hands shot up and grabbed his arm. The domed head changed from crimson to pale blue. Austin shrieked, but he felt no pain. The grip was soft, and the haptic touch soothing. Austin was instantly transported back to the narthex, when he was lost in that mist—consigned to suffer with his demons for all eternity—when out of the nothingness came Virgil. This was his friend, and if anyone could help, it was him.

"I was praying for the souls in Saudi Arabia," Virgil said in his sweet voice. "That they may have repose."

"The Pilgrims have to stop, Virgil," Austin pleaded, looking into Virgil's dome with a mixture of desperation and hope. "They have to stop now while there are still people left to save."

"The war will be complete in approximately twenty-eight minutes," Virgil replied, the rhythm of his voice noticeably slower. "Then Michael will declare a peace."

Austin pulled his arm out of Virgil's grip.

"This isn't war! It's a slaughter," Austin yelled. "Children, Virgil. You're killing children! I saw it with my own eyes."

Virgil remained kneeling. "I know, Austin. All we can do

now is pray."

A metallic taste filled Austin's mouth. "Pray? *That's* your answer to mass murder?"

Virgil was silent, only the pale blue glow of his head an answer.

"Now, Virgil! You need to stop the killing now!"

"I cannot, Austin." Virgil stood up. "That is not my choice. It is Michael's, and he is firm."

Austin's legs began to move, his anger driving them onward. "Then tell Michael he has to nunc desinere!" Austin yelled. "You're violating the Commandments—remember 'Thou shalt not kill'? He is making himself—no—he's making *all* of the Pilgrims into hypocrites."

Virgil drooped his domed head. His movement sent a spark of hope through Austin that he might be getting through to him.

"God have mercy on us if he is," Virgil replied, unmistakable sadness in his voice.

"What do you mean 'if'? Millions of innocent people just had their lives snuffed out. If Michael believed in God, he would stop this instant."

"It is war, Austin." Virgil raised his head back up. "To kill is the nature of war."

Austin's hand raised, the primal urge to strike his friend strong, but he resisted. "This isn't war; it's vengeance! A crazy prince killed your pope, and so you're slaughtering his innocent subjects as payback."

"No, Austin." The pleading in Virgil's voice was like a splash of cold water on Austin's face. "It is not vengeance. It is defense. Quadrillions of souls are at stake."

"Quadrillions?" Austin seethed.

"Yes, Austin." The pale blue in Virgil's dome shifted, playing a video. Austin tilted his head, caught off guard by this seemingly new ability on Virgil's part, but as the image moved his eyes focused, trying to discern what he was seeing.

Thousands of little black dots appeared in front of a red-orange sun, small shadows against its nuclear furnace. As the image zoomed in, Austin realized that the little dots were an uncountable number of space stations, each with ornate rotating portions. Small ships raced between the stations, or at least Austin thought they were small until the image zoomed in further and he saw how immense they were.

"This is the Pilgrim home system. From our moons to our Lagrange points, it is filled with life."

Austin's clenched hands loosened as he stared into Virgil's dome. The video had zoomed into the closest rotating habitat. He was now looking at an electric blue ocean, so crisp that he could almost feel the waves lapping on his arms. The water was crisscrossed by an archipelago, the land a swell of color. Zooming in on one of the islands, Austin could see that it was covered in flora that stretched as high as the tallest skyscraper, with leaves that had more colors than a rainbow. At the base of those trees were thousands of structures, made of the same silvery metal as Virgil, that connected directly into the ocean, as if the water was their bloodstream, breathing life into the buildings.

"The Pilgrims never had religion. God was a mere philosophical concept. An explanation for the continued existence of reality—a primal cause—but nothing more. But when we saw the data from Earth, we were confronted with a difficult truth."

The image changed to Pilgrims gathered around a hologram, reviewing the video of the Resurrection Austin had seen in the chancel.

"The Creator and Sustainer of the cosmos was a proximal reality. And the Pilgrims had been ignoring Him, devoting themselves entirely to their pleasure, neglecting the state of their souls."

Austin could now see a massive gathering of the Pilgrims standing on a grassy plain somewhere on one of their rotating habitats. Their pale skin was pigmenting in various shapes and figures all in unison, all of them speaking as one. Then, one at a time, they knelt and made the sign of the cross.

"Our only hope was to reconcile with Him, to travel to His Church and partake in the sacraments, thereby saving our souls from perdition."

Austin blinked as Virgil's head returned to a pale blue.

"But now the Church is in danger. Its very existence jeopardized. That is why Michael wages war."

He had forgotten his anger amid his awe. To see the Pilgrim home system, to realize that the massive ship in orbit was but an insignificant fraction of this ancient race—it overwhelmed him. There were so many questions Austin wanted to ask, so many mysteries he wanted to have revealed, but then the image of the dead girl staring up into the security camera came back into his mind.

"How many thousands died in the time it you took to give me that speech?" he said, the metallic taste growing in his mouth.

"Too many," Virgil replied.

"Then stop!" Austin stormed toward the couches by the fireplace.

"We can't stop, Austin." Virgil followed Austin across the room. "Prince Khalid was not alone. He had confederates. They killed the pope and half of the college of cardinals, but they wanted to destroy the entire apostolic succession by murdering all the bishops. If they succeeded, the connection to the sacraments would be severed forever. Humanity, Pilgrimkind—all sapient life in the universe would be consigned to darkness. An uncountable number of souls separated from God. Michael felt he had no choice but to act."

"By killing innocent people?" Austin seethed. "By killing children?"

"The neurotoxin is painless," Virgil said, seeming to shrink from Austin. "They felt nothing. We took care to spare those who repented, those who knew Christ or turned toward Him at the end."

Austin's vision started to go red. He wanted to rush at Virgil, pummel him, but he took out his rage on the Victorian sofa instead, flipping it over as he let out an animal roar.

"They *felt* terror. You could see it on their little faces!" Austin shouted. "Right up to the minute of their death. They felt a horror no human should feel."

The outburst extinguished his rage, leaving him nothing but the ashes of despair. He collapsed to the ground, exhausted, as the fight left him.

"I know, Austin," Virgil said, his voice low. "There is no good way to take life. No matter how sophisticated the technology."

Curling his knees into his chest, tears poured from his eyes. The futility of what he was trying to do was catching up with him.

"Why do it?" Austin sobbed. "Why not just kill those responsible for Rome? Why hurt those children?"

Virgil glided over to Austin and sat down next to him on the floor.

"It was considered. But Michael is firm, and he thought it would only embolden other malcontents, knowing that there was such a limited price to pay for imperiling all sapient life in the universe."

Virgil's words fanned the embers of Austin's still-smoldering rage. "Limited? Michael thought it would have been *too limited* to spare the children?"

"Yes," Virgil replied as he lowered his domed head. "Before the Pilgrims found the Lord, and learned the error of our ways, the Pilgrims had war. *This* is how war was fought from time immemorial, leaving none of the opponent alive."

Austin was almost too stunned to respond. "But now you found the Lord. Isn't that right, Virgil? How does Michael justify total annihilation now?"

Virgil sat there, silent.

Austin waited, but the robot still didn't speak, like he was holding something back.

"Tell me, Virgil! How do you justify genocide now?" Austin shrieked, the spit from his exhortations landing on Virgil's pale blue dome.

"Michael says humans are a primitive species, that they only know force. And so, he issued the command."

"What command?"

Virgil pointed his dome at Austin.

"Tell me!"

Virgil spoke, his usually steady voice cracking. "'Arabia delenda est.'"

The words sucked the air out of Austin's lungs.

"Arabia must be destroyed . . ." Austin could barely say it. "Do you agree with this, Virgil?" he asked, a chill going up his spine.

Virgil turned his entire body toward Austin, as if he were looking him in the eye.

"No," Virgil replied firmly. "If the good thief who was crucified next to our Lord and Savior can come to know Him even at the last moment of his life, then there is always hope that man can have a change of heart, that he can repent. And so, we must preserve life, endeavor to protect it unless all other means of justice are exhausted."

Relief flooded through Austin at his friend's words. He may have only been a machine, but he knew goodness. And just like Austin, he was a victim of the same soul-crushing circumstances. "Then plead with Michael. Tell him to spare those who remain, even if it's just the children, before it's too late."

Virgil again lowered his domed head once more. "I have tried, Austin. Many, many times. But he is firm." Virgil's voice was fleeting, resigned. "There isn't anything I can do."

As Austin looked at his friend, realization began to sink in. Virgil was a robot, built to serve the Pilgrims, and no matter how magnificent his capabilities, he was still just a pawn, forced to do what his betters told him to—just like Austin.

"Is there no one who could have saved those people?" Austin asked rhetorically, not expecting a response.

"His Holiness, Pope Stephen," Virgil answered, the hopelessness dripping off his words. "But Prince Khalid killed him; may God rest his soul."

So this was it. Michael, a creature with unlimited power, bound by nothing, orbiting Earth. General Fergusson's warnings echoed in Austin's head. He'd seen this coming, the inevitable consequence of unbridled power. Austin had been too blinded by his budding friendships to recognize what was really at stake. "There really is nothing to be done," Austin said, feeling empty.

"We must pray, Austin. Pray for the souls in Saudi Arabia. And pray for our own."

Gracefully resuming his kneeling position, Virgil made the sign of the cross and then clasped his hands.

Austin stood up and looked at his friend, this beautiful creature, its artificial mind somehow managing to be much wiser and gentler than the wicked minds that created it. He thought about the vile Pilgrims, an advanced race of murderers, wrapping themselves in the cloak of God.

As Austin exited the living room, he knew that there was only one path forward: to disempower the mighty and lay them low, as low as Austin felt now in the pits of futility and despair.

Austin would finally become what General Fergusson had always been sculpting him to be—his righteous weapon—and no mercy for the wicked would be had.

PART IV

30

You were right." Austin looked through the two-way mirror at the central monitor. The map of Saudi Arabia was back on the screen, and there was no tan left: the whole country was red, the blood of forty million Saudis staining the land. "All they care about is power."

General Fergusson stood next to Austin, his arms behind his back. "Power is all anyone cares about, DeSantis."

A heavy silence hung in the command center, every person in the room staring at the map in anguish. The Pilgrims' brutality had made them all hollow. Austin would be, too, if it weren't for the rage he felt.

"They thought they were being humane," he said. "Using a painless neurotoxin, sparing the Christians."

"Humane?" General Fergusson scoffed. "Terror is the most brutal kind of pain. At least when we nuked the Japs, they didn't see it coming."

Austin recalled seeing old images of Hiroshima, the mushroom cloud rising over the city, the shadows permanently imprinted on the walls, the horribly burned people looking for help that would never come. It occurred to him that Rome must be in a similar state right now; he'd been too busy watching a genocide in Saudi Arabia to have seen the aftermath of that nuclear blast—just one horror stacked on top of another.

"Good killing, bad killing," Austin said with a sigh. "It's all just killing."

There was quiet between the two men, the carnage they had witnessed taking the place of words, but after a moment General Fergusson spoke.

"Why did you come here, DeSantis?"

Austin steeled himself for what he needed to do. "I'll do it."

"You'll do what?"

"I'll be your weapon."

General Fergusson met Austin's eyes.

Austin expected to see the feline smile, but the general merely gave him a shallow nod, his expression inscrutable.

"What now?" Austin asked.

"That depends," General Fergusson said. "How did you leave it with the robot?"

Austin thought back to the Victorian living room, sitting on the floor with Virgil, anger and despair crushing them both. "I don't know."

"What do you mean you don't know?"

"I yelled at him. I told him the Pilgrims were evil, that

they're hypocrites."

The general raised an eyebrow at him. "Did you call the robot a hypocrite?"

Austin could see Virgil's pale blue head drooping, his metal body hunched over. "No. He said that he opposed the attack. He even tried to convince Michael not to do it."

"That's good," General Fergusson said. "We still might be able to finish the job."

Austin tilted his head, not sure he liked the sound of that. "Finish the job?"

"Yes," General Fergusson said, resolute. "I aim to settle this once and for all."

"How?"

Stepping back, General Fergusson turned his whole form to face Austin, then began unbuttoning his shirt, each movement deliberate, until his shirt was open, his emaciated frame exposed.

The entire left side of his torso was a dermic wasteland, the flesh swollen and necrotic, streaks of brown-red punctuating the skin, making the wounds look fresh and raw.

"Green on blue, DeSantis," General Fergusson said, calling back to their conversation in the wrestling room, his eyes locked on Austin's. "That's how."

"Afghanistan?" he said, fighting the waves of nausea that urged him to look away.

General Fergusson nodded. "They used an IED, ignited

a fuel dump. Took out fifteen of our best people. Those who lived"—he touched the tortured flesh with his right hand and winced—"look like some version of this."

Austin grimaced, the image of a young General Fergusson on fire filling his mind. "You want me to plant a bomb on the Pilgrim mother ship?" he said skeptically. "Take out a few dozen Pilgrims in retaliation?"

"No," General Fergusson said, his waiflike fingers starting to re-button his shirt, hiding the scars from view. "Not just any bomb. A nuke."

"A nuke?" Austin laughed nervously. "You're joking, right?"

"Power only responds to power, DeSantis. Anything less won't do."

"Okay." Austin drew out the word for effect. "I guess I'll just carry a nuke up to the ship in my pocket, just like that damn camera."

"No," General Fergusson said, ignoring Austin's sarcasm. "Our miniaturization programs are not yet that advanced."

Austin studied the general's unyielding face. "You're actually serious?" he said.

"Have you ever heard me tell a joke, DeSantis?"

Austin had not; he'd only ever seen the feline smile. "How do I get a nuke on board?"

"Simple," General Fergusson said. "If you can come up with an excuse to bring an object up, we can disguise it in that. We have nuclear devices that are totally analog—nothing digital, nothing electronic."

Stepping away from the mirror, Austin began to pace around the observation room, his mind racing. "Will a nuke be effective?"

"Yes, the alien craft over Rome was destroyed in the blast. They're not invincible."

"Why not just fire our nuclear missiles, the ones on the orbital launch platform? You've been talking those things up on TV for years."

"They're useless," General Fergusson said dismissively. "Even if we launched at the optimum spot in orbit, it would take hours for the missiles to impact the alien mother ship. The aliens would have plenty of time to intercept or avoid the inbound missiles. It would be like dodging a punch you know is coming from miles away. I only ever talked it up to keep the public calm, make them think we had a chance."

Austin stopped pacing. "It was another noble lie?"

General Fergusson nodded.

Austin shook his head, beginning to see the logic of General Fergusson's plan. "If I sneak it aboard, there's no travel time. They won't have any time to avoid it."

"That's right."

"You are asking me to kill them all—the millions of Pilgrims aboard the ship?"

From where General Fergusson stood in front of the

two-way mirror, the red map of Saudi Arabia framed his face. "When I told you you'd be my weapon, what did you think I meant? This would restore the balance of power. Save countless human lives."

Austin imagined the giant explosion inside the Pilgrim ship, shattering it into a thousand pieces. As the flash of the bomb went off in his mind, he was back in the shop, the kind old man looking up at him from the ground, pleading for Austin to help before the Fedcoin machine came crashing down.

It was all too much. In his anger with the Pilgrims, he hadn't fully appreciated what being General Fergusson's weapon would entail. Now he was finding out again that he had no way out.

"I can't do it," Austin said as he flopped onto the observation room floor opposite General Fergusson. "I can't kill again."

Austin readied himself for General Fergusson to scream, to tell him off. Instead, the general crossed the observation room to him.

"As Sun Tzu said, 'The greatest victory is that which requires no battle.'" He took a seat on the floor next to Austin. "We didn't beat the Soviets by firing our missiles. We beat them by wearing them out, never allowing them to have the upper hand. That's how you win a war without a battle: you take away the enemy's power, make it so they don't want to fight."

Austin perked his head up. "You mean like a cold war?"

General Fergusson nodded. "When you get the nuke up there, it'll be on a dead man's trigger. If the aliens attack again or try to remove the bomb from their ship, the nuke will go off." General Fergusson placed his hand on Austin's shoulder. "They'll have lost their monopoly on power. We'll have peace."

Austin felt like he finally saw a light at the end of the tunnel, a way out of the corner he'd found himself in. "How does the dead man's trigger work?"

"Extremely low-frequency radio waves," General Fergusson said. "The wavelengths are so long they can go right through a massive solid object, like the thousands of feet of rock outside the alien ship. If the signal ever turns off, the bomb will detonate. We used a similar system for our nuclear submarines patrolling deep under the ocean during the Cold War. If the signal ever went off, it meant America was under attack. They would surface and release their ordnance. It's the same principle here."

"The idea is to create the *threat* of attack?" Austin asked. "The point is to never actually set off the bomb?"

"That's right. After you return from the ship, I'll let the Pilgrims know there's a bomb on board that we can set off at any second—deterrence achieved."

"No killing?" Austin looked into General Fergusson's eyes.

"No," General Fergusson said. "Not unless they find you with the bomb."

Austin frowned. "What happens then?"

The general's eyes never wavered. "You die a warrior's death."

Austin pictured it, the Pilgrims killing him, throwing him out into the vacuum of space. To his surprise he felt nothing. He couldn't feel anything when all he could see was all those dead bodies in Saudi Arabia. "Well then I guess they'd better not find it," he coolly replied.

This was it, then: the plan they needed to prevent what had happened in Saudi Arabia from ever happening again, hatched on the floor of a lonely observation room. Austin tried to get up, but, despite the cortisone shot, he struggled when he put weight on his bad ankle. Before he could try again, General Fergusson's hands were helping him to his feet.

"It's all quite simple in the end," General Fergusson said. "The only trouble will be getting an object onto the ship. Michael will be on high alert. If I were him, there's no way I would allow anything on board."

Austin looked through the two-way mirror to Saudi Arabia covered in red. "I know how to get something up to the ship."

General Fergusson tilted his head.

"We give them the one thing they want." Austin turned to General Fergusson and met his gaze. "The thing they traveled across the galaxy to get."

31

S arge closed the door behind Austin. The air inside the trailer was thick as if the men in search of absolution had left a miasma in their wake, their fear and guilt lingering like a hot fume. Father Ambrose was kneeling on the ground, hunched over the small cot, a rosary wrapped around his fingers, his body as still as the dead.

"Father?" Austin asked nervously.

A wave of relief crested over Austin when he heard the shallow snores emanating from Father Ambrose's mouth.

Moving closer, he shook Father Ambrose's shoulder. The priest's head shot up in surprise.

"Austin?" he said, his voice worn down to nothing. He started to stand up, but his knees locked, sending him falling over sideways.

"Father!" Austin grabbed him just before he hit the floor and then hoisted him up onto the cot.

"I'm fine." Father Ambrose rubbed his knee. He looked

sallow, his skin so pale it looked like the blood had been drained out of him. "Just not as young as I used to be."

Once the priest was settled, Austin said, "Have you heard?"

"Depends," Father Ambrose said, clearing his throat. "About Rome or Arabia?"

"Arabia." Austin winced as he said the name.

Father Ambrose reached into his pants pocket and pulled out a phone, flicking one of his fingers to unlock the screen. "One of the soldiers gave me this last night." A live news stream appeared on the screen, depicting a reporter stepping over dead bodies as she made her way through the silent landscape of Riyadh. The chyron at the bottom of the screen read: "The Arabian Apocalypse."

"I tried to stop it," Austin said, tears welling up in his eyes.

Father Ambrose pulled Austin into an embrace.

"I failed," Austin said. "Virgil said Michael had already made up his mind."

"It's not your fault," Father Ambrose soothed. "If there is anyone to blame, it's me."

Austin released himself from Father Ambrose's hug. "Don't be ridiculous, Father. Michael is to blame for this, no one else."

"No, Austin. I am called 'Father' for a reason." Father Ambrose took off his glasses and rubbed his temple. "That isn't some empty word. It means I'm supposed to be a spiritual rock for the faithful. To help them grow. To guide them. Show them how to come into the fullness of a life in Christ—

just like a loving father would. But if this is what the Pilgrims think Christianity entails"—Father Ambrose gestured to the news stream on his phone—"then my efforts and those of my fellow priests have been in vain."

The camera was panning over the corpses in Saudi Arabia when the image abruptly changed to a fireball over Rome. The nuke had caused a firestorm, sucking people and debris into its fiery maw with hurricane-force winds. Even outlying neighborhoods that had survived the blast would soon be turned into ash, the nuke's thirst for death not yet quenched.

Tearing his gaze away from the phone, Austin said, "Come on, Father. Is Catholic guilt really so bad that you blame yourself for other people's sins?"

"Ah yes, Catholic guilt." Father Ambrose's voice was low. "The great oppressor of happiness, the scourge of the modern man. It's good we've eliminated all self-accusation from our lives, turned our vices into virtues, wear our failings like awards. Because now we can have the wrath of Prince Khalid, the vengeance of Michael; as long as we don't have to look in the mirror and confront how broken we really are."

The twinkle was gone from Father Ambrose's eyes. His friend needed space, healing, and care, but there wasn't time for that; there was a mission to complete.

"You can still teach them," Austin said. "Show them the correct path."

"If only they'd listen," he said, defeated.

"They'll listen if you say a Mass."

Father Ambrose raised an eyebrow. "A Mass?"

"Yeah, up on the ship. There's no way they'll say no to that. You can teach them how to be good Christians, make sure there are no more tragedies like the one in Saudi Arabia. Put this madness to an end."

Father Ambrose tilted his head, his forehead creasing. "Are you being serious?"

"I am," Austin replied.

"Austin," Father Ambrose said, speaking slower, as if he was trying to let Austin down gently. "After what the Pilgrims did, that isn't something I can do on a whim. It's frankly a matter for the next pope to decide."

"How long until there's a new pope?" Austin asked, his anxiety growing.

"I don't know. There'd have to be a new conclave. Before that could happen, the surviving cardinals would have to decide on a new place to gather now that the Vatican is gone. That won't be easy. It will take months, maybe even years."

"We don't have time for that!" Austin stood up. "There might be another attack. Michael might order—"

"I'm leaving, Austin." Father Ambrose's voice was sharp now. "I'm heading back to Arizona."

"You can't." Austin took a step back. "You'd be a fugitive."

Father Ambrose managed to stand up, the pain visible as he straightened his legs. "I think the government has bigger things to worry about than me. They'll probably just deduct a hefty fine from my Fedcoin account and be done with it."

Austin moved back until he was touching the kitchenette. His plan was all falling apart, dying at the feet of a priest unwilling to conduct a Mass. "How will you get off the base?"

"Simple." Father Ambrose walked over to the tiny mirror affixed to the wall and started tidying his beard. "John offered to sneak me out in a supply truck in an hour. With the Regulars banned from the base, the Black Shirts are spread thin, and discipline is falling apart."

Austin's heart began to race. "I saw the crowd here last night," he said, trying to hide the desperation in his tone. "The soldiers on the base need you. You can't turn your back on them."

Father Ambrose pulled a bottle of water out of the minifridge, opened the lid, and took a sip. "Is there a crowd out there now?"

Other than John still standing guard at the door, there had been no one when Austin arrived. "No."

"That's because, after waiting for hours, most of them decided to see if they could find a priest at a local parish. We are in the middle of a major American city, not some desert outpost in central Asia. If they desire it, these troops have pastoral care at hand."

Father Ambrose raked his fingers through his hair, restoring a semblance of order to his salt-and-pepper locks.

"You can't leave, Father," Austin pleaded. "This is your

chance to go up to the Pilgrim ship and pray for the souls of the people they killed. Rub their alien faces right in what they did."

Father Ambrose frowned at Austin. "You mean conduct a Mass out of spite?"

"Exactly," Austin replied.

Father Ambrose shook his head. "I can see I haven't been a good teacher to you either if that's what you think the Mass is about."

Austin's heart beat faster. "You're running away," he said. "Just like in the nave."

"That was different."

"No, it's the same. With everything that's happened, you're scared. That's only natural. We're all scared, but do you think the saints would turn tail and run when things got bad?"

"I'm not running, Austin, I'm acquiescing—acquiescing to God's will. It seems He has other plans for me, that it's someone else's calling to show the Pilgrims the way of a true Christian life. Someone more capable than me."

He was losing Father Ambrose, the whole mission going to pot, and there was only one card left to play, the most manipulative thing he could think of. "Then don't do it for the Pilgrims." Austin got down on his knees. "Do it for me."

Father Ambrose's eyes went wide. "What are you saying?"

Austin's heart constricted, the weight of guilt settling in. "I'm saying that in the midst of all this darkness, your faith has been the only light I've been able to see. If you leave, if you can't rise to this challenge, then I'm sure that little spark of faith inside me will be extinguished."

Father Ambrose's face fell. "The Mass . . . it would be for you?"

"Yes, Father," Austin said, his heart in so much pain it felt like it was splitting in two. "I *need* this."

Before Austin could say anything else, Father Ambrose pulled him back up to his feet. "I'm sorry, Austin. You've been so coy about your faith, I didn't know."

"It's hard for me to talk about," Austin said, the pain in his heart so intense he was barely able to utter the words.

"I'll put together a list of things I need." Father Ambrose reached for his phone. "When do we leave?"

"Tomorrow at noon," he said.

"If you can get these things by then," Father Ambrose said while typing on his phone, "that should work."

"Of course, Father," Austin said, waiting for Father Ambrose to be in the deepest depths of distraction before pressing home the most important point of all. "And I'll make sure to get you an ambo. I remember the chancel didn't have one."

"Thanks, Austin." Father Ambrose barely looked up from his typing. "That'd be good."

Austin tried to smile but couldn't, the pain in his chest too strong. He just had one more thing to do to complete his plan, and that would be the hardest part of all.

32

Austin found Virgil where he'd left him: on his knees praying on the Persian rug, the couch still overturned, his dome glowing a deep crimson.

"If you don't stop praying and talk to me," Austin said, "I'm going to leave."

Almost immediately, Virgil stood up with the grace of a dancer and his head turned pale blue. "Michael did not want you to enter."

"Why?" Austin's snapped. "Is Michael afraid of a little human like me?"

"Yes," Virgil said. "He is afraid for the Church, and now that he sees that some humans will stop at nothing to destroy it, he looks at you all differently."

Crossing his arms, Austin said, "Tell him the feeling is mutual."

Virgil turned and picked up the sofa, lifting it like it was a pillow and placing it back where it was before.

"If he's so afraid, why did he let me in?"

"I asked him to," Virgil replied, gliding over to stand in front of Austin. "I am your host; I am responsible for you."

"So you did it out of obligation?"

"No," Virgil said. "I asked him to let you in because you are my friend."

A tightness shot through Austin's chest. He was doing this to save humanity; manipulating his friends was a necessary evil. The thought didn't get rid of the guilt, though.

"I didn't come to visit you. I came to pass along a message."

To Austin's surprise, the barb landed, Virgil's head drooping in manifest sadness. The sight made the pain in Austin's chest grow more severe.

"What is the message, Austin?" Virgil asked.

"Father Ambrose," Austin said, trying to regain his resolve, "wants to offer a Mass for the victims of the slaughter in Saudi Arabia inside the Pilgrim church."

Virgil's head shot bolt upright. "Father Ambrose would confect the Eucharist on the Pilgrim ship?"

"Yes."

"Praise God!" Virgil made the sign of the cross and turned his dome upward. Austin felt a twinge of delight; after everything that had happened, he still couldn't help but enjoy seeing his friend happy.

After a moment, though, Virgil unclasped his hands and lowered his dome to face Austin. "Why are you delivering this message?" Virgil asked. "Why hasn't Father Ambrose made this request himself?"

"Father Ambrose is busy."

"Too busy to discuss the first Mass celebrated on an alien vessel?"

Austin's mind raced for an answer. He thought the Eucharist would be enough, the Pilgrims' desire for it too strong to resist, but he'd miscalculated. He strained for a plausible explanation but found none; Father Ambrose's absence from this discussion was too glaring. Austin turned to the one thing he had left—raw anger—hoping it would carry the day.

"You're right. He's not too busy," Austin sneered, letting bitterness seep into his words. "He's too disgusted to come and face you! You pretended to be Christians, convinced him of your faith, but now he sees that the Pilgrims are just butchers—hypocrites down to the core." Austin stalked around the room, his anger driving his feet. "I offered to spare him the pain of facing you by delivering the message myself."

The rage was real, but it swirled in self-doubt. He feared that some imperceptible tick or body expression would reveal him for what he was: a liar. Yet he had no other choice, bluffing his only recourse. He planted his feet and buried his panic, pointing an accusatory finger at Virgil's torso, right where a human heart would be. "And you, Virgil. He's upset with you most of all."

Virgil's head drooped again, and regret washed over

Austin. He hated causing his friend pain. But this was scorched earth. This is what needed to be done.

"So?" Austin said. "What's it going to be?"

"Michael does not trust you," Virgil said, his voice weak.

"Trust?" Austin growled. "Michael wants to talk about trust? He's got the blood of over forty million people on his hands! What does he know about trust?"

Virgil lifted his domed head. "It is just so strange that Father Ambrose is not here to make the request himself."

"Fine." Austin turned around to face the mahogany wall. "I'm leaving, then. The Pilgrims can wait another two thousand years to get what they want."

"Stop." Virgil reached out his arm toward Austin. "We have not given you our answer yet."

"Oh, yeah?" Austin said coolly, his heart beating so fast he was sure it was almost audible. "What's taking so long?"

"We are in an argument."

"I know we are."

"No," Virgil replied. "Michael and I."

Austin tilted his head. "Who's winning?"

"Michael."

Austin stopped breathing, too afraid to make a sound. The fate of humanity rested on the shoulders of an alien machine that was in an argument with the most powerful being in the solar system, and he didn't dare move lest he do something that tilted the argument the wrong way.

After what felt like forever, Virgil turned his whole body to face Austin. "Michael has made a decision," he said.

It took all Austin's concentration to hide the fear in his reply. "And?"

Virgil's expression remained unreadable, save for the pale blue glow of his dome. "He has agreed."

Relief surged through Austin. "Good," he said, trying to sound nonplussed. "It's the least he could do."

"Michael did not want to do it," Virgil replied, "but the Pilgrims are insistent. This would be the culmination of an over-thousand-year journey."

"I'm glad Michael listens to public opinion," Austin said.

"No, Austin, that was not decisive. Ultimately, it was my insistence that you and Father Ambrose are trustworthy, that you are my friends."

The words cut Austin's chest like razor blades, the sting so bad he had to fight the urge to double over. This was the price of being the general's weapon, the price of peace.

"Let's talk logistics," Austin said, choking down the pain. "Father Ambrose will perform the Mass tomorrow after he's had a day to rest. We'll bring everything we need with us, including an ambo, which Father Ambrose said your chancel lacks."

Virgil tilted his head. "As I explained on the ship, Austin, the missal is projected into the presider's eyes by directed beams of light. There is no need for an ambo to hold a book."

"Father Ambrose wants one," he abruptly replied.

"Then we can build him one. It will be ready in plenty of time for the Mass."

Austin felt sweat pooling in his armpits despite the perfect temperature control in the room. After all he'd accomplished, he couldn't stumble here, right at the finish line. He dug down again, past the tumorous ball of anxiety and fear, to where the fire of his anger burned.

"No, Virgil. Just no!" Austin pointed his finger at Virgil's torso. "We're doing it Father Ambrose's way or no way at all. He's already made arrangements to get one. I'm not going back and forth like a message boy. He's bringing his stuff, or you can just forget about the Mass. Your call." Austin was huffing as he said his final lines, hoping that Virgil would see only his burning anger and not his all-consuming fear.

"Father Ambrose may bring whatever he desires," Virgil replied.

"I thought you'd say that," Austin said dismissively. "He also said no Pilgrims at the Mass. Things are still too touchy right now. I'll be the only one in attendance. The Pilgrims can watch a broadcast remotely, but they can't be present in the church."

Virgil's head drooped for the third time. "May I attend the Mass?" Virgil asked, the longing in his request unmistakable. Before Austin had time to think it over, he reflexively agreed.

"Thank you, Austin." Virgil glided forward, wrapping

Austin up in a hug. "You are a good friend."

As Virgil squeezed him, he felt the haptic response, the warmth of Virgil's true friendship. He had saved Austin, had come searching for him, worried for him. And now Austin had returned the favor by making his friend a pawn in a war neither of them wanted as he prepared to strike the final blow.

33

s that the ambo?" Father Ambrose asked, his face scrunched up.

The crate towered two feet over their heads. General Fergusson had assured Austin his people could get a nuke inside an ambo. Now, standing outside the cylinder and waiting for Virgil to arrive, Austin wondered if this plan was dead on arrival, the Trojan horse too big to fit through the city gates.

"I hope it's smaller than it looks." Father Ambrose inspected the crate, rubbing his hand along the wooden slats.

Sensing that Father Ambrose was wavering, and worried he might suggest they just leave it behind, Austin snapped, "The Pilgrims traveled across the galaxy. I'm pretty sure they can carry a simple podium."

Father Ambrose's face fell, the bite of Austin's temper hitting its mark. He stopped touching the crate and awkwardly fiddled with the black leather case containing Mass supplies. The pain in Austin's chest grew. He hated browbeating his friend, but all he could see was the little girl staring into the security camera on the central monitor, her dead eyes like anchors, dragging him down into a sea of despair. He had to make this work, so that there would be no more children like her.

"Let's go. Get it open before the robot arrives," General Fergusson barked, sending three Black Shirts to attack the crate with crowbars.

As the soldiers worked to open the crate, the walls of the cylinder began to fold away, revealing Virgil, his pale blue dome glowing in the dim December sky. The sound of guns being cocked rang out, the surrounding Black Shirts on edge, Saudi Arabia fresh on their minds.

"Father Ambrose," Virgil said in his sonorous voice as he glided over to him. "I am blessed to be with you again."

"I wish it were under better circumstances," Father Ambrose replied, not hiding his sadness.

"As do I," Virgil said.

A wooden side of the crate fell to the ground with a soft bump, drawing everyone's attention. The ambo was as big as he'd feared. It was over seven feet tall, covered in white marble with a large gold cross inlaid on the front. In the back were three marble steps so the speaker could ascend to the lectern. Even to Austin, who had no experience with ambos, it was clear this was abnormally large.

Nausea gripped him as he realized that General Fergusson

had let him down. His "people" were far less capable than he'd been made to believe, and now Father Ambrose was shaking his head, clearly displeased with the monstrosity. Austin tried to think of something to say to justify taking the ambo with them, but his mind was blank, no more bluffs left to play.

"Goddamn it, DeSantis!" General Fergusson roared. "All this for a fucking Mass?" The general got right up into Austin's face. "I don't know what line of bullshit you fed to Secretary Ramirez, but this stinks to high hell!"

In a sudden surge of fury, General Fergusson lunged toward Virgil, flinging his bony frame at the machine. "You are giving these *things* a goddamn Mass when they deserve a bullet between the eyes!" The general slithered over to Father Ambrose, whose face was now tight with ire. "And it's not enough for you to find them a priest, you had to find them the gaudiest fucking book stand I've ever fucking seen!"

General Fergusson then made his way back to Austin and looked him right in the eye. "And you, DeSantis, you alien-loving, booze-swilling, no-good sack of shit. You're useless, worse than useless. You're a festering sore whose very existence is a blight on the whole human race."

The general leaned in so close that Austin could feel his hot breath on his face. "Those five seconds when we thought you might have been good for something vanished into irrelevance the instant that robot spoke English. Yet here you are, hanging around like a skin tag, contributing nothing, no better than a worm."

General Fergusson's narrow eyes were crisp and unyielding, and his tirade was hitting its mark, stripping Austin down to his core. "You're nothing, DeSantis. Nothing to me. Nothing to the army. Nothing to this world." Austin felt wetness welling up in his eyes. "We should have never plucked you up from your dead-end job and brought you here. We should have let you rot, left you wallowing in your worthlessness until the bathtub hooch did you in."

Austin went to wipe the tears from his face, but as he did, General Fergusson grabbed his arm, holding it tight. "If you had any decency or sense of obligation to your fellow man"— General Fergusson traced his withered finger up Austin's forearm—"you'd do us all a favor and slit these wrists from north to south, end the miserable little saga you call your life."

"Silence, you cretin!" Father Ambrose bellowed, barreling over to Austin. "I've had enough of your bile!" General Fergusson ducked back, shrinking away as the priest positioned himself in front of Austin like a shield. "Now be gone, and torment us no more!"

General Fergusson shot Father Ambrose the vilest look, as though his mere existence were cancer. Father Ambrose stood taller, General Fergusson's darkness no match for his light. Without a response, the general marched away, the slightest hint of a feline smile on his face as he passed close by Austin.

"Are you okay, Austin?" Father Ambrose asked, resting a

compassionate hand on Austin's shoulder.

"I am, Father." Austin wiped the tears from his face, the nature of General Fergusson's misdirection dawning on him.

"You are loved, Austin," Father Ambrose said, "just like General Fergusson is loved. But that's what you become when you reject that love, let yourself turn into a wellspring of bitterness and hate."

Austin knew the words were meant to comfort, but the pain in his chest returned, the ache rising to a yawning swell.

"Austin?" Virgil asked as he glided over. "Do you still want me to take the ambo?"

Austin looked into Virgil's pale blue dome, the color bathing him in its soothing light. He wanted to be different from General Fergusson, more like the kind priest before him, someone not consumed by bitterness and hate, but he felt the weight of the dead pulling on him, tugging on his sleeve. This would be his only chance to avenge them, make things right.

"Yes, Virgil," he said, driving the dagger deeper into his friend's back. "Please take the ambo."

Virgil stood still, taking a second before he replied. "As you wish, Austin." He glided over to the ambo and picked it up as if it were as light as air.

As Virgil carried it into the cylinder, Austin and Father Ambrose followed behind. When they had crossed the threshold, a sled appeared like the ones they had seen on the Pilgrim ship. Virgil carefully placed the ambo on top of it and then continued walking, the sled now carrying his load.

Austin looked back out through the threshold, taking in his home world one more time. The Black Shirts were shuffling nervously, glad to see the alien robot returning to its cylindrical lair. Austin's eyes caught General Fergusson's, his face straining as if he was suppressing a look of rapturous delight. Austin had become his weapon, just as he'd said he would.

And now came the final battle, one Austin would have to face alone.

34

The ambo sat there like a bruise, marring the intricate beauty of the Victorian living room with its cheap marble facade, its indecorous trim. Even the golden cross that adorned its front was wrong, its lines not intersecting at a right angle, causing the cross to have a faint slant. It was almost like a final indignity—the threat of nuclear annihilation contained therein not punishment enough.

"Father," Virgil said in his sweet voice, "I have prepared blanquette de veau with heritage champignons de Paris—it was your favorite of all the dishes I prepared. Would you like to have some now?"

"No, Virgil." Father Ambrose stared blankly into the crackling fire as he sat on his usual sofa. "I'm not hungry."

"I see, Father." Virgil moved closer to Father Ambrose. "Are you well?" Virgil asked, concern in his voice. "Shall I dispose of the food?"

Father Ambrose looked at Virgil. "Am I well?"

There was an acid in Father Ambrose's voice that Austin had never heard before, the very sound of it enough to make the hairs on the back of his neck stand up.

"Yes, Father." Virgil's voice was earnest, seemingly oblivious to Father Ambrose's mood. "Your well-being is of utmost importance to me."

"My well-being?" Father Ambrose's cheeks flushed. "What about the well-being of all the innocents in Arabia? How important was their well-being to you?"

Virgil's posture remained unchanged. "Michael took great care to make sure the neurotoxin was painless and that none of our Christian brethren were harmed. It was the most care we could offer under the circumstances."

Father Ambrose muttered something under his breath, as if he were barely managing to suppress a swear-laden outburst. Steadying himself, he took a deep breath before speaking. "Murder is against the Commandments, pain or not, Virgil."

"It was war, Father." Virgil's tone had finally changed, his exasperation evident. "Even the catechism accounts for war."

Father Ambrose stood, facing Virgil squarely. "Was it war when you killed women and children? Was it war when you killed millions of people who knew nothing of Prince Khalid?"

"Prince Khalid was not alone, Father. He was merely the beginning." Virgil's pale blue dome changed, turning into a video. Austin was sitting too far to see the details, but he spotted text messages floating by and images of people on video calls. "We see the messages humanity sends, the hundreds of millions of people that do not want us here, their disdain only fueled by our witness to the risen Lord."

The video shifted to an angry red-headed man. Austin couldn't tell what he was saying, but the graphic said "End the Church—End the Aliens."

"The idea has been circulating on the internet for some time. If humanity destroyed the apostolic succession, then there would be no more valid sacraments. The Pilgrims would have no reason to stay."

"A crackpot idea from the dark corners of the web," Father Ambrose sneered. "You'd have to kill hundreds of thousands of priests and bishops in order to do that. And if the Pilgrims haven't learned by now not to take everything they hear on the internet so seriously, then—"

"That is fewer people than were killed in the blast in Rome, Father." Virgil raised his voice. "Prince Khalid's attack was enough to make millions around the planet think the stratagem was possible. Thousands of separate attacks were set in motion. We ran trillions of simulations, Father, imputing all the variables we could into our most powerful computers. The conclusion was the same: there was a 7.18 percent chance that the apostolic line would be severed, that the individual mayhem of the disaffected would succeed, dooming the universe to spiritual darkness. Michael felt the need to act, a show of force strong enough to stay the hand of those who would imminently commit violence, thus saving the apostolic line."

Father Ambrose eyes narrowed. "You said you ran trillions of simulations, is that right, Virgil?"

"Yes, Father."

"In those trillions of simulations, what variable did you impute for God's Providence?"

"We would not . . ." For the first time, Austin heard Virgil dissemble, bumbling his words. "That is not something we would do, Father. One cannot begin to try and quantify such a—"

"Do you not trust in God's Providence, then?"

Virgil quivered, his silver metal frame, usually the paragon of grace, vibrating like a car choking on bad gasoline.

"Of course we do, Father. We trust our Lord with all our heart, with all our mind—"

Father Ambrose's brow furrowed, his eyes boring into Virgil's dome. "Yet when our Lord and Savior said that the gates of Hell would not prevail against His Church, you chose not to believe Him? You chose to substitute that with your own simulations?"

"Of course not, Father." Virgil's voice cracked, melting under the cross-examination. "But God's Providence is not an excuse for inaction."

"Nor is sin the way to salvation!" Father Ambrose bellowed with such force that Austin almost thought he saw a shock wave. "'For wide is the gate, and broad is the way that leadeth to destruction, and many there are who go in thereat!'"

Virgil fell to the floor, his domed head all the way on the ground, gripping Father Ambrose's feet. "You are right, Father! Sin only leads to death and annihilation! Forgive me. Forgive us all!"

Virgil continued to shudder at Father Ambrose's feet, but the priest maintained his stern pose. "Before I left Rome, the cardinals were debating whether the Pilgrims were fallen, burdened with original sin. I think after what happened, there can be no question—the Pilgrims are fallen, just like man."

"You are right, Father," Virgil wailed. "The Pilgrims *are* fallen, riddled with sin. That is why we thirst for the sacraments so."

Austin could hear the tears in Virgil's voice, the machine that had picked up the ambo like it was air made feeble. Father Ambrose remained unbowed, the authority of his teaching an unseen force, bending the universe around it.

"The Pilgrims may thirst for the sacraments, but it's clear to me that the Pilgrims still have a lot of formation to do before they can participate in them." Father Ambrose sat back down on the sofa while Virgil remained kneeling at his feet. "So much formation, in fact, that I've reconsidered offering a Mass. When we get to the ship, I will say some prayers outside the church for the departed souls of Saudi Arabia and Rome and then return to Earth. There will be no Mass today."

When Austin realized what Father Ambrose was saying, he stood up in a panic.

"I understand, Father," Virgil replied, his voice filled with resignation.

"But wait!" Austin interjected. "You promised me you'd have a Mass."

Father Ambrose's face softened as he turned his attention to Austin. "I want to support you in your faith journey, Austin," he said softly, "but it just wouldn't be right."

"That doesn't make sense," Austin said. "You agreed."

"I shouldn't have," Father Ambrose said. "I didn't have my wits about me when you asked."

Austin could barely manage to contain the shock of watching his plan blow apart at this late stage. He racked his brain, trying to find something that would change Father Ambrose's mind. "You're being unfair to the Pilgrims," he said.

"How so?" Father Ambrose's tone was skeptical, almost mildly amused.

"The Pilgrims' hearts were in the right place; they were just trying to save the universe." It took all of Austin's willpower not to choke on his own words—defending the indefensible.

"Their 'hearts were in the right place'?" Father Ambrose nearly spat out his reply.

"They're aliens, Father. They were bound to make some mistakes," he said with a shrug, amazed that he didn't gag. "The one person they would have turned to for guidance—the pope—was murdered by Prince Khalid along with hundreds of thousands of other innocent people in Rome."

"The death toll in Rome is over one million people," Virgil added, still prostrating himself at Father Ambrose's feet.

Father Ambrose looked down at Virgil and again back at Austin, still perplexed. "You said it yourself, Austin. The Pilgrims traveled across the galaxy. They're a highly advanced race. They didn't need the pope to tell them killing innocent people is wrong."

Austin's abdominal muscles began to squeeze. He knew what Father Ambrose was saying was true, and it made it nearly impossible for him to summon up an argument opposing him, but he had to do something. "What about all of the innocent Pilgrims?" Austin managed to say. "Not all of them agreed with Michael. Isn't that right, Virgil?"

Virgil lifted his domed head, but remained kneeling. "That is correct, Austin. Out of the approximately seventy-five million Pilgrims aboard the ship, about twenty-nine million objected vehemently to the war strategy. But Michael is our leader, and he is firm."

When Austin's mind processed the number, his stomach churned. There were almost twice as many Pilgrims on the ship as there were in Saudi Arabia, and he was about to place a nuclear weapon right in the center of it, just one push of the button away from becoming a mass murderer at twice the scale of which he set out to avenge.

"What about the twenty-nine million?" he asked, shoving this new realization down as deep as he could. "You're depriving them, too, by not saying a Mass in their church."

"I'm glad they objected," Father Ambrose replied, his words laced with unwavering conviction, "but 'I was just following orders' is not an excuse for genocide."

Austin's stomach knotted. He was failing. A terrible thought occurred to him, one that intensified the ever-present tightness in his chest. "What about Virgil?" he asked.

"What about him?"

"Michael didn't just let us walk in here. Virgil argued with Michael, recruited a bunch of Pilgrims to his cause, and demanded that the Mass happen. He went out on a limb for this. And now, halfway to the alien ship, you change your mind? Getting all of the Pilgrims' hopes up just to pull the rug out from under them?"

Austin was barely breathing now as he studied Father Ambrose's expression to see if he'd made a dent.

"I told you. I shouldn't have agreed in the first place," Father Ambrose replied, a flicker of doubt trickling into his tone.

"But you did," Austin pressed, seizing the moment and feeling even more terrible for it. "How do you think that will make Virgil look? It could be the last straw of a malfunctioning AI—enough of a mistake to get him deleted."

Austin could see the look of shock on Father Ambrose's

face as he internalized what Austin was saying. "Virgil, is this true?"

Virgil remained kneeling, taking a moment to reply. "I have sacrificed what remained of my credibility and reputation in order to organize this Mass, Father. My fate is tied to it."

The words hung heavy in the air, another dagger to Austin's battered chest. Virgil's fate was tied to the Mass, a Mass that would be the Pilgrims' downfall, and it was all Austin's fault, not Father Ambrose's, even though he was making the kind priest feel bad for it now. But this was Austin's chance. He had to push hard and make sure that Father Ambrose couldn't turn back.

"Would you betray him, Father?" Austin had to strain to get out the words. "Condemn him to death?"

Father Ambrose looked down at Virgil, still kneeling on the floor in front of him, the glow of his pale blue dome reflecting off his glasses. A pained expression had crept into his eyes when he looked back at Austin. He opened his mouth, and Austin braced himself, the fate of humanity hanging on his next word.

35

Father Ambrose had been silent since they'd arrived on the ship. He said nothing as the mist lapped against their sled in the narthex; he was still as they basked in the polychromatic majesty of the nave. When the whispers came in the transept condemning Christ to death, he did not stir. Only at the foot of the cross did he disembark the sled and say a prayer.

But now, adorned in his vestments, Father Ambrose was a man transformed; a mild-mannered astronomer no more—replaced by a soldier of God festooned for battle, his flowing white robe his armor, the Gospel he carried his sword.

"Virgil, could you please sing a gathering hymn?"

The chancel thrummed like the golden walls and ceiling were alive, throbbing with anticipation at the prospect of a holy Mass finally being performed on its sacred altar. Austin stood just a few yards back from the altar rail, and with each pulse, a pang of self-satisfaction rippled through him. He'd failed at so much in life, but somehow he'd bested all the obstacles that were thrown his way, and now he was on the cusp of completing the most important mission in human history while tens of millions of Pilgrims watched remotely via broadcast. Only afterward, once Austin was safe back on Earth, would they realize that their triumph was actually their downfall, justice for all the innocent blood they'd shed.

Yet the cost weighed on him. He wanted so badly to spare his friends from his betrayal, but he couldn't; the nuke was the only way to make things right.

"Adoro te devote," Virgil sang from next to him, the melody flowing out of the robot like a dream, drowning out the hum of the chancel. "Latens Deitas, quae sub his figuris vere latitas: tibi se cor meum totum subiicit, quia te contemplans totum deficit."

Austin translated in his head.

Hidden God, devoutly I adore Thee, truly present underneath these veils: all my heart subdues itself before Thee, since it all before Thee faints and fails.

Father Ambrose proceeded to the altar, taking his time with each step, the gold embossed Gospel above his head, Virgil's music filling the air. As he approached, the altar rail melted away, allowing him to walk unimpeded up the two steps to the pink altar table, where he bowed deeply and venerated it with a kiss.

"In cruce latebat sola Deitas," Virgil continued, "at hic latet simul et humanitas; ambo tamen credens atque confitens, peto quod petivit latro paenitens."

On the cross was veiled Thy Godhead's splendor, here Thy manhood lies hidden, too; unto both alike my faith I render, and, as sued the contrite thief, I sue.

As he translated in his mind, Austin thought back to the Victorian living room, when Virgil had revealed that his singing was not up to the standards of the Pilgrim choirmaster. It had seemed like a joke then—a machine *singing* rather than just playing a song. But the music coming from Virgil could be called nothing less than singing—a singing so sweet Austin thought he might split in two.

The memory pressed on Austin's heart, asking it to throw open the gates. In the power of the moment, Austin felt himself turning toward Virgil, who still sang, ready to tell him the truth, to stop his assault on his friend's virtue and begin to make amends—the mission be damned.

Then another flash of memory shot through his mind.

He was back in the command center, standing next to General Fergusson. They were watching the video of the hospital, the spider robots singling out the Muslims, condemning them to death because they did not worship in the "correct" way.

Bitterness filled Austin.

He had no choice; he needed to stop that from happening ever again.

Virgil finished the song.

"In the name of the Father, and of the Son, and of the Holy Spirit," Father Ambrose said.

"Amen," Virgil replied.

"The grace of our Lord Jesus Christ, and the love of God, and the communion of the Holy Spirit be with you all."

"And with your spirit," Virgil replied again.

"Now, let us call to mind our sins so that we may prepare ourselves to celebrate the sacred mysteries."

The old man flashed into Austin's mind—his broken skull, his desperate gaze—followed by so many other misdeeds. But he wasn't the only murderer here. The Pilgrims had exponentially more blood on their three-fingered hands. They were far worse than him, and they would pay for everything they'd done.

After a moment, Father Ambrose began again. "You were sent to heal the contrite of heart: Lord, have Mercy."

"Lord, have mercy," Virgil replied.

"You came to call sinners: Christ, have mercy."

"Christ, have mercy."

"You are seated at the right hand of the Father to intercede for us: Lord, have mercy."

"Lord, have mercy."

"May almighty God have mercy on us, forgive us our sins, and bring us to everlasting life."

"Amen."

With each call-and-response between Father Ambrose

and Virgil, Austin felt the chasm between him and his friends grow wider. The ambo had been delivered to the center of the alien ship, his mission a success. Yet the victory tasted bitter. Despite the righteousness of what he had to do, he knew he would lose his friends forever for it.

"Glory to God in the highest," Virgil sang. "And on Earth peace to people of goodwill."

Austin stopped paying attention after the first line, his mind wandering. He stared at the ambo as he thought about "peace." Peace was merely an epilogue, the denouement of violence. That ambo was the only way to bring peace, carnage to stop carnage.

"A reading from the book of Exodus."

Father Ambrose's voice brought Austin back to the Mass. The priest stood on the ambo with a book opened in front of him. Austin tried to listen to the reading, but he couldn't look away from the slanted cross, the ugliness of the thing swallowing his friend.

"Alleluia . . . alleluia . . . alleluia."

Virgil's singing brought him back again, the sound of his voice so magnificent it nearly made him weep. When Virgil stopped, Austin looked at Father Ambrose, curious to see if the singing had had the same effect on him, but to Austin's surprise, Father Ambrose's eyes were narrow.

"The Lord be with you," Father Ambrose said.

"And with your spirit," Virgil replied.

"A reading from the holy Gospel according to Matthew."

"Glory to you, O Lord." Virgil made little crosses with his fingers. Twice on his head, and once on his torso where a human's heart would be.

Father Ambrose read, "'You have heard that it was said, "You shall love your neighbor and hate your enemy." But I say to you, love your enemies, and pray for those who persecute you, that you may be children of your heavenly Father, for He makes His sun rise on the bad and the good, and causes rain to fall on the just and the unjust.'"

Father Ambrose's voice cut through the air—sharp and steadfast.

"'For if you love those who love you, what recompense will you have? Do not the tax collectors do the same? And if you greet your brothers only, what is unusual about that? Do not the pagans do the same?'"

Father Ambrose paused, his hands gripping the side of the ambo. As he held himself there, the ambo seemed to grow smaller, shrinking underneath his feet.

"'So be perfect!'" he thundered, his voice echoing across the vast landscape of the room. "'Just as your heavenly Father is perfect!'"

Virgil fell to his knees as if struck by a shock wave.

"The Gospel of the Lord."

"Praise to you, Lord Jesus Christ," Virgil choked.

Taking a deep breath, Father Ambrose waited a beat,

letting the words sink in.

"Here in the Gospel," he eventually began, "we hear one of our Lord's most sacred instructions, that we must love our enemies like ourselves. But what does it mean to love your enemy?"

Father Ambrose leaned forward. "Does it mean raining death down upon them?"

Austin shifted nervously where he stood.

Father Ambrose leaned closer still. "Does it mean forcing mothers to watch their children die?"

He peered around as if looking his unseen audience in the eye.

"Does it mean annihilation?" He punctuated each syllable of the word "annihilation" with a staccato viciousness. "Who among the witnesses of the risen Lord would say *that* is loving your enemies? Would you, Michael?"

Father Ambrose asked the question quietly, almost gently, but it hit like a truck. Virgil, still kneeling, began rattling like a man pulled from a frozen lake.

Understanding suddenly dawned on Austin; this was Father Ambrose's idea of justice. He would preach the truth directly to the Pilgrims from the center of their ship, their technology powerless against the might of his words.

"You are all called to be perfect!" Father Ambrose boomed. "Like the Father in Heaven is perfect!" His eyes narrowed to slits. "And woe to those who fail to follow our Savior's words."

Father Ambrose held his glare. Each second passed like an hour in the silence. After what felt like forever, Father Ambrose stepped down from the ambo and walked to the opposite side of the altar, taking each step deliberately, forcing the Pilgrims to wallow in their sin before he moved forward with the Mass.

Austin had tricked the priest into coming here, but Father Ambrose had turned the betrayal into a victory, ensuring that on this momentous occasion—the first Mass held aboard the Pilgrim ship—they would have to look their great sin in the eye and cower before the admonitions of a small bespectacled human.

As the Mass continued, Austin marveled at his friend's bravery, too caught up in the splendor of it to pay close attention to the creed and the series of prayers for those who had died in Saudi Arabia and Rome that Virgil and Father Ambrose uttered. The whole time Virgil did not stand, remaining prostrate on the ground, quivering, as if broken by Father Ambrose's sermon.

"Austin," Virgil eventually whispered after he had finished singing a hymn. "You must kneel. For our Lord—the Creator and Sustainer of the universe—will soon be with us."

Austin complied, sinking to his knees next to Virgil on the hard chancel floor. His heart ached for his friend, who felt such guilt for the atrocities committed by Michael, the cruel leader he was in no position to stop. Once Virgil realized what he'd done, Austin was certain he would never want to see him again. The thought tore at Austin, like he was destroying a part of himself, and it took all his concentration not to start weeping right there on the chancel floor.

"You are indeed holy, O Lord, the fount of all holiness," Father Ambrose prayed. "Make holy, therefore, these gifts, we pray, by sending down Your Spirit upon them like the dewfall, so that they may become for us the Body and Blood of our Lord Jesus Christ."

Father Ambrose then took the wafer and raised it up to his head. "At the time He was betrayed and entered willingly into His passion, He took bread and, giving thanks, broke it, and gave it to His disciples, saying: 'Take this, all of you, and eat of it, for this is my body, which will be given up for you.'"

As soon as the priest stopped speaking, the room went dark, and a deafening horn filled the air, shaking the room.

Panic seized Austin, and his arms shot out into the void—but he felt nothing but darkness. A scream clawed at his throat as terror threatened to consume him, but before it tore free, the ground stopped shaking and the light returned. The chancel was now filled with the same all-encompassing fog as the narthex. There was a small clearing where he knelt with Virgil, and a clear line of sight to Father Ambrose up on the altar, but the rest of the space was bathed in murk, making it impossible to see the golden ceiling and walls.

"In a similar way," Father Ambrose continued, seemingly unbowed by the shaking and the darkness. "When supper was ended, He took the chalice, and, once more giving thanks, He gave it to His disciples, saying: 'Take this, all of you, and drink from it, for this is the chalice of my blood, the blood of the new and eternal covenant, which will be poured out for you and for many for the forgiveness of sins. Do this in memory of me.'"

The darkness, the shaking, and the horn resumed, this time so violent that it threw Austin onto the ground. He clung to the floor as he thrashed about.

After a few moments, the light reappeared, and the shaking stopped. Austin got back onto his knees next to Virgil, but out of the corner of his eye, he noticed something.

A forty-foot-tall silhouette in the mist was moving toward him.

"Through Him, and with Him, and in Him," Father Ambrose sang, oblivious to the towering figure approaching Austin. "O God, almighty Father, in the unity of the Holy Spirit, all glory and honor is Yours, for ever and ever."

Fear paralyzed Austin as the massive being drew near.

"At the Savior's command," Father Ambrose continued, "and formed by divine teaching, we dare to say: Our Father, who art in Heaven, hallowed be Thy name."

Austin looked to Virgil to see if he noticed the shape in the mist, but he was standing up now, calmly reciting the Lord's Prayer. Meanwhile, the figure grew closer, and by instinct, Austin leaned toward Virgil, like a child clinging to his father's legs.

"Thy kingdom come, Thy will be done on Earth as it is in Heaven."

Finally, the figure emerged from the mist into the clearing: a Pilgrim towering over Austin on its tripod legs, its skirt of tentacles wriggling.

"Give us this day our daily bread, and forgive us our trespasses, as we forgive those who trespass against us."

Drawing close to Austin, the Pilgrim bent its three legs and lowered its face as low to the ground as it could. Austin found himself staring into its black eyes, each one like a puddle of ink.

"And lead us not into temptation, but deliver us from evil. Amen."

Up on the altar, Father Ambrose was just now noticing the Pilgrim in their midst.

The pigment on its body was changing, displaying all manner of shapes and symbols. He was talking to Austin, saying *something*, but Austin had no idea what.

The three of them remained there in silence, the Mass on pause.

The Pilgrim then stood up, revealing its true height. With a graceful stride, it moved to the altar, made the sign of the cross, and lowered itself in a deep and reverent bow. Then, in one swift motion, it picked the ambo up and disappeared into the mist.

A chill descended upon Austin as the realization hit him: he'd been discovered. The Pilgrims knew he had a weapon, that he had betrayed his friends.

He felt the air leaving his body.

"I'm sorry, Austin, but I wanted to say goodbye to you in my own words, in my own way," Virgil said, breaking the silence. "I had to act now. I couldn't let the nuclear bomb detonate."

"Detonate?" Austin stammered. "It's not going to detonate . . ."

"It is a time bomb, Austin. It will detonate in approximately ten minutes. I had to remove it from the ship."

Dizzy, Austin reached out to Virgil for support.

"Austin, you didn't," Father Ambrose said from up on the altar.

"It was meant for deterrence," Austin stuttered, "in case the Pilgrims attacked again. America could threaten to detonate it. It was to preserve peace. All I wanted was peace."

"The device is not capable of remote detonation." Virgil's voice was calm. "The trigger is mechanical. There is no way to disarm it once it is engaged."

Austin clung to his friend's shoulder, his panic intensifying. "Engaged?"

"It was engaged back on Earth," Virgil said.

Austin fell away from Virgil into the edge of the mist. His skin cried out as the mist enveloped him, the nothingness of it like an entity. He thrust himself in the opposite direction, toward the altar. "General Fergusson said they would use extremely low frequency radio—"

"General Fergusson is a liar, Austin," Virgil said, his tone soft. "There is no way to get a signal into our ship. He sent you here with a time bomb."

"You trusted that loathsome man?" Father Ambrose said, his voice full of pity. "How could you?"

In that moment, Austin realized that General Fergusson had been honest with him all along. He *was* making Austin his weapon, and just like the mortar explodes on impact, so, too, was that to be Austin's fate. It was a suicide mission—always had been—and he'd been too naive to see it coming.

"Virgil?" Father Ambrose asked with sudden concern. "What did you mean when you said you 'had to say goodbye in your own words'?"

Virgil joined Austin in front of the altar, feet from the rail.

"You and Austin, Father—you have now seen my true form."

"That was you? You're a Pilgrim?" Austin sputtered. "That can't be . . . you're not one of *them*. You're an AI, a machine!"

Austin stepped toward the altar rail. Instead of melting away from him, it stayed solid. As he pressed into it, he realized he had nowhere else to go.

"No, Austin," Virgil said. "As I told you back in the nave, humans have many misconceptions about artificial minds, as if computation alone is enough to create one. The mind is a singular thing, and I am Virgil, a Pilgrim born over three thousand years ago. This body you are speaking to is merely an avatar, a device I pilot so I can more easily interact with you."

Austin cowered within arm's length of what was just a drone, his friend on the other side. Virgil was not a robot; he was one of the Pilgrims Austin had come up here so thoroughly despising.

"Virgil, if that's true, then where are you going with that bomb?" Father Ambrose asked.

"I am taking it off of the ship to detonate in space," Virgil replied in his sweet voice. "The ship will not be damaged."

"Will you be able to get back to safety before it detonates?"

"No, Father."

"But why, Virgil? Can't you launch the ambo off the ship?"

"The ambo has a safeguard, Father. If it touches the vacuum of space, it will detonate. It must be ejected by sending it away inside a small spacecraft."

"Then pilot the spacecraft remotely. Surely you can do that."

"I'm sorry, Father," Virgil said, his voice still sweet. "It is not a matter of means but one of justice."

"Justice?"

"Yes, Father," Virgil replied, his voice gentle. "That bomb brought violence into our most sacred space. This is one of the most serious transgressions in Pilgrimkind. For that, I must pay with my life."

"*What?*" Father Ambrose cried. "This wasn't your fault."

"No, Father." Virgil's tone was kind. "As I have told you, I am your host, and I am responsible for you. My life was forfeit as soon as I let you bring the ambo onto the elevator. It is our way."

Austin doubled over, falling at the feet of his friend Virgil's robot body. "You knew?" he gasped. "You *knew* it was a bomb, and you still let me bring it on?"

"Yes, Austin." Virgil reached down a hand and rubbed it reassuringly on his back. "We traveled across the galaxy. Our sensors were more than capable of seeing all the items you brought on board."

Austin looked up at Virgil's dome, peering into the pale blue glow. "Even the cam—"

"Yes, Austin. Even the camera."

Virgil had known all along, had always seen Austin for what he truly was—a philanderer, a murderer, and a liar—and he loved him anyway, rescuing him in the mist, traveling to Washington, DC, to find him when he'd gone missing, and now dying for him.

"But why?" Austin pleaded. "Why did you let me take it on and kill you?"

"Love," Virgil said. "Love of God and His creation."

"I don't understand," Austin choked.

Virgil knelt, his dome now at Austin's level. "When we arrived at Earth, I was number three in the command structure. When Michael died, I became number two. I opposed

Michael's plan to wage war on Saudi Arabia, but the majority of the crew sided with him, and so the decision was made." Virgil gestured to the altar table. "But my brethren have seen the sacrifice I have made in order to bring them to the Lord. Because I have surrendered my life, He sits there now on our ship, all of our greatest hopes and dreams fulfilled. Their hearts have been moved by my actions, including Michael's, and he has promised never to wage war like that again. And Michael will honor his promise because he is true of heart."

"Humanity is safe?" Father Ambrose asked.

"Yes, Father."

"I'm so sorry, Virgil." Tears poured out of Austin, landing on the golden floor in a pool. "I didn't mean to kill you. I thought what I was doing was right."

Virgil patted Austin on the back. "I forgive you."

Austin looked up into the pale blue dome, its unwavering light shining down on him.

"How can you?" Austin writhed. "I betrayed you. I killed you. I destroy everyone who is kind to me." Sobs racked his body as Austin hunched over Virgil's feet.

"I know, Austin," Virgil replied, his voice full of warmth. "But I forgive you."

"How?" Austin demanded. "How can you possibly do that?"

"Because love transcends all." Virgil reached out and took Austin's hand in his own. "It is fundamental to all of reality. It is God Himself."

"But I've done nothing to deserve your love," Austin said between sobs.

When Virgil didn't move, Austin wondered if he had won the argument, convinced his friend to withdraw his forgiveness, condemn him as he ought to be condemned.

"I know how you feel, Austin." Virgil squeezed Austin's hand, sending a haptic response up his whole arm. "I lived for a thousand years for myself, existing in an empty universe with nothing but my pleasure to fill the void. There was no meaning for me or my kind. Then the data came back from Earth." Virgil tilted his dome up, as if looking into the sky. "God had come into His creation. He had taken on the form of a lowly bipedal creature, one enslaved to passion, allergic to reason, a mere insect when compared to the sophisticated Pilgrim race. And He allowed Himself to die a horrific and humiliating death, not one mercy shown to Him, the Creator and Sustainer of all things. And for what? For the sinful and uncaring Pilgrims? For the depraved and vicious man? That they may both share in an eternal life with Him? To what did we owe this grace, this truly undeserved gift?"

Austin felt the blue of Virgil's dome washing over him, the same blue as Mary's eyes.

"It was love, Austin. That was how great God's love was for His creation and the sinful creatures in it. It was so great He offered Himself to be tortured and killed for us. So we may live."

As Austin looked into Virgil's dome, for the first time in weeks, he felt the tightness in his chest loosen.

"So I try to love you like our Lord loves you. I love you despite your sins. And I love you for bringing me back to Him. For on that altar sits our Lord, and I have waited thousands of years to be near Him."

The tears burst forth anew as Austin reached out and hugged Virgil, needing to show him how much he loved him back.

"I don't deserve that kind of love," Austin said, clutching his friend.

"None of us do," Virgil replied, his voice carrying a mixture of understanding and compassion, "but He gives it nonetheless."

Not wanting to let go, Austin held Virgil tight, but he soon felt Virgil's hands gently pushing against him, letting him know it was time.

"Father, I have exited the ship. I am traveling away with the bomb. You are all safe. Please, finish the Mass before it explodes."

Father Ambrose's beard glistened with tears as he nodded to Virgil.

"Oh, Sacrament most holy," Virgil whispered as Austin embraced him. "Oh, Sacrament divine. All praise and all thanksgiving, be every moment Thine."

Father Ambrose raced through the rest of the Mass as

Austin held his friend. After what felt like too soon, Virgil beckoned Austin to stand.

"The Lord be with you," Father Ambrose said.

"And with your spirit," Virgil replied.

"May the almighty God bless you, the Father, the Son, and the Holy Spirit." Father Ambrose made the sign of the cross in the air.

"Amen." Virgil, too, made the sign of the cross.

"The Mass has ended. Go in peace, glorifying the Lord in your life."

"Thanks be to God," Virgil replied.

Father Ambrose ran down from the altar, his arms wrapping around Virgil tightly. "We are blessed to have known you, Virgil," Father Ambrose said.

"It is I who am blessed, Father."

They all embraced for a moment until Virgil broke the silence.

"Father?"

"Yes, Virgil?"

"Will you do me one final grace?"

"Of course, Virgil."

"Will you pray with me in these final moments?"

Father Ambrose backed up to look at his friend while tears flooded his face. "How long do we have?"

"Seconds, Father."

Father Ambrose's mouth quivered, but he took Virgil's

hands in his and began. "Hail, Mary, full of grace, the Lord is with thee."

"Blessed art thou among women," Virgil said in his sweet voice, "and blessed is the fruit of Thy womb, Jesus."

Austin moved closer to Virgil, hugging him. Holding his friend to the last.

"Holy Mary, Mother of God, pray for us sinners, now and at the hour of our death. Amen."

With that, the pale blue of Virgil's dome faded away, Austin's friend gone forever.

36

Virgil was gone, but his robot avatar stood in the corner of the Victorian living room, its head glowing a deep crimson—some new and nameless Pilgrim now behind the wheel, escorting them back to Earth.

"I thought I was doing the right thing." Austin wept. "I didn't want him to die."

Father Ambrose stared into the fireplace, silent, as he had been since Virgil died.

"I never should have trusted General Fergusson. How could I have been so stupid?"

A log crackled, sending a small ember onto the marble hearth. Father Ambrose remained motionless, the flames dancing in his glasses.

"Now he's going to kill me."

For the first time since they'd left the chancel, Father Ambrose's sad eyes connected with Austin's own. "He tried to blow you up—blow us all up—and he failed. Virgil saved you.

He saved humanity. It's over."

Austin felt the tightness in his chest amplify at the sound of Virgil's name. "No, Father. He won't stop there. I failed him. He'll have me executed."

Father Ambrose's face scrunched up. "I've heard the rumors of the extrajudicial killings, too, Austin, but this is still America. They can't just—"

"The rumors are true, Father," Austin interrupted. "I've seen it happen with my own eyes."

Father Ambrose shook his head, his face more anxious than before. "They'd kill you? For what? For failing to annihilate tens of millions of Pilgrims? For not throwing another genocide onto the pile? I don't think so, Austin. It was a senseless plan. Even if it worked, do you think this will be the last Pilgrim ship? There must be others on their way here as we speak. Imagine what position the US would be in if they'd succeeded in destroying the first. And that's to say nothing of the asteroid fragments that would've likely rained down on Earth, the damage from which would exceed—"

"I killed a man, Father," Austin said, a hollowness to his voice. "That's why they'll kill me. That's why they were always going to kill me."

Father Ambrose's eyes widened in shock. "When?"

"Before the Pilgrims arrived, I was part of a robbery gone bad. I could have saved a man's life, but I did nothing. I froze. I watched him die." Austin could feel the tightness in his chest loosen as he told the truth, no more rotten parts of himself left to hide.

"That's why they picked you as a translator? You were a condemned man?"

"Yes," Austin said. "General Fergusson needed a nobody, a washed-up Latin teacher no one would miss. Someone too stupid to see through his lies."

"Someone clever enough to cajole his friend into saying a Mass he didn't want to give," Father Ambrose added with a raise of his eyebrows. "Someone sly enough to get him to unwittingly read the holy Gospel from atop a nuclear bomb."

"I'm so sorry, Father," Austin said, hanging his head in shame. "You're one of the only people in the world who's ever been kind to me."

Father Ambrose was still, only the sound of the fire crackling between them. "You're a killer and a liar. That's the real you. Is that right, Austin?"

"Yes, Father."

"Yet Virgil gave his life for you—a killer and a liar. Why do you think he did that?"

"Because he's good, Father. Truly good," Austin said. "I could live for thousands of years like he did and still never be a fraction as good as him."

The fireplace popped, shooting another ember onto the marble hearth.

"Do you even *want* to be?" Father Ambrose asked.

Austin looked back at the priest, confused. "What do you mean?"

"Do you want to be good?" Father Ambrose repeated, his question hanging in the air without a trace of irony.

"Of course I do. That's what I've always wanted. But it's too late now. I can't change the past."

"That's true." Father Ambrose's eyes were piercing under his glasses, focusing intently on Austin, not about to let him wriggle away. "But you can change the future."

"I have no future," he sullenly replied.

"You're still breathing, aren't you? You still have some time left. And in that time, ask yourself who you would rather be like: General Fergusson and his ilk, the ones who focus on *this* world like it is everything there is . . . or like Virgil, who aimed toward the transcendent, trying to align his will to God's, devoting himself entirely to Him—to goodness itself?"

Austin felt his throat tighten at the sound of Virgil's name. "It's obvious," he replied.

"Ha, obvious!" Father Ambrose took off his glasses and pointed them at Austin. "If that's the case, why isn't everyone like Virgil? Why aren't you?"

"I don't know." Austin sniffed. "I really don't know."

Standing up, Father Ambrose approached Austin. "I've been thinking about those two Black Shirts who were guarding my trailer. The ones who said that if the Pilgrims were on God's team, they wanted to be on the opposite one."

"I remember," Austin said.

Father Ambrose stood at the foot of Austin's couch, the fireplace behind him, his body backlit by its orange glow. "Before the Pilgrims, we had ambiguity," Father Ambrose continued. "A thin excuse that God was some distant thing, something for philosophers and theologians to argue over. Not one of the important things, like my mortgage, or the Super Bowl, or what I'm having for dinner, or why that girl didn't text me back."

Father Ambrose leaned closer.

"Never mind that that was all hogwash and that God is everywhere. In morality, in logic, in the predictability of the laws of physics. Or in the stillness of a sunrise, when you wake up before everyone else and have the whole thing to yourself, all of its splendor and beauty, like it was made for you, so that you know that you are loved."

Austin heard a pop from the fireplace, a log burning down, the others crashing into its place.

"I can see how some people missed God, thought He didn't apply to them, that life had more pressing concerns. That way, when their life fell into the pits of sin, there was at least some element of accident, an ignorance that fueled the thing."

Austin tried to look away but couldn't, the tightness in his chest as searing as the flames at Father Ambrose's back.

"But now that the Pilgrims have brought incontrovertible evidence of the risen Lord, that thin reed of ignorance is stripped away. Now, when we sin, it can no longer be chalked up to ignorance; we're opposing Him, we're opposing God—goodness itself. Just like those two Black Shirts outside my trailer."

"I don't oppose God ..." Austin said, not knowing if he was trying to convince Father Ambrose or himself.

Father Ambrose moved closer to Austin, his body blocking the hearth from view, standing between him and the fire.

"You might have been able to say that before, Austin, but not anymore. God's hiddenness was a mercy, a compassion in disguise. But now, in His infinite wisdom, He's pulled away the veil and made Himself as plain as that couch you're sitting on."

Despite Father Ambrose standing in front of him, Austin could feel the heat of the fire, the burning on his skin.

"And so you need to pick a side, Austin. Either repent and be like Virgil, align your will with God's, or ..." Father Ambrose stepped aside, the fire blazing in the hearth. "Or be who you've always been. The choice is yours."

37

The cylinder wall folded away, revealing a sky that had opened up, a cold December rain coming down in fat droplets, stealing all the heat from whatever object it touched. General Fergusson was standing on the now-muddy fairway, the platoon of Black Shirts next to him looking grim in their soaking wet uniforms.

"DeSantis," General Fergusson snarled. "What did you do?"

Without saying anything, Austin stepped through the threshold onto the fairway, not even flinching as the raindrops wet his shirt. He'd exhausted all his feelings up in the church and on the elevator ride down, and only numbness remained.

"We saved you from making a terrible mistake," Father Ambrose said when Austin didn't respond.

General Fergusson looked Father Ambrose up and down as if he were examining a blister. "You saved nothing," he sneered. "Now we're powerless against the aliens and—"

"It was your lust for power that caused this, General." Father Ambrose stepped out of the cylinder and into the rain. "When are you going to see that?"

General Fergusson furrowed his brow, his thin frame unmoving, even though Austin saw one of the Black Shirts next to him shivering. "You two have doomed humanity with your misplaced loyalties and your silly ideals."

"You're wrong," Austin said with a shake of his head. "You've always been wrong."

His deep-set wrinkles contorting in disgust, General Fergusson glared at Austin. His gaze broke only when a Black Shirt jogged up to him and saluted.

"Sir," the Black Shirt said. "Advance elements of the Eighty-Second Airborne have passed through the park cordon."

"Tell the perimeter squads to send them back." General Fergusson scowled. "Regulars are banned from this installation on my orders."

"The perimeter squads tried, sir, but SecDef is traveling with them. She countermanded your order. She's on her way here now, and she's got the whole division behind her."

General Fergusson turned toward Austin. "I save you from the executioner, and this is how you repay me, DeSantis? You make me look like a fool?"

Austin shook his head—not knowing how he was supposed to respond to a man who chastised him for failing to blow himself up with a bomb. He could see the man so clearly now that he wondered how he could have missed it before. "The only fool was me," he said, his voice steady. "I should have known better than to ever trust you."

General Fergusson took a step forward, his eyes narrowing. "You killed a man, DeSantis. A good man, one with a family—all so you could hire a prostitute."

Austin winced, water running into his eye. He could still see the kind old man, the pain of what he'd done still sharp.

"That's right, I always knew about her: your perverted obsession." General Fergusson's lips curled upward, as if fueled by Austin's pain. "And I knew that you'd do anything to get what you want, no matter the cost." General Fergusson tilted his head, a tiny puddle of water falling off his service cap. "You're just like me, DeSantis. You're just a weaker version. One who doesn't know how to get what he wants; one who doesn't deserve to live."

"That's enough, you—"

Austin touched Father Ambrose's shoulder before he could continue.

"You're right, General." Austin's voice was level. "You and I are the same. I see that now." He glanced at Father Ambrose, the priest's eyes encouraging. "The only difference is that I wish I was different; whereas you …" Austin looked back at General Fergusson, not bothering to hide the pity in his gaze. "You don't want to change. You just wish you had more control."

"Wish you were different? That's adorable." General

Fergusson chuckled. "You won't be around to *wish*. We're going to erase you, DeSantis. End your sorry life and any memory of you. And I'm going to watch." The general gestured, and two Black Shirts headed for Austin.

Austin watched them approach, the two black shades his gathering doom. He knew that he deserved what was coming, just punishment for what he'd done to Virgil and the kind old man. But still, every part of him desperately longed to be spared.

"Max!" At the sound of the woman's voice, the two Black Shirts stopped—a dozen yards short of Austin.

"What the hell happened?" Secretary Ramirez stormed toward them, her heels sinking into the muddy ground. A colonel was holding an umbrella over her head as a squad of Regulars followed close behind, the rain rolling off their body armor. "POTUS wanted you at the White House an hour ago."

General Fergusson twisted to face Secretary Ramirez. "I was busy," he said dismissively.

"Busy?" Secretary Ramirez walked out from under the protection of the umbrella to stand right in front of the general. When the colonel with the umbrella tried to follow her, she waved him back. "Our satellites showed a multi-megaton nuclear detonation outside the alien mother ship. Isotopic readings indicate it was one of ours. And you're the only field commander who hasn't reported in for his arsenal audit."

Her tone was cutting, accusatory, but General Fergusson

only folded his arms behind his back, seemingly unbothered. "I did what I had to do to protect my country."

"Max." Secretary Ramirez shook her head. "You were in the briefings. POTUS said no retaliation. And after what they did to Saudi Arabia, I was sure that you—"

"For five fucking years we said 'an attack on one is an attack on all.'" General Fergusson closed in on Secretary Ramirez, looming over her as the rain soaked her hair. "But as soon as the weak-willed politicians are faced with the alien might, they cower. It was time for the warriors to step up."

"Warrior?" Secretary Ramirez scoffed, leaning toward the general. "You think you're a warrior? You're a goddamn talking head, a cable-news rodeo clown we trotted out to keep the people calm. To think, an empty suit like you tried to take the country's fate in his hands."

General Fergusson's eyes narrowed as thunder clapped in the distance. "While you all panicked, I wrote the book on great power asymmetric warfare. I gave us a lifeline to cling to." General Fergusson put his finger in Secretary Ramirez's face. "And I executed on that plan. I used the enemy's trust against them. I got an agent into the heart of the alien ship. I nearly destroyed them!" Spittle shot from General Fergusson's mouth and landed on Secretary Ramirez, mixing with the raindrops, but it didn't shake her look of steely resolve. "What have *you* done besides fill the president's diversity quota on his cabinet?"

As the two argued, hundreds of Regulars poured into the

barricades and took their stations behind Secretary Ramirez, hands on their rifles. The Black Shirts behind the general followed suit, their eyes wary.

Austin could feel Father Ambrose shuffling next to him, nervous at the prospect of an internecine fight.

Austin peered into the crowd, scanning the new arrivals. After a moment, he spotted a familiar face. Lieutenant Wu was standing twenty yards behind Secretary Ramirez, rifle in hand.

"Oh, yes, I forgot, your brilliant plan . . ." Secretary Ramirez looked Austin up and down. "Pinning your hopes on this buffoon."

Austin could barely hear the secretary; his attention was focused solely on Lieutenant Wu. No matter what happened here, he was going to die and all the pain, all the trauma—it started with *her*. If she hadn't done that tech check at the muster, or if she had shown just a little bit of mercy to the kind old man, Austin wouldn't be here. He'd have gotten to his Latin class on time and then seen Aurelia. No kind old man dead, no Virgil blown up by a bomb.

"It was a plan as pathetic as you are." Secretary Ramirez shoved her finger in General Fergusson's chest. "No wonder it failed. It never had a chance."

"No, you failed, Madam Secretary." General Fergusson stood up straight, a feline smile curling up his face as water dripped down the side. "You failed when you and POTUS did nothing. When you revealed yourselves as cowards. I'm the one who fought back—the one who did something. The American people will worship me for it. I'll be a hero in their eyes."

Lieutenant Wu met Austin's gaze, and a flash of recognition shot across her face. He stared back, unblinking even as lightning crackled across the sky overhead. He knew her secret: she likely had her cell phone in her pocket right now, every piece of data on it being read by the Pilgrims.

"You're going to have some trouble doing cable-news spots from the cell we're going to stuff you in," Secretary Ramirez shot back. "General Fergusson, you are hereby relieved of duty and placed under arrest." She waved to a nearby Black Shirt. "Take General Fergusson into custody."

The Black Shirt didn't move.

The air became taut as Austin held his stare on Lieutenant Wu. It was a cell phone, a measly cell phone, and if she'd just been lenient, then there would have been so much less pain, so much less suffering, and Austin wouldn't have to die.

"Corporal," the secretary said to the unmoving Black Shirt. "You are receiving a direct order from the secretary of defense."

"I've bled with these men, Madam Secretary." General Fergusson grinned. "Do you really think your title is more important than that?"

The troops cradled their guns, Black Shirts on one side and Regulars on the other, but it wasn't enough to break Austin's attention. How could he forgive her for what she'd done?

"What you're going to find out," General Fergusson said as

he leaned menacingly close to Secretary Ramirez, "is that you can win a few battles and still lose the war."

Austin could see Lieutenant Wu was filled with fear, fear she'd be in a firefight, fear he'd betray her secret.

But he had a choice.

Father Ambrose had made that clear.

He could be like General Fergusson, or he could be like Virgil.

And if Virgil could forgive Austin after he'd lied to him, after sending him to his death, he could forgive her, the mother to a young daughter with Down syndrome, guilty only of doing her job.

Austin smiled and gave her a nod, letting Lieutenant Wu know with every ounce of his being there was no score to settle, no revenge to attain. She was free, just like Austin had been set free. And in that moment, when their eyes met, he could see she understood, knew she was safe.

"Are you done?" Secretary Ramirez asked, the mascara starting to run from her eyes, but her gaze no less defiant.

"For now." General Fergusson put his arms behind his back and looked upward at the alien craft far above them. He laughed, a cackle, as if amused by some unheard joke. He then strolled away, the Black Shirts not daring to touch him, the Regulars too hesitant to act as well.

"Ma'am, should we go after him?" the colonel asked.

"No," Secretary Ramirez said. "We'll get him later."

The colonel gestured at Austin and Father Ambrose. "What about these two, ma'am?"

The secretary beheld Austin and Father Ambrose standing there in the rain for a few moments.

"Cut the priest loose," she said. "He's here on trumped-up charges. As for the translator, process him for homicide."

This time the Black Shirts obeyed readily, and the two who had approached Austin earlier continued making their way toward him.

"I'll pray for you, Austin," Father Ambrose said, tears mingling with rain on the cheeks of his wet face.

Austin nodded, prepared to meet his fate, but as Austin and Father Ambrose exchanged a final glance, a horn blared so loudly that it caused everyone to stagger and cover their ears. When the horn finally stopped, Austin looked up to see a deep crimson glowing above him, a Diplomat standing at the opening to the cylinder wall.

"Nunc consistite!" the Diplomat bellowed in its deep bass voice.

"It's saying to stop now!" Austin yelled to the crowd, the two Black Shirts sent to arrest him just a few feet away.

"Augustinus DeSantis praesidio Michaelis protegitur. Si eum nocueritis, bellum indicetur," the Diplomat bellowed again.

Austin couldn't believe what he was hearing.

"What did it say?" Secretary Ramirez demanded.

Still in shock, Austin steadied himself. "It said, 'Austin DeSantis is under Michael's protection. Harm him and it is war.'"

Secretary Ramirez's eyes went wide, and the soldiers around her leveled their rifles in his direction. Austin turned around to see what they were looking at: a swarm of spider robots scurried around the Diplomat's legs.

"Get back! Leave him alone!" Secretary Ramirez screamed.

"Votum enim erat morientis, quem vos Virgilium vocastis, ut Augustinus amicus suus salvaretur. Et Michael constans est, sed corde fidus," the Diplomat bellowed as the wall of the cylinder slowly folded closed.

All eyes were on Austin, waiting to hear the translation, but he was too overcome to speak. His friend, the one he'd betrayed, the one whose long and glorious life he'd cut short, had saved him yet again.

"He said," Austin translated, his voice breaking, "'For it was the dying wish of the one you called Virgil that his friend Austin should be saved. And Michael is firm, but true of heart.'"

38

The brakes let out a hollow squeal as the cab stopped in front of Glen Meadows Phase IV.

"That'll be two hundred and fifty grand." The driver handed the Fedcoin machine to Austin.

He accepted it, feeling the weight of the machine in his hands. The old man was dead, Austin as guilty as Cynthia for his demise, but Austin had a future now, a lifetime full of choices, and if he lived like Virgil, perhaps this time he could do it right.

The driver nodded after the Fedcoin machine let out a soothing ding. Five million dollars courtesy of Uncle Sam: the price of Austin's silence. It was not enough to change his life, but it was enough for him to pay back his mother, enough for him to start again.

He closed the door, and the cab drove off, no luggage to retrieve from the trunk. The smell of old paint filled his nose as he entered the lobby.

He was home.

"Austin!" Mr. Washington had his hand in his mailbox, his jaw nearly on the floor. "You're back?"

Austin smiled. "I am."

"For good?" Mr. Washington peered over Austin's shoulder like he expected a squad of Black Shirts to be behind him.

"For good," Austin said.

Mr. Washington put the mail down and shook Austin's hand. "I told Monica everything would be all right, that the army just wanted you for your Latin. She wouldn't hear it. She was convinced you were in danger. But look at you now. You're in one piece."

Austin nodded, trying not to reveal with his body language all the scars he carried with him. "Is she home?" he asked.

"She is," Mr. Washington said, his tone becoming grave. "Hardly ever leaves her apartment."

"How bad is she?" Austin asked.

Mr. Washington looked down. "It's good you're home, Austin."

Austin stood there a moment, unsure what to say, before excusing himself. He continued through the lobby and up the six flights of stairs to his mother's floor.

"We can't keep doing this, honey."

Austin exited the stairwell to find Mrs. Armstrong in the hallway, her husband grabbing the suitcase she held in her hand.

"Let go! You saw the news," Mrs. Armstrong protested. "The French detected a nuclear explosion outside the Pilgrim mother ship. They say it's one of ours. We need to get out of here before the Pilgrims attack."

They were too absorbed in their argument to notice Austin coming down the hall.

"You said that after Rome and Saudi Arabia, and we're still here," Mr. Armstrong said. "Now put that suitcase down and come back inside before—"

"Austin?" Mrs. Armstrong said, cutting her husband off.

Austin waved as he passed, not wanting to slow down. "Hi, Mrs. Armstrong."

"But I thought the Black Shirts…" Mr. Armstrong's voice trailed off as Austin reached his mother's door.

As he drew closer, he saw a pink piece of paper affixed to the doorjamb, big black letters that spelled "Notice to Quit" along the top. She was being evicted, the consequence of him spending all of her meager savings on Aurelia. But he was back now with a few months' worth of overdue rent in his Fedcoin account. It wasn't enough to solve all their problems—not even close—but it was enough to buy time, maybe even enough time to make it right.

Not wanting to prolong his mother's suffering any longer, he knocked loudly. It took nearly a minute for him to hear motion, and then the sound of her unlatching the lock and opening the door.

"Austin!" His mother wrapped him in a hug so tight he lost his breath. "They never told me what happened to you," she said, weeping. "I wrote letters. I called. I even had Mr. Doherty in 9-B reach out to some old army buddies, but I heard nothing."

"I know, Mom." Austin squeezed her back. She was thinner now, her threadbare clothes that much more like paper to the touch. He released the hug, and his gaze landed on the cheap brass cross she was wearing around her neck.

"I prayed for you, Auss," she said, touching the necklace. "I prayed for you every day, pleading with God to save you and bring you back to me. I didn't know what else to do."

He could see the look on her face. It was love, pure love, and his chest ached with guilt for all the things he'd done. But he was different now. Virgil had shown him what he'd been missing all along.

"And now I'm here," he said. "I guess He listened."

Wiping a tear from her eye, she pulled him inside. "You must be exhausted." The smell of his old life flooded into his nostrils. "And hungry. I can make a grilled cheese for you. I know you love grilled cheese, and I think I have a slice of cheese left."

"I'm okay, Mom."

"Nonsense," she insisted, pulling him into the front hall. "There's no way the food in pris—" She cut herself off and looked at him apologetically. "I'm sorry, Auss, we don't need to talk about why they had you. I shouldn't have brought it up."

Austin's chest grew tighter. He didn't want to hurt her more, not after everything she'd been through, but he didn't want to lie to her anymore, either. "I did some bad things, Mom. But I'm back now, free and clear."

She smiled; no more explanation needed, the both of them knowing they could get to the remainder of his tale in their own time—time he now had thanks to Virgil.

"I love you, Auss," she said, hugging him again. "I love you so much."

"Mom," he said after she loosened this second hug. "I'm going to change. Is that okay?"

"Of course. I left your room exactly the same. I always knew you'd be back."

Austin hugged her again, then walked to his bedroom door. As he entered the dim space, there was a heaviness in the air, the smell of body odor and hopelessness still lingering. When he stepped in, he knocked over an empty liquor bottle. It rolled across the floor and came to a stop on a pile of dirty clothes. This was his old life, who he used to be.

Going to the bed, he grabbed one of the shirts piled on top. It was a button-down, one of the many he'd considered wearing for his rendezvous with Aurelia. He looked at it like a curiosity, as if it were an artifact from another age.

Rather than put the shirt on, he went straight to his ancient laptop, still whirring from having been left on all this time. With a few clicks, he began a factory reset, formatting the hard drive, destroying all the pictures he'd saved of her, all the videos of her body he'd used for his pleasure. He couldn't look at her like that anymore, like an object meant to serve him—that was how General Fergusson looked at people in this world.

Turning to the window, he drew aside the curtain, letting the daylight stream into his dark cave. The Virginia sky was a clear blue made pale by the low winter sun. He thought about what Father Ambrose had said: there would be other Pilgrim ships coming, trying to be close to their Lord.

They'd changed everything, changed the world—changed Austin.

Thanks to one of them, he had time, he had a choice. And he knew what he finally needed to do.

He got down on his knees, still looking at the sky, the same color as Virgil's dome.

"God," Austin said, not sure if he was doing it correctly. "I'm sorry," he said, tears bursting forth in a stream down his face.

His heart seared in pain. He was sure he couldn't go on, but he looked at the pale blue sky, its light washing over him, reminding him of his friend, and he found the strength.

"Help me to be like Virgil, Lord," Austin whispered, wanting it with every part of his soul. "Don't let me be like who I was."

In an instant, the tightness evaporated, his heart transcendentally light. He was at peace, for the first time in as long as he could remember. The emptiness that had plagued him, the emptiness he'd tried so mightily to fill with worldly things, was gone, replaced by an eternal hope. And he knew in that moment that his prayer had been answered, his heart no longer restless now that it was resting in Him.

Austin stood up, transformed, finally understanding why Virgil was the way that he was. And as he made his way back to his mother in the kitchen, he knew he would never be the same again. He had time now; he had a choice.

And, by God's grace, this time, he would do it right.

I hope you enjoyed *Pilgrims*!

Please don't forget to give this book a quick review on Amazon. This is my first novel, and I want to share it as widely as possible. That means it needs engagement. Even just a two-word review helps so much. Thank you in advance!
And Austin's story is not over . . .
To keep up to date, sign up for my mailing list at www.MRLeonardauthor.com.

ACKNOWLEDGMENTS

First, I want to thank my wife who has spent over a decade listening to me, talking to me, and being interested in the things I have to say. She was interested enough to insist that I write this book. She was interested enough to bear with me as I underwent the trials of a debut author. She was even kind enough to like the raw, early versions of this manuscript, an opinion that can only be chalked up to the delusions of love. I couldn't have done any of this without her, and for that I'm eternally grateful.

I want to thank my children, who are too young to read but who remained my North Star throughout this process. For if they are to be my only readers, this whole odyssey will have been worth it.

I want to thank Kevin Johns—writing coach extraordinaire. There is no better person in the world to teach a rookie writer what it takes to go from an idea to a finished book. Any aspiring writer would be wise to look him up.

I want to thank my copy editor, Parisa Zolfaghari, who helped make my prose sing, and my proofreader, Hanna Richards, who brushed the manuscript clean. And I want to thank my design team at Cover Kitchen, who made the final product look so damn good.

I want to thank my many friends who supported and encouraged me along the way, especially those who took the time to read my manuscript twice.

I want to thank Jeff Hays and the team at Soundbooth Theater who transformed this text into one of the best audio books ever made. If you enjoyed this story, then get the audio book and experience it in a whole new way. You won't regret it.

And finally, I want to thank God almighty, without whom none of this would be possible.

Fiat voluntas tua.

Michael Leonard has had a strange and varied life that has brought him from the banks of the Yangtze River in China to the halls of MIT. He resides in Massachusetts with his wife and two young sons, and he can be found discussing his next novel with his eight-pound dachshund.